MARY'S SONG

A sequel to

Charles Dickens'

A Christmas Carol

Dixie Distler

ACKNOWLEDGMENTS

I am grateful for the editorial assistance of Willy Mathes.
www.bookeditorcoach.com

Cover design by Robin Ludwig Design, Inc.
www.gobookcoverdesign.com

I also thank my husband, family, and friends who encouraged me
to keep writing so this story could finally be told.

Most importantly, I acknowledge Mr. Charles Dickens, who
brought us *A Christmas Carol* through his mastery of storytelling.
His timeless classic has set the Christmas tone for generations.
I am humbled to expand on his masterpiece with
Mary's Song.

Prologue

"Mary, my dearest," he whispered as he watched her delicate fingers close around his hand. "I feel your strength returning. It won't be long now, and you'll be your old self again, skipping merrily through the garden with the children."

"No, my precious brother. Not this time." Her voice trailed as she strained to talk.

"But you will get better, you *must*. I cannot bear the thought of life without you. I need you. We *all* need you." Tears fell from his cheeks as his face drew nearer to Mary's.

"Hold me."

He released her hand to slip one arm under her shoulders, lifting her head to rest against his heart.

"Hold me!" she insisted.

"I *am* holding you, Mary," he replied tenderly.

"Hold me tighter; I can't feel you."

Cradling her against his chest, he could feel her skin twitching, as if she were shivering from a sudden winter rain.

"I'm cold, I feel so cold," she said with a tremble in her voice. "Say my name."

"Mary."

"The name you gave me. The name I love to hear, dear brother. Say it over and over so it will be the last words I hear."

He pressed his cheek against her auburn hair and laid his mouth next to her ear, whispering, "Mary-... Christmas." Her body quivered in his arms as he continued, "Mary Christmas." Her breaths became rapid and short, but her dying wish was all that mattered now. "Mary Christmas, Mary Christmas." His words grew louder so he could be sure she heard him over the sounds of her panting.

Suddenly, all was silent. Mary's body stopped shaking. He relaxed his hold and gently rested her head on the pillow. It took a few moments for him to realize the sobbing he heard in the room was his own. He found within himself the strength to say, one last time, the nickname he had given the carefree girl years before; this girl who loved and lived Christmas all the year, every year; this girl who was never without a kind word or warm thought for anyone, rich or poor.

"Mary-... Christmas."

After closing the lids of her eyes and positioning her to appear as an angel at rest, he slipped the ring from her middle finger and slid it onto the smallest finger of his right hand.

Chapter 1

The morning after Christmas Day was unlike any Robert Cratchit had ever known. Something miraculous indeed had melted the icy heart of his employer, Ebenezer Scrooge. So much so that the man was a completely different person, and a far better one from his clerk's perspective.

Bright and early, the two men walked side by side through the frigid London streets. One shopkeeper after another unlocked their doors and removed their shutters, as the wintry city opened for business. From every street corner came the boisterous shouts from street peddlers, religiously out at the crack of dawn selling their goods for another day's trifle earnings. If the sight of Scrooge walking next to him wasn't enough to astonish Robert, Scrooge's genuine warmth and goodwill indeed were.

"Good morning, madam! Top of the morning to you, sir," Scrooge said with a song in his voice and tip of his hat, as they passed an elderly couple.

"And to you as well, sir," replied the gentleman with a slight nod.

Suddenly the couple stopped and looked at one another. "I dare say. Wasn't that Ebenezer Scrooge?" asked the man of his wife.

"Certainly not," she chuckled. "Ebenezer Scrooge has never worn a smile in public, at least not one I have been privy to."

Between greetings, Scrooge was like a long-lost friend toward his loyal clerk. "Tell me, Bob, have you ever known a finer morning than this?"

Robert took a deep breath, filling his lungs with the cold, crisp morning air, trying not to wake up from what he felt must undoubtedly be a heaven-sent dream. "No, sir. I must say, this is an amazing morning indeed, in more ways than I can count."

Suddenly, two popping sounds interrupted their morning stroll, the first coming from a snowball hitting Scrooge on the back and the second sending his hat flipping from his head. Robert braced himself for the rage he believed would inevitably erupt from Scrooge, but the man once again showed his new character. "Stand back, Bob! I've got this. I used to have quite an arm when it came to a snowball fight with the lads from my school."

Turning quickly, Scrooge targeted the two boys who threw the snowballs. Scooping up a double handful of snow, he pressed it into a ball and heaved it toward the pair of rascals. "Ha, I got you!" Scrooge proclaimed, even though only a fraction of his snowball came anywhere near the boys.

As Scrooge retrieved his hat from the curb, Robert asked, "Sir? Are you alright? Do you want me to go have a talk with those boys?"

Scrooge laughed again, a sound that still seemed so extraordinary to Robert's ears. "No talk needed, Bob. I'd say their aim was pretty good."

If nothing else could convince Robert he was dreaming, he stopped to watch Scrooge cross the street to drop a coin in the tin cup of a young, blind beggar.

"Praise the day," Robert whispered as Scrooge returned to resume their morning stroll. "Yes, praise the day, indeed."

As they approached a vendor selling a fragrant mulled wine, specifically a smoking bishop, Scrooge enthusiastically said, "Top of the morning, sir! We would each like a bowl of your most delicious concoction."

"Aye, sir," said the old man, flashing a toothless grin. "Ain't nut'n like a hot bit'o spices and port on an icy morning."

"You are quite right, my good man," answered Robert with a smile, catching a tantalizing whiff of orange and cloves rising from the steaming kettle.

Both men pulled bowls from their coat pockets, and the vendor ladled into each a healthy portion of the traditional Christmastime drink. After Scrooge paid for the two bowls of punch—with a significant tip for the vendor—they stood on a nearby corner, both eager to enjoy the first hot sip. "Ah, warms you to the bones, eh, Bob?"

Robert watched the ice cycles hanging from eaves over the walkway, glistening in the morning sun as they began to release droplets of water. "Yes, sir. I must say it warms you inside and out. Thank you for this tasty treat, Mr. Scrooge. 'Tis a taste of the season, I must say." The pair walked slowly back to the office, so as not to spill their drinks. The previous day's hazy sky that brought a Christmas snow had given way to what promised to be a bright day of new beginnings. After stepping in through the doorway and hanging up their coats and hats, Scrooge declared, "Now, that's a warm stove! What say ye, Bob? Let's sit by the fire and toast the day."

Robert followed his employer's lead and listened to the tone of his voice as it brought great pleasure to his heart. The day had seemed surreal to him, having been so accustomed to serving a wretched, miserable miser whose only delight could be found in the suffering of others or the weight of coins in his own pockets.

As they each moved a chair to be near the stove, Robert asked the question that had been burning inside him since first arriving at the office. "Mr. Scrooge?"

Scrooge turned, looked straight into his longtime employee's eyes and, raising his hand to interrupt, spared him from the awkward effort of finding the right words. "Bob, you want to know if I have flipped my wig, right?"

"Yes, sir-... I mean no, not at all! I mean-... Sir, are you alright?"

Scrooge stared at Robert for a moment, contemplating what he wanted to convey; just how much of the ghostly encounters from the night before Christmas he should divulge. Striking a more serious demeanor, he said, "Bob, I am completely well and sober—better, in fact, than I have been for quite some time. Throughout Christmas Eve, an old acquaintance of mine showed me the person I had become, and it terrified me. I don't want to be that person anymore. I wish to return to the carefree days of my youth, filled with love and respect for my neighbors. I want to have-… friends."

"Yes, sir, I understand. My father called it *the ripples*. Our acts of good or evil, directly and indirectly, affect those around us, making us the person we become."

"Your father was a wise man, Bob. I don't know what my future holds, but I *do* know it will be quite different from my past."

"Mr. Scrooge, for the first time since I have known you, I can see the light inside you, and I pray it will never extinguish."

Steering the subject of the conversation away from himself, Scrooge said, "Mr. Cratchit, I believe there is the small matter of the proposal I made before we went out for this wonderful bishop. Let me begin by offering you a belated Christmas gift." Extending his hand to shake Robert's, Scrooge passed a guinea to his clerk and said, "Merry Christmas, Bob."

Robert looked at the coin in his hand and froze for a moment. "Mr. Scrooge, thank you, sir. Thank you very much, indeed!"

"There are many past Christmases in that coin, sir. More still, your salary, as of this moment, is raised to fifty shillings a week."

Robert sprang to his feet. "Mr. Scrooge, sir!"

Scrooge stood as well, with both men placing their bowls on the coal-burning stove. That which began as a hearty handshake quickly became a heartfelt embrace.

As they sat once again, Scrooge continued. "Bob, I am a changed man, this I promise and can only prove with time. I want you to help me, in the course of this business to *serve* our fellow men for the common good. I can't do this without you."

"Oh, Mr. Scrooge, it would be my honor, sir."

"Good, Bob. Good! Together we will make this city a finer place to live."

Motivated by Scrooge's sincere desire to restructure his business, the two men talked well into the afternoon, exchanging ideas and plans for the days and weeks to come.

The walk home from work was far different from any day since Robert's first, as a young apprentice. His shoulders no longer bore the weight of the world. Still, he continued to doubt his senses while reviewing the day's events in his mind. Knowing Scrooge as a kind and gentle man seemed to him more difficult to accept than did the years of torment he'd suffered as an apprentice to him and his former business partner, Jacob Marley.

Walking into his home, Robert appeared distant, nearly in shock, as he greeted his family, "Good evening, my dears."

His good wife, Emily, lifted the large spoon out of the pot in which she had been stewing the bones from their Christmas turkey and hurried to her husband's side when she saw the faraway gaze in his eyes, "Robert? Are you ill? You don't look well."

"No, no, my dear, I'm quite well."

"Then, what is it? You seem as though you're looking right through me." Gasping with both hands covering her mouth, she concluded, "Oh my stars! He fired you, didn't he? The stingy old coot actually did it."

Robert looked around the room and saw his children—except Martha, who was not yet home from her job—facing him with concerned looks following the premature announcement from Emily. He sat in his chair at the table and motioned to his children for them to sit with him. Turning to Emily, who was already showing tears, he said, "Rest assured, my dear, Mr. Scrooge has not dismissed me. To the contrary, he was kinder to me than any man since my father, God rest him. I truly don't know where to begin."

Thinking still about how he could explain his experiences that day and sound believable, Robert reached into his pocket and pulled out a coin, which he laid on the table.

"A guinea?" Peter said.

"Where did you find it, Father?" asked Richard.

"Find it? I dare say I did *not* find it. Indeed it was a gift, and if you can believe me, a gift from Mr. Scrooge himself."

The entire Cratchit clan erupted in disbelief at what they imagined must surely be a prank. "Robert?" Emily asked with a suspicious tone, "Are you speaking truly?"

"I am, my dear. I must say that if I did not have this guinea in my pocket, I would have serious doubts of my own faculties. It was the most amazing miracle I have ever witnessed, Em. The Mr. Scrooge I saw today was not the Mr. Scrooge I have known all these years. He was gentler than any man you could find on the streets of this fair city, I'm quite certain."

"Oh, but I can't believe it! He must have been pulling your leg," challenged his wife.

"I understand your reservations. I must confess it took me *hours* before I could lower my guard in his presence. Still, I have not even told you the best part."

The entire Cratchit family wanted to hear more, with each asking him to continue. Raising both hands to lower the voices around the table, Robert explained, "Mr. Scrooge, for no apparent reason, raised my salary to fifty shillings-... *every week.*"

The Cratchit children stood up and surrounded their father, giving him both hugs and pats on the back. As their celebration eased, he looked at his wife, who was now hiding her face behind her hands. "Emily?"

She shook her head back and forth, and slowly lowered her hands. "Robert, this *can't* be true. There *must* be something more than meets the eye. Things like this don't happen to people like us."

Again the children spoke all at once, this time to their mother, encouraging her to trust their father's good fortune, as though it would not be real until she believed.

"Emily, my love, it *is* true, I have seen it with my own eyes. Something miraculous happened over Christmas that changed Mr. Scrooge into the finest, and I dare say most generous gentleman in all of London."

"That must be it, Father," Tiny Tim said, as he ambled with the aid of his crutch toward his father.

"What's that, my boy?"

"Christmas happened, Father. You said it yourself."

Robert put his arm around his crippled son and hugged him close, "I'm sure you're right, Tim, as sure as I am that on this day, I have witnessed a Christmas miracle of the grandest proportion."

When first light broke through their bedroom window, Robert rose earlier than usual to get ready for work. For the first time in his life, he found himself anxious to begin a new day at Scrooge and Marley's. To reassure himself he wasn't waking from a cruel dream, he reached into his pocket and pulled out the guinea.

In the dim morning's light, while the rest of the Cratchit family was still asleep, he wrote a note to his wife and placed the coin on the paper in the center of their dining table.

My Dearest Em,

Take this guinea and our blessed children to the market. Buy yourself, and each one of them gifts to satisfy your heart's desire. For me, I already have the gift of a new friend.

Love, Robert

As he hurried through the streets to begin a new day and a better life, Robert fondly remembered the conversation he and Scrooge shared the previous day. *I charge you, Bob Cratchit,* Scrooge had said, *with the responsibility of overseeing this office and upholding the highest moral fortitude.*

If there was any doubt remaining in Robert's mind concerning Scrooge's sincerity, it immediately faded when he stood outside the office and read the freshly painted sign above the door:

Scrooge and Cratchit

Chapter 2

"Good morning, Mr. Cratchit!"

As Robert entered through the door, he couldn't help but feel somewhat peculiar hearing Scrooge's enthusiastic greeting, even knowing of his recent turnaround. Immediately, however, he noticed how warm and inviting the room felt, partly from the extra coal on the fire, but more so, he surmised, from Scrooge's cheerful demeanor.

"Good morning, Mr. Scrooge, sir."

After Robert hung up his coat and hat, he took his place at his writing table and opened the ledger that had remained closed since Christmas Eve.

Watching from his office, Scrooge interrupted Robert's work, even before he could uncover his inkwell. "Mr. Cratchit? A moment of your time, please?"

Robert hurried to his usual spot in front of Scrooge's desk. "Relax, Bob. I just wanted to know why my business partner is sitting at the *clerk's* station and not sitting here at my *partner's* desk?" Scrooge gestured at the desk to his right.

"Me, sir? Partner?"

"Did you not see the sign outside? You *are* Bob Cratchit, are you not?" Scrooge chuckled.

"Why, yes sir, I am indeed. But Mr. Scrooge, this was Mr. Marley's desk."

"This is the desk of one of the partners in the counting-house of Scrooge and Cratchit. Besides, I have it on good authority that Jacob would be honored if you took your place at his desk."

"Yes, sir. If you don't think I'm being disrespectful, *I* would be the one who is honored to take a seat at your side."

He's quite sincere, Robert thought, as he gathered his work and belongings from the clerk's writing table and settled into the desk next to his former employer—now, partner.

As Robert began working, Scrooge once again interrupted him before the ink started to flow, "Bob, tell me about your son."

"Peter?"

Scrooge shook his head.

"Richard?"

Again, he shook his head.

"Tim, sir? Tiny Tim?"

Scrooge smiled and nodded. "Yes, Tiny Tim. How is he?"

"Oh, quite well, sir," Robert answered slowly, trying to remember when he had mentioned Tim, or anyone from his family for that matter, in Scrooge's presence.

"Quite well, eh? Good, that's good, yes." Scrooge suddenly adopted a serious tone and asked again, "Now, Bob, tell me the truth. How is Tiny Tim?"

Robert paused to consider Scrooge's question. "Well, sir, Tim has suffered poor health since birth. His right leg has not developed properly, so he walks with a crutch. He cannot hold much food in his stomach, so we give him small portions throughout the day, yet his body seems weaker with each passing year."

"Thank you, Bob. I needed to hear that. Now, I want you to hear this. You and I are going to do *whatever* it takes to spare that boy's life. No matter what the cost, Tim will live. Are we in agreement, sir?"

"My goodness, Mr. Scrooge. Yes, thank you! And indeed, we *are* in agreement." Robert stood to shake Scrooge's hand. "Bless you, sir. God bless you!"

"Good. Then with your permission, I would like to arrange a meeting with a doctor I know from the London Exchange."

"By all means, sir."

"Now, our next course of business, Bob, is we appear to have a vacancy where my clerk used to sit."

"Oh, no worries, Mr. Scrooge. I will continue to fulfill my clerk duties as well. I dare say it is the least I can do, considering everything you have done for my situation."

"Nonsense, Bob, you and I have a business to run. I will make it my personal goal to have an apprentice clerk within a fortnight. After all, I think I made an excellent choice with the last clerk I hired," Scrooge concluded with a wink.

As the two men continued talking, a timid gentleman entered the office with his hat in hand. "Pardon me for interrupting."

Rising to greet the man, Scrooge extended him a friendly handshake. "Come in, sir, please come in. How may we serve you?"

"Jeremiah Adkins, sir. I'm here to see if I could possibly get an extension on this month's rent, sir. I humble myself to your good will, Mr. Scrooge, and I promise to make amends and be on time next month."

Scrooge walked around his desk to retake his seat, before exerting the effort to appear disturbed. "My good sir, did I ask you for more time to provide your accommodations?"

"No, sir, you didn't."

"Then, I have no recourse but to turn your request over to my partner," Scrooge replied, struggling to hold back his laughter.

"Sir?" Mr. Adkins replied, knowing full well Scrooge's partner had died seven years earlier.

"Yes, Mr. Cratchit will show you how the firm of Scrooge and Cratchit deals with people who are unable to fulfill their obligations." Looking at Robert with a wink, Scrooge passed the responsibility. "Go ahead, Mr. Cratchit. Explain to Mr. Adkins how we handle late payments."

Robert smiled at his partner and turned to address the man, who was now feeling even less comfortable than when he walked in.

"Mr. Adkins, please relax, sir. Everyone has trouble now and then. Do you know when you will be able to make good on your debt?"

"I need only a week, kind sir. Ten days at the most, but I will be able to satisfy half of the duty in just a few days' time."

Robert smiled as he responded, "Your solution is perfectly acceptable. There will be no penalty accessed with your account if you are able to fulfill your commitment." Opening the ledger that was already on his desk, he made a note and said, "I have registered our agreement, Mr. Adkins. You are in good standing."

"Oh, thank you, Mr. Cratchit. Thank you, Mr. Scrooge." After nodding to each man, Mr. Adkins turned to make his way out, only to find himself being followed to the front door.

Before the man could exit, Scrooge shook his hand again and wished him a good day. After their client left, Scrooge turned to Robert and asked, "Tell me, Bob, why did we excuse the late payment, instead of forgiving the entirety of the month's liability?"

Astounded that Scrooge was seeking his advice, Robert thought for a moment before responding, "Mr. Adkins did not come here to seek our charity. He is a proud man and a good provider for his family. All he asked for was our patience, so that is how we responded. Besides, sir, had we forgiven the debt, we would have been swarmed by half of London within the hour, all of them looking for the same sort of charity."

Scrooge dropped back into his chair behind his desk with a heavy sigh. "I never imagined being happy could be so exhausting."

The two men laughed heartily.

Suddenly, Scrooge looked concerned. "So little time," he declared.

"Time, Mr. Scrooge? Time for what?"

Scrooge took a deep breath before answering, "I'm not a young man, Bob. Not that I'm afraid of dying, mind you. But I *am* afraid of dying before I've made amends for my former self. You see, the dear friend who I told you about showed me what you have known all these past years. I now realize that the way we treat our fellow man follows us through our days. There's so much I can do. So much I *will* do, I *must* do. I dare say I have barely slept a wink these past few nights, just considering the possibilities."

Within the hour, Scrooge stood to put his coat on before stepping out into the brisk winter morning. As he wrapped his scarf around his neck, he noticed Robert standing alongside him, holding his hat as he had always done. Scrooge smiled and accepted the hat from his new partner, realizing old habits take time to break. "I have a number of errands to run this fine morning, Bob. Will you keep the wheels turning while I'm out?"

"Yes, sir, I shall indeed."

Scrooge held his hat before exiting and turned back to Robert. "Please remember, sir. We are partners in business, now. You have as much right to make decisions for our company as I do. I trust your intuition and your integrity."

"Yes, sir, I will do my best. Thank you, Mr. Scrooge."

As Scrooge strolled through the London streets, everyone knew they were walking past a fine, kindhearted gentleman. Every street beggar received a coin, a thoughtful word, and a warm smile. Every lady received a greeting with a tip of his hat. Every man, regardless of stature or class, with whom he spoke, parted with a warmed heart. Even those who'd encountered Scrooge before, promptly realized this was not the man they thought they knew.

Scrooge's first stop of the morning was to re-register his business with the London registrar under the new name, *Scrooge and Cratchit.*

After concluding the paperwork, Scrooge proceeded to the office of Dr. Jonathan Cecil, who was known well in London as a pioneer of medicine and surgical techniques. Aware that this doctor was rightfully thought of as the best of the best, even amongst his colleagues, Scrooge considered no other to treat Tiny Tim.

When Scrooge returned to the office, well after the noon hour, he greeted Robert boisterously. "Bob, invite me to your home for dinner tonight!"

"Sir? I mean, yes, by all means, Mr. Scrooge, would you care to-…"

"I'd love to, Bob!" Scrooge interrupted. "I dare say I don't believe I have *ever* had the pleasure of meeting your good wife. I can only imagine she and I will each have a pleasant surprise, eh, Bob?"

Both of them chuckled at the possibilities.

By mid-afternoon, Scrooge suggested they close the office early to begin preparing for dinner. "After all," Scrooge added, "it may well take an extra hour or so for Mrs. Cratchit to allow me past her front door."

As the two partners walked toward Camden Town, they paused to note the fragrant aroma of hot, spiced gingerbread. "Do you smell that, Bob? I haven't had gingerbread since I was a schoolboy, eating in the dining hall with my friends." Guided by his fond memories and nose, Scrooge led Robert to a street vendor standing at the corner.

"Good afternoon, gentlemen," the plump, bearded peddler said. "Interest you in some ginger treats?"

"A loaf of your finest and freshest, if you please," Scrooge replied.

"And will you be eating this today or tomorrow, if I may ask?"

"Why, *today*, my fine fellow. Within the hour, if all goes well."

"Then you'll be wanting yesterday's bread."

"Day old?"

"Oh, *yes*, sir. You see, gingerbread is at its best when time allows the flavors to blend."

Scrooge looked at Robert, who nodded in agreement with the vendor. "Then may we have a loaf of your finest, and don't be trying to slip me anything that came from the oven today," he said with a wink while patting the man's back.

"Yes, sir. Quite right," the jolly man said, nimbly wrapping a thick golden loaf in paper.

"This will be a delightful surprise," Robert said, as they resumed their journey. The street and walkways were randomly dotted with piles of snow, shoveled to clear shop entrances. The pure white of a fresh snowfall had given way to gray mounds, a mixture of coal ash and horse manure, all frozen into an icy pile of dirty snow. Ruts were carved through the slushy streets by countless wagons, making their walk a slow and treacherous exercise requiring great effort and determination. Through the holes in the bottom of his shoes, Robert felt the chill of the cold water stabbing his feet with painful needles.

Upon reaching the Cratchit home, Scrooge waited just outside the door, while Robert stepped inside to announce him. When the elderly guest stepped in a moment later, the household was stunned into silence at the sight of the man who all had known by name and reputation alone—Ebenezer Scrooge.

With his hat in his left hand and loaf of bread under his arm, Scrooge humbly approached Emily. "Good evening, my dear. I am Ebenezer Scrooge. I beg your pardon for the intrusion this evening, but your husband was rather insistent that I come for dinner."

Scrooge gave a quick wink to Robert, gently kissed Emily's hand and placed the freshly wrapped gingerbread in her arms. As she stood in silent shock, the stillness was broken by the slow and rhythmic shuffle and clop of Tiny Tim's feet and crutch, as he walked up directly behind the stranger in the room and tugged on his coattails for attention. "I'm Tim Cratchit. I'm pleased to meet you, Mr. Scrooge."

The sight of Tiny Tim warmed the old man's already cheerful heart. Scrooge gently released the hand of Emily Cratchit, to shake that of Tiny Tim. "Well now, I am very honored to meet *you*, Timothy. I think you and I are going to become great friends." Scrooge gazed at the face of the eleven-year-old boy who looked no older than seven.

"I think so, too," Tim agreed confidently, working his way over to his chair by the fire.

Emily shook her head slightly to make herself blink, before finding her voice. "Yes, Mr. Scrooge, my goodness—where are my manners? Please give me your coat and hat, and do have a seat. It's a long walk from your office, I'm quite sure."

Robert smiled while watching Scrooge charm his wife with his gentleness. Each and every Cratchit, in their own way, and in their own time, began warming to the man who seemed more like a jolly old uncle than the spiteful, mean-spirited soul who had once detested every man, woman, and child. While the conversation around the table welcomed him to be part of the family, their simple meal of hearty oyster stew was like a feast for Scrooge's senses, who gladly accepted a second bowl. To everyone's delight, dinner was followed with a slice of delicious gingerbread for dessert.

After the dishes were cleared, Scrooge sat at the table with Robert and Emily for a private conversation. "I wish for the two of you to consider my most urgent request," Scrooge began with a strong sense of purpose. "This afternoon, I scheduled an appointment for your son, Timothy, to be evaluated by Dr. Jonathan Cecil. He is a wonderfully skilled surgeon, one who is recommended above all others. If you are both willing, I would be grateful if you would allow me this opportunity to help you and your son. I have already taken the liberty to instruct the good doctor to bill me directly for any and all services."

"Oh, Mr. Scrooge!" Emily gushed. "I have prayed for this day to come for *years*. What a loving and generous offer." Looking at her husband, and then back to Scrooge, she responded, "Yes—yes, with a grateful heart, our answer is *yes*."

"Bless my soul," Robert said. Taking Emily's hand in his, he gently kissed it.

Walking around the table, she embraced Scrooge, who stood to greet her. "Dear sir, you are truly the answer to a mother's prayers."

Hearing her sincerely spoken words and feeling the warmth from being held close, Ebenezer Scrooge felt a single tear roll down his cheek. "Then it is settled," Scrooge concluded. "On the second day of the New Year, Mrs. Cratchit, please be at our office no later than one o'clock with Timothy, to take your husband from his business duties and proceed directly to Dr. Cecil's office. It is important that you both agree with the doctor's prognosis. If you do not, if you are in doubt, then we will try another and still another, until you are convinced you have found the best doctor for Timothy. Please understand this must be *your* decision, not mine."

Emily nodded while holding both hands over her mouth, looking at Tiny Tim as she listened to Scrooge's instructions.

"Emily, are you alright?" Robert asked.

Through tear-swollen eyes, she nodded before saying, "I'm trying to imagine Tim walking without a crutch."

The new year brought renewed hope for the fate of the youngest Cratchit. Robert lowered Tim from his shoulder, as he and Emily stopped outside the doctor's office to talk briefly before he went back to work and she took their son home. "We can talk more about it tonight, Em, but I must say I'm inclined to follow Dr. Cecil's recommendation."

"But you heard what he said as clearly as I did, Robert."

Standing between both parents for warmth from the cold, gusty wind, Tim expressed his feelings, as well. "I'm not afraid Mother, Father. I'm not afraid."

Robert studied his youngest child, observing the ever-present dark rings around his sunken eyes, surrounded by an ashen complexion. He kissed his wife and gave her an extended hug, realizing the two of them had a life and death decision before them, and that this conversation was best held away from the ears of their son.

As he sat behind his desk, Robert barely noticed Scrooge watching his every move. Finally, Scrooge broke into his thoughts. "Well, sir? Does Dr. Cecil believe he can help Timothy?"

"Indeed he does, Mr. Scrooge, but what he suggests is quite risky, at least in my opinion. He said there are two problems. For one, Tim's foot is lame because a tendon has not developed as it should, which has caused his foot to turn inward as it grows. This, he said, can be solved by cutting the tendon. Tim would then wear a metal brace for about a year as the foot heals and strengthens."

"Excellent! And the second?"

"The *second* problem is precarious. Dr. Cecil believes there is a blockage, or possibly a kink, in Tim's intestine. He said Tim was likely born with this condition and it would require cutting into his abdomen to find the problem. Five years ago, he said, there would not have been any means to perform such an operation, but now there is a new chemical called *ether*, which allows him to make a patient sleep while he operates. He assured us Tim would feel no pain during the operation."

Scrooge rested against the back of his chair as he considered the gravity of the situation, "Cut open the belly of a child while he is asleep?"

"Dr. Cecil has no experience with the use of this chemical," Robert continued, "but he told us there is a doctor from France who is giving medical lectures in London next week on the use of ether. He is going to contact this French doctor to see if he would be willing to administer the ether, while he himself performs the operation.

"Given there are so many variables, Mr. Scrooge, all of which seem quite perilous, I truly don't know what to do. According to Dr. Cecil, if Tim gets too much ether, he will never wake up. Not enough and he will wake during the surgery. Then, there is the risk of dying from the operation or from an infection afterward."

"And if he does not operate? Is there a chance Timothy will get better on his own?"

"If he does not operate, he told us Tim would most certainly die before next Christmas."

Sunday service at the Keystone Church of Camden Town presented Robert and Emily with an opportunity to pray for wisdom and to seek guidance from their minister, Reverend Potts, for Tiny Tim's wellbeing.

The Reverend was a tall, lanky man with deep wrinkles above his brows that were exaggerated when he glared, which was often. Also prominent was the way his mouth seemed to hold a permanent frown, which made his face appear long and sinister.

After the congregation sang an opening hymn, Reverend Potts stood behind the podium in silence for a moment, studying the faces in the pews. Clearing his throat forcefully, he set his bible down and began to speak. "Brothers and Sisters," he began, "this past December was most disturbing to my colleagues, and to me." His voice raised and cracked, and soon he was bellowing his ominous message of condemnation toward anyone who did not heed his warnings.

"I have sat idly by for *many* years now, while members of this congregation partake in the pagan festivities of Christmas. I am here to tell you that it *must* stop, and it must stop *now*! Caroling and gifts do not enhance the message of this Church; rather they diminish it. Feasts on December the twenty-fifth are *blatant* sins of gluttony. Never again will the bells of this tower ring on the pagan holiday and any one of you who still partakes will be *banished* from this hall of worship and shunned by those of us who are the true believers."

His attack on Christmas did not end there. Reverend Potts yelled, stomped his feet and slammed his fist for over an hour that Sunday. As his fiery message was not uncommon for the time and place, many in the congregation were nodding in agreement. However, the Cratchits, who occupied the majority of the third row, remained shocked in their silence. At the conclusion of the service, after the closing hymn was sung and the parishioners were dismissed, Robert could not bring himself to discuss Tim's operation with the Reverend, as he had planned. The best he could muster as he shook the Reverend's hand after passing through the front doors was a polite, "A vigorous sermon, Reverend Potts."

The Reverend held Robert's hand tightly as he replied, "I hope you will not disregard today's message, Mr. Cratchit. I understand you and your family are among those who have been known to participate in the pagan practices of the Old World. As I said in my sermon, it is not only *this* church, but churches all across this city and these great lands that are coming together in unity to put an *end* to sinful celebrations."

Upon leaving Reverend Potts at the church entrance, Robert, Emily, and the five Cratchit children proceeded to the cemetery behind the church, just as they did most Sundays, to visit the graves of Emily's parents and Robert's mother and sister. As they rounded a corner of the church, Emily stopped abruptly, to avoid stepping on a small plant in the pathway. Pulling it from the ground, roots, bulb, and all, she walked quietly up to a weathered headstone and pushed it into the soft earth above the grave of Rebecca Cratchit.

"What's that plant?" Richard asked his mother.

"It's called a Winter Aconite. It will bloom a small yellow blossom, even in the winter. I've actually seen them open while surrounded by snow. When we come here a year from now, we may see the tiny flower right here on your grandmother's grave."

Disturbed by the morning sermon, Peter asked, "Father, does this mean we won't celebrate Christmas anymore?"

Still shocked by the day's events, Robert said, "I don't know, Peter. If Reverend Potts has his way, and I dare say the way of other churches, from what he claims, Christmas may no longer be considered a religious holiday."

Chapter 3

Walking down the crowded streets on his way home, Scrooge gratefully thought to himself, *It was not so very long ago that so many of these people would have angered me, just by their mere presence. But now, I feel a sense of belonging I've not known since my apprentice days at Mr. Fezziwig's, or in the arms of my beloved Belle.*

Suddenly, his sentiments were interrupted by a gang of boys running by him on either side. In his startled state, Scrooge spun around, as one of the boys accidentally brushed his arm in passing, causing him to fall to the cobblestones. In the confusion, his top hat landed on the street, just out of reach.

Immediately, the boy who had knocked Scrooge off his feet, the tallest in the group, returned and fetched his hat.

"Well?" the rather annoyed Scrooge asked, "Are you going to help me up or just stare at an old man sitting in the street?"

"Sorry, guv'nor," the young fellow replied. "We meant you no harm."

"Whether you meant it or not, you certainly caused it."

"Again, I'm sorry, sir. Me and the boys, we like to be at the back door to the bakery before he tosses the scraps. If we aren't fast, the dogs will beat us to 'em."

"Eh? Help me up then. It seems like the least you could do," Scrooge demanded, reaching his hand forward. After standing,

Scrooge did not release the boy's hand, even as the scruffy teen eased his grip.

"What's your name, boy?"

"David, sir. Can I go now? I have to catch up-…"

"David what?"

"Just David. I ain't got no last name."

"Where do you live, just David?"

"I ain't got no home, either."

Suddenly Scrooge realized he was face-to-face with that which he had feared the most; poverty, and here in its lowest form. A young man who survived, more than lived. To Scrooge, the drawn up flesh of the boy's malnourished face seemed hauntingly familiar.

In an instant, the painful memory returned. David's face reflected the face of the boy beneath the robe of the Ghost of Christmas Present—one of three spirits who had not long before visited the former tyrant—the face of the boy named *Ignorance*. Looking now into the large brown eyes that resisted looking into his, Scrooge wished only to comfort him.

"Pardon me, guv'nor; can I have my hand back now?"

"What?" Scrooge realized he was still holding David's hand tightly with his own. "Oh-… yes," he said, releasing his grip.

As the young man turned to run after the other boys, Scrooge spoke directly to him, recognizing any hesitation would cause the opportunity to be lost forever. Motioning with a tilt of his head to the restaurant next to where they stood, he asked, "David, would you allow me to buy you lunch?"

David looked at the eatery, and then back to the old man who was now brushing off his hat.

"Unless, of course, you find bread scraps more appetizing," Scrooge added, slightly grinning.

"And what's in it for you?"

Scrooge smiled. Although David was much older than the child who clung to the leg of the ghost that night, a teenager for sure, still he saw in him the same need: the yearning to belong. "What's in it for me is a chance to share a meal, and perhaps a chance to make a friend. What say ye, David? No one ever died from a good meal before, at least no one I've ever known."

While Scrooge nibbled away at the light lunch he'd ordered, he thoroughly enjoyed watching David ravage half a chicken and two whole boiled potatoes. "David, where do you stay when you're not running about the streets?"

Despite his mouth being too stuffed to answer, David shrugged his shoulders and said, "Here and there."

"Are you employed?"

"Odd jobs, guv'nor."

"Do you earn enough to eat on?"

"Sometimes, but mostly I just find what I need. It's a crying shame the amount of food a place like this will toss out their back door."

Scrooge studied the young man, who was obviously wise to the ways of street life, by the fact that he had survived on little more than his wits and ingenuity. "Would you be interested in doing some work for me?"

David stopped chewing with a half-eaten chicken leg still held firmly in his grip. "What sort of work?"

"Jobs around my home, jobs around my business. If you do well, we will see where it goes from there. I will give you a warm place to sleep and food to eat. If you work hard for me, I will pay you, as well. If you steal from me, I will turn you loose, simple as that."

After a moment of contemplation, David began bobbing his head, then reached his greasy hand across the table to shake that of his new benefactor. "Deal, guv'nor."

"Scrooge is my sir name."

David continued the handshake as he restated, "Deal, Mr. Scrooge."

As the door to the business swung open, Robert returned his quill to its holder before looking up to see Scrooge standing in the doorway waiting to gain his partner's attention. "Bob, come and see who I ran into, or more to the point, who ran into me."

Robert walked toward the door, stopping just in front of his old clerk's table and stool to see a young man, nearly as tall as Scrooge, wearing tattered and patched clothing, whose hands and face were smeared with dirt and coal, and whose hair was unkempt and scraggly.

"Meet my new friend, David," Scrooge declared.

Robert reached forward and shook the stranger's hand, "A pleasure, David."

Scrooge continued the introduction, "David, this is my business partner, Bob Cratchit."

"Guv'nor," David shyly replied, momentarily mesmerized by the office's shelves filled with books and ledgers. He inhaled deeply, relishing the smell of old paper and wood shelves, seasoned with age. "Blimey, did you gents read all these books?"

"More writing than reading, I'm afraid," Scrooge replied with a chuckle, placing a hand on David's shoulder. Switching his attention to Robert, he said, "Bob, I have decided to take a chance on this fine fellow by offering him some odd jobs around here, and around my home."

"Splendid, Mr. Scrooge," Robert replied, still astonished each time Scrooge displayed genuine, kind-hearted generosity.

"Come to think of it," Scrooge continued, "I *am* taking a big chance on our young protégé. We know nothing of his character or morals." Turning back to David, he said, "I'm going to call you *Chancy*, to remind us of the day I took a chance on a boy who didn't know me any more than I knew him. How does that strike you, sir?"

"You can call me anything you like, Mr. Scrooge, as long as you hold up your end of the bargain."

"Good!" Scrooge declared. Then he reintroduced the young man. "Bob, I'd like you to meet my new friend, Chancy. He is going to board in my home in a bedroom that I feel certain he will find more accommodating than the shadowy back alleys of

London. He will work around here as we need him, and around my home when we don't."

Robert managed a partial grin that showed his reservations, "Mr. Scrooge, sir, are you quite certain you-..."

"I am certain, Bob. And someday, I will explain how I know the rightness of this."

Robert nodded in acceptance and grabbed the boy's hand to shake it once again. "Welcome, Chancy. I hope you appreciate the opportunity Mr. Scrooge is offering you."

Chancy smiled. "It's a lot to take in, I grant you, Mr. Cratchit. I must say, it will be a nice change to wake up without rats that crawled in my coat overnight for warmth."

"Speaking of coats," Scrooge said, "let's go get you cleaned up and some proper clothes."

He promptly turned to Chancy and steered him to walk out of the building and into the cold afternoon air, just as a father might with his son.

"Mrs. Dilber?" Scrooge inquired, after finding her crouched over to add coal to the cooking stove in his kitchen. "Please allow me to introduce you to Chancy."

The charlady, herself nearly Scrooge's age, with more holes in her smile than teeth, rose to greet the visitor. "Pleased to meet you, Master Chancy."

"The pleasure is mine," Chancy responded.

"Now that we are all well acquainted, Mrs. Dilber, I have a favor to ask. Chancy will be boarding here from this day forward, and as you see is carrying some new clothes we purchased within the last hour. However, before he wears them, I would like you to scrape away the layers of grime and ash that have caked on him to see if you can find an actual boy."

"Oh, dear me," she said more to herself than in response to Scrooge's request. "Yes, indeed it will take my strongest lye soap to do the job, I have no doubt. You leave it to me, Mr. Scrooge. I'll find the fellow who's lurking underneath."

"What?!" Chancy protested. "You want to bathe me-… naked?!"

Ignoring his concerns, Scrooge added, "And Mrs. Dilber, if his clothes can be cleaned, donate them to anyone who could make use of the scraps. If not, just burn them."

"Indeed I will, Mr. Scrooge. I'll have him looking presentable in no time."

With that, Scrooge took his leave after assuring Chancy he was being left in capable hands.

While heating water in her three large pots, Mrs. Dilber drug the copper tub over next to the stove and said, "Now, young fellow, take off those rags and pile them in the corner."

Chancy clinched his shirt to protect the buttons and shook his head, while slowly stepping backward.

Mrs. Dilber, who was not about to ask twice, approached him and said, "Now, see here, Master Chancy. I have a husband and two sons, all of whom are older than you. And you ain't got *nothing* I haven't seen a thousand times."

To speed the process, she began pulling layers of clothing off of him, including his shoes, which were filled with scraps of leather to keep the water away from his bare feet.

As instructed, he stood in the center of the tub, given it was not large enough for him to sit in. He shyly kept his hands cupped in front of him until Mrs. Dilber pulled them away to expose his last sense of privacy. With her bar soap in one hand and a scrub brush in the other, she scraped and burnished until she uncovered the body of what she guessed to be that of a seventeen-year-old boy.

"There you are, good as new!" she proclaimed.

After stepping away from the tub to dry himself with a towel that had been hanging to warm above the stove, Chancy watched as Mrs. Dilber pulled the bath toward the back door to dump the water outside.

"I ain't never seen wash water that black," she said after returning. "Now, let me look at you," scanning the boy from head to toe, who now stood before her with a towel wrapped around his waist.

Chancy remained as still as he could be, for fear she might choose to expose him to more humiliating tortures.

Mrs. Dilber stared at him as if he were a sculpture she was creating from a solid lump of clay, but was still not satisfied. "No," she finally said, "the hair."

With that said, she instructed Chancy to pull on his new trousers and kneel with his head over the tub. Once again, she threw herself into scrubbing and rinsing until she could at long last pull her fingers through his hair without getting them stuck in knots and tangles.

Then Mrs. Dilber sat him in a chair and relished the terrified look on his face at the sight of this portly woman holding her kitchen shears in one hand and a razor-sharp blade in the other. She proceeded to cut his scraggly beard as close to his face as she could, and then used the razor to scrape down to his bare skin. This was followed by numerous snips of his hair, in order to shape a nicely groomed appearance. With an expertly tied knot, she pulled his hair back into a ponytail to fully expose Chancy's previously unseen, charming facial features.

Finally, she paused and stepped back to enjoy her creation. "Stand up, please." This time, it brought a smile to her face to study the young man who showed little in common with his former self. "By heaven, Mr. Scrooge," she said, though he was not yet home, "you were right. There really *is* a handsome young fellow under all the grime. This *boy* you brought me is in truth, a young *man*."

The following morning, Scrooge came to work at his usual time, taking his place behind his usual desk beside Robert's, who was already intently writing. "Well, Mr. Cratchit, what do you think of my new friend?"

Robert stopped writing and began asking the questions that had provided him with a restless night's sleep. "Mr. Scrooge, as much as I appreciate your willingness to help a young man who is down on his luck, I must say I'm concerned you may be extending a helping hand, only to have it bit off. You just met Chancy yesterday, and today you give him free run of your house. After all, what do you know about this boy?"

"Bob, Chancy and I have an understanding. I will help lift him from poverty if he takes only what I have to offer. The moment he crosses me, I will send him back to the streets from whence he came. I am his benefactor, not his bank."

"But how did you find him? And what convinced you so quickly that he is worthy of your trust?"

"You'll probably laugh when I tell you. Yesterday, I was walking down Market Street when a group of boys ran past me. One passed so closely that he knocked me off my feet. When I gathered my senses, I looked up to see that one, and *only* one, of the boys, had returned to apologize and check on my well-being."

"Chancy?"

"Yes. We got to know each other better over lunch. That young man has no family and no home. He seems bright enough, but has had no formal education. I don't know how better to say it than-… it felt right."

Robert leaned back in his chair, somewhat relieved, and feeling a bit foolish for doubting Scrooge's instincts. "That's good enough for me, Mr. Scrooge."

"Besides, I seem to remember taking a chance on a young boy once before. That boy stole from me, and yet I kept him on. He turned out to be the best clerk-… no, the best *friend* a man could ever have."

Robert blushed at the compliment. "Is Chancy our new clerk?"

"Time will tell, Mr. Cratchit. Time will tell. But this much I know for certain. Chancy has not benefited from parents such as you or yours. If he is to become our clerk, we will need to begin with the basics. It will be for us to teach him to read and write. His math skills are nonexistent."

"I will talk to Emily when I get home, and if she's willing, he could go to my house for an hour or so each day. Emily, Martha, Peter, we could all teach our strengths, if he is willing to learn."

"An excellent suggestion, Mr. Cratchit! Chancy will certainly put our skills to the test."

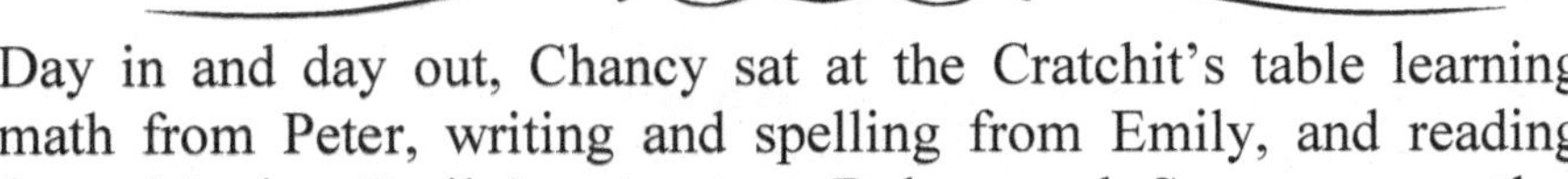

Day in and day out, Chancy sat at the Cratchit's table learning math from Peter, writing and spelling from Emily, and reading from Martha. Emily's report to Robert and Scrooge was that Chancy soaked up knowledge like a sponge absorbs water. "Never in all my days have I known a boy so eager and willing to learn. We can barely keep up with him."

Chancy's afternoons around the office of Scrooge and Cratchit were filled with chores, while evenings were in the company of Scrooge at his residence. In a matter of weeks, he had earned the trust and admiration of Scrooge, as well as discovering a family life with the Cratchits, the likes of which he had never known.

Chapter 4

"He's not breathing," Dr. Martin declared in his thick French accent, lifting the ether-laced cotton away from Tiny Tim's face.

"Should I stop?" Dr. Cecil asked of his operating partner, as he pulled a black string through Tim's abdominal surface layer.

"Keep working!" Dr. Martin focused all of his attention on the young patient lying on the table. The white linens beneath Tim's lifeless body were now blood-soaked on both sides of his torso. The six-inch cut across his abdomen, that minutes earlier had exposed his small intestines, was nearly closed. Dr. Cecil continued to add stitches, nearing the end of a demanding, uncertain surgery.

"Tim! Tim Cratchit!" Dr. Martin called loudly near the boy's ear, simultaneously giving several slaps to his pale cheek. Bending over him, he watched hopefully for a sign, *any* sign, of chest movement, while a bluish hue began crossing Tim's lips.

After finishing the final stitch, Dr. Cecil stared helplessly, as Dr. Martin frantically struggled to resuscitate the unresponsive child. Eventually, though, he stopped, and a numbing silence consumed the entire room. Surveying the corpse, covered with blood and reeking of alcohol, utterly motionless there before him, a wave of helplessness overtook Dr. Cecil. Frustrated by the prospect of facing the parents who waited for promising news just beyond the surgery doors, he slammed his fist on Tim's small chest in a fit of anger.

Dr. Martin, who had been standing over Tim, slowly sat back down on his stool next to the boy to reconcile the inevitable in his mind. "We lost him." He stared into the dead boy's face, then moved closer, inexplicably drawn in by Tim's innocence and tender features.

With a tone of defeat, Dr. Cecil muttered, "It's a shame, it is. And I think we should *both* talk to his parents. This lad fought a good fight, God bless 'im."

"You did everything perfectly, Jonathan. It was *me*. I must have administered too much ether."

In the midst of consoling one another, both men were startled when they heard a faint whimper. As soon as they stopped talking and looked over at the boy, they both witnessed a slight movement of his chest.

"He's breathing!" hollered Dr. Cecil.

Returning to the operating table and gently slapping Tim's cheek, Dr. Martin cried out, "Tim! My God, Tim! Can you hear me?"

After Tim acknowledged him with a weakened moan, the two surgeons looked at one another and spontaneously hugged in a jubilant embrace.

In a brightly lit room with six beds, three per side, where Robert sat on one side of the bed and Emily on the other, Robert leaned over his son and quietly asked, "Tim-... Tim, my boy, are you awake?"

Just as the bells from a nearby church tower announced the noon hour, Tim slowly opened his eyes, narrowly, through mere slits, to see his parents. "Father? Mother?"

"We're here, Tim," Emily replied.

"Where's Mary?"

Five days passed, as Tim embarked on the long and difficult road to recovery in the hospital ward. One spoon at a time, he consumed his mother's chicken broth. "No solid food for another week, Tim," Emily reminded him. "Doctor's orders, you know." Little did she mind though, as evidence in his bedpan convinced her the operation had indeed been a success. She cherished his slowly growing appetite and marveled at his resilience.

"You're getting stronger every day, my boy," Robert reassured Tim, squeezing his hand affectionately. "I declare, when you get back on solid food, you'll grow to be taller than *me* one day."

Tim smiled at his father, feeling too weak to say much, but turned to his mother as she said, "And I dare say I'm going to have to start cooking more food. The doctors told me you would be eating like a *horse* before long."

The boy grinned at his mother's encouragement, but when he saw the man approaching the foot of his bed, his eyes grew wider. In an excited, yet understandably croaky voice, he cheered, "Uncle Ebenezer!"

Scrooge smiled at the reference. "Oh, *Uncle* Ebenezer is it now, Master Timothy?"

"Do you want to see it, Uncle Ebenezer?" Without waiting for a response, Tim pulled his nightshirt up to expose a horizontal slit across his belly, sewn together with black thread, like two pieces of leather.

"My word!" Scrooge exclaimed. "I believe that is the biggest scar I have ever seen. Dare I say *no one in London* will be able to boast a larger one. Well done, Timothy. Well done, indeed!"

Tim smiled at the idea of impressing his new uncle with such a dramatic wound, before lowering his shirt. Over the course of the following week, he became a proud trophy on display, as Dr. Cecil escorted one colleague after another to his bedside to explain the medical significance of his remarkably successful operation.

Chapter 5

Within a week of being released from the hospital, Tim was able to sit up in bed and eat small bites of toast with butter. As time progressed, Robert and Emily were overjoyed to watch him consume an entire meal without vomiting. The doctor told them to keep him walking as much as possible, so brothers and sisters alike served as his "crutch," walking him around the home and out on the narrow Camden Town streets.

"Are you tired, Tim? Would you like to rest?" Robert asked as they walked side-by-side on a pleasant stroll one Sunday afternoon.

"Yes, Father, I *am* feeling tired and would very much like to sit down."

The two found a bench near the entrance of Regent's Park, and soon Tim began fidgeting. "Father, can I tell you about what happened to me?"

"Yes, certainly, my boy."

"When I was in the hospital, I left for a while."

"I don't know what you're trying to say. Left what, Tim, the hospital?"

"Yes, well, in a way. I saw the doctors operating on me. Dr. Martin was slapping me and calling my name."

"Oh, Tim. You probably heard him, but you were asleep. You couldn't have actually seen him."

"But I wasn't on the table. I saw the doctors from across the room. They were both worried because I was not breathing at all."

"You were obviously *dreaming*, son. The operation was very much on your mind when they put you to sleep and so you dreamt about it."

"And then I saw you, Father. I saw you and Mother in the next room."

"All part of the same dream, I'm quite sure."

Yet Tim persisted, trying to help his father understand, trying to make him believe. "Mother had her head on your shoulder. She said that if I died, she would never forgive herself."

Robert turned to see the sincerity in Tim's face, "How do you know that, Tim? Did your mother tell you she said that, because I know I never did and we were alone in the room, waiting for word from the doctor?"

Without answering his father's question, Tim continued, "It made me sad to hear that she would never forgive herself. Then I saw your prayer."

"You mean you saw me pray?"

"Yes, but I also saw your prayer. It was a colorful beam of light that went straight up from you. Sort of like the way you see a sunbeam coming through a window in the afternoon, your prayer went all the way up to heaven. And what you prayed was lovely, Father—you prayed that while we were apart, God would carry me on His shoulder, just as you had always done."

Robert sat speechless, unable to find the words that would explain away his son's dream. "How-… how do you know these things? That *was* my prayer, indeed, but it was a *silent* prayer, from me to God."

"I told you, Father, something happened to me during the operation."

Six weeks later, Tim was back on Dr. Cecil's surgery table for the operation on his foot, once again breathing through cotton soaked in ether. The procedure to sever the undeveloped tendon was minor in risk compared to the last, but according to the doctor, the recovery period would be much slower.

After the procedure was over and seeing Tim was safely awake, Robert left the hospital to go to Scrooge's office and let him know his son was doing fine, while Emily stayed at his bedside. Tim was groggy at first, and he passed in and out of sleep for several hours. Once he revived fully, the effects of the ether left him temporarily feeling nauseous. By that evening, however, he was sitting up in bed relishing a hearty meal. His foot was wrapped in bandages and throbbed horribly, but as Tim explained to Dr. Cecil when he came to check on him, "It hurts because it's growing longer."

After work, Robert returned to the hospital to stay with Tim overnight, while Emily went home to care for their other children. "Father, do you remember what I told you happened to me during my last operation?"

"I do, Tim. I think about it a lot, but I don't understand how it can be true."

"You don't believe me?"

"I don't know what to believe, my boy. With all my heart, I believe you would not make up such a story, but what you said was so fantastic, I don't know how-..."

"There's more, Father," Tim said, interrupting him. "There's so much more to tell you. When you prayed for me, I looked up to follow your prayer. I mean, the ceiling opened up, and I saw the sky. And then through an enormously beautiful light, I could see into Heaven."

Robert leaned forward and sharply protested. "Tim, you must stop this!" Looking side-to-side to make certain no one was listening, he lowered his voice. "If people hear you talk such nonsense, they will denounce you and accuse you of heresy."

Tim's eyes filled with tears. "But Heaven is not evil."

That night in the hospital, the pain Tim experienced in his foot was minor in comparison to the pain he felt in his heart.

One week after his foot operation, Tim was back in Dr. Cecil's office to be fitted for a child-sized leg brace. "Now, Tim," Dr.

Cecil began, "I'm not going to lie to you. This is going to be painful. Every week, just as you think it's feeling better, your parents are going to turn these screws tighter, in order to straighten your foot, and it will hurt all over again. Do you understand?"

"Yes sir, I do. But please don't worry. It won't hurt too much."

Doctor Cecil smiled and said, "I wish my grown-up patients were as brave as you."

Turning his attention to Emily, who sat in a chair next to Tim, he gave her further instruction, while pointing to different regions of the elaborate metal brace. "Mrs. Cratchit, once a week Mr. Cratchit will need to turn these two screws one half a turn, and *this* one a quarter of a turn. I ask that Mr. Cratchit make these adjustments so you can comfort your son through the process. If you notice any infection or smell any unpleasant odors, please come see me at once."

"I understand, Doctor," she replied while holding her young son's hand.

"All is well, Mother," Tim said, as though she was more in need of comfort than he. "I'm quite certain I will not die this time."

"Oh *my*, Tim. What would make you say such a thing?"

"What do you mean by that, Tim?" Dr. Cecil asked.

"When you first operated on me, I died during the operation."

"Tim!" Emily interrupted. "I'm sorry, Doctor. He has been making some outrageous claims since that first time we brought him home from the hospital. I *do* hope he hasn't offended you with his-…"

"It's quite alright, Mrs. Cratchit. Go on, Tim. What else do you remember?"

Tim looked at his mother, then back to the doctor, pleased that the doctor was willing to listen to him. "I stood near the door watching you and Dr. Martin. You were standing next to the table where I was lying, pulling black thread through my stomach, but Dr. Martin was upset with me. He kept calling my name. I tried telling him I was here, but he couldn't hear me. Then I saw my parents in the next room, holding hands. I could hear my father's prayer, even though it was silent. And then the ceiling opened up, and I found myself next to a woman—a very pretty woman. We talked for a while, but she eventually told me it was time to go back. That was when I felt something hit my chest, and she was gone."

Dr. Cecil sat back in his chair and said, "Tim, some people have very vivid dreams during an operation such as yours. I believe it is your brain's way of suppressing the pain your body is experiencing. Try not to dwell on the dream or make any false claims because of it. The operation is over, and you're going to be fine."

Tim looked down, disappointed once again that he was not believed.

"Would you please wait in the hallway, Tim, so I can talk to your mother privately?"

Tim winced as he walked with his crutch, each step as painful as the one before, and listened to the clanking sounds his new leg brace made while he searched for a bench near the doctor's office door.

In the privacy of his office, Dr. Cecil said, "Mrs. Cratchit, it is your and your husband's decision how you handle Tim's memories of the operation. We are treading on new territory, and I don't want to pretend that I know all of the answers to the mysteries of this world, or the next. But I feel compelled to tell you something I should have told you and Mr. Cratchit earlier. During the abdominal operation, Tim stopped breathing."

Emily gasped and cupped her hand over her mouth.

"Actually, Mrs. Cratchit, his heart stopped, and his color changed to a very pale blue. In my opinion, Tim did, indeed, die. He was correct when he described the situation. Dr. Martin was calling his name and slapping his face. After several minutes, we had all but given up on ever seeing him breathe again. I was angry, mostly with myself, and in my exasperation, I slammed my fist against his chest. Moments later, as we prepared to bring you and your husband the difficult news, he started breathing again. I checked, and Tim's heart that *had* been silent was once again beating."

"Dr. Cecil, are you saying Tim's dreams were real?"

"No, Mrs. Cratchit. I'm saying Tim died as he claims, but-… beyond that, I'll just say medicine cannot resolve a theology issue. Have you noticed any other changes in him?"

"Well, Doctor. I didn't want to say anything before, but he seems different to us somehow."

"How so?"

"It's hard to put my finger on it really. Timmy's mood changes are greater. When he's happy, he's *very* happy. But when he's sad, he's *very* sad. It concerned me when I overheard him telling his brothers that he has no fear of dying, almost as if he *welcomed* it. Yet somehow, he seems wiser than his years. Sometimes, it's as if he can see my very soul."

"That's a fascinating analysis. There *is* one more thing I should tell you, Mrs. Cratchit."

"Yes, what is it?"

Dr. Cecil walked from behind his desk to sit in the chair next to Emily while searching for the right words. After releasing a deep breath, he said, "I convey this to you so you and your husband can prepare yourselves. Tim's heart is not strong."

"But he will live, won't he?" she asked nervously.

"He will live, but I don't know for how long. Please don't let him over exert himself. It could happen tomorrow, or it may happen ten years from now. We have no way of knowing when, but eventually, his heart will give out."

Chapter 6

The office door swung open, and Robert was delighted to see his wife stepping inside. "Emily, my love. What brings you?"

Scrooge, too, chimed in his gladness, especially seeing the basket in her hands. "Mrs. Cratchit, what a pleasant surprise!"

Opening the basket before them, she laid some fresh mincemeat tarts on a nearby table. "It was such a lovely day, I just decided I had to bring my two favorite gentlemen some of my best tarts, fresh from the oven."

"Very kind of you, my dear," Robert said, standing up and kissing her on the cheek.

"Yes, indeed," added Scrooge. "I dare say you spoil us with kindness. Won't you stay and join us?"

"No, not today, I'm afraid. I have other matters to attend." As Emily stepped toward the door, she stopped and turned, "There is just one more thing I nearly forgot to mention."

Before enjoying the first bite, both men set their tarts down and gave her their full attention.

"Mr. Scrooge, do you remember a number of months back, around Christmas time, I believe it was. You came to dinner at our home and nearly sent me into shock. Do you remember that, sir?"

Scrooge smiled timidly, seeming somewhat confused. "Yes, I remember."

Robert, just as perplexed, asked, "Emily, what-…?"

She raised her hand toward Robert to silence him before continuing. "As I recall, you waited outside my door so that you could make your rather dramatic entrance, isn't that right?"

Scrooge nodded warily.

"Well, sir, I am not without surprises myself, you know."

Emily opened the door and took the hand of a woman standing just outside to lead her in. As the woman raised her head, she smiled and said, "Good afternoon, Mr. Scrooge."

Robert recognized the midwife who had delivered all of his children, but Scrooge saw only his former fiancée, from whom he had walked away so many years before.

"Belle," he whispered, as his face flushed with anticipation. Approaching her slowly and cautiously, Scrooge reached for her hand, leaning forward to kiss the top of it in a most gentlemanly fashion. Her hair had changed to a grayish silver hue, and the skin on her face had wrinkled some, but in the deep blue stillness of her eyes, he could only see the delicate young beauty he'd once treasured.

"Get on, out with you two!" Emily urged, smiling as she walked the couple through the door and into an open carriage, which was waiting just outside with a horse and driver to take them on a private ride through the streets of London. "You two have a lot of catching up to do, and I don't have all day to stand around here and chaperone you."

As the couple climbed aboard the carriage and the driver beckoned the horse to walk, Emily returned to the office to answer the inevitable stream of questions from her husband.

"There, I got them together at last. The rest is in God's hands, now."

"Emily, what just happened here?"

"It's a long story with what I hope will be a happy ending. Back when I was in labor with Tim, Belle was talking to me between contractions and just asked me, matter-of-factly, what *you* do for a living. When I told her you worked for Scrooge and Marley, she turned pale and asked if that would be Mr. Ebenezer Scrooge. I said, 'Why, yes it is. Do you know him?' Then she said, 'I should say I do. We were engaged to be married once.'"

"I tell you, Robert, I nearly shot poor Timmy out across the room when she told me that. I said to her, at the time, I despised the man. She said she didn't hate him, but she *did* pity him. Apparently, when Scrooge was a young boy, he was very much as he is *today*: kind, benevolent, even joyful. Belle explained to me that he slowly began turning cold toward her and the world, as he warmed to money and greed. The more he earned, the more he wanted until eventually there was no room left in his heart for her."

Robert sat quietly, slowly processing Emily's tale. "Mr. Scrooge was engaged-… to a woman as sweet and kind as Belle?"

"Unbelievable, is it not? So, after Mr. Scrooge's startling conversion last Christmas, for what reason I suppose we'll never know, I remembered what Belle had told me about him. And then I began thinking lately, how could I ever begin to repay the sort of generosity and endearing affection he has given us with Tim's operations? The only gift that could reward such love is love itself."

"So you went to see Belle."

"Yes, I went to see her this morning. At first, she wanted no part of it, but when I told her the sort of man Mr. Ebenezer Scrooge had been these last months, she agreed to meet him, *if* he was willing."

"But Emily, how did you know he would be willing to meet her after all this time? Certainly, you couldn't know whether or not there is bad blood between them. I dare say you took a big risk surprising him this way."

Emily approached her husband with a grin and put both hands around his neck. "Mr. Cratchit, you may know many things about business and finances and such, but I know a thing or two about romance-… and I *know* when a man needs a woman in his life."

Leaning in toward her, Robert kissed Emily and yielded to her better instincts. Shaking his head with a laugh, he settled back down behind his desk and asked, "How was Tim's appointment with Dr. Cecil? Did he get his leg brace?"

"He did, indeed. The doctor is pleased with the way the incision on his foot is healing, and he showed me how you and I need to adjust the brace every week, but-…"

"But what, my dear?"

Emily's eyes became glassy as tears began to swell. "The doctor pulled me aside to say he is concerned about Timmy's heart. He made a point to warn us there may come a day when his heart simply stops beating."

"Oh my! After everything our Tiny Tim has been through, we could *still* lose him? Did he think this would happen sooner rather than later?"

"He has no way to know. We should keep a close eye on him and pray wholeheartedly."

"And pray we shall. We shall indeed."

Silence filled the room as Robert contemplated the gravity of the doctor's warning. "Was anything else said?"

"Well, Tim started talking about his dreams again, only this time in front of the doctor."

"Oh dear, oh dear. I was hoping he would have put those ideas aside by now."

"Let's talk with Tim tonight when you come home. And one more thing. Have you noticed Martha acting peculiarly of late?"

"No, I can't say I have. For that matter, I don't think I've seen much of Martha in these past few weeks. Why, Em? Is something amiss?"

Emily frowned and replied, "Nothing I can put my finger on. Just my intuition acting up, I suppose. Probably just growing pains. Now, eat your lunch, Robert. I need to get home to start dinner."

With one more kiss, Emily turned to leave for home, concerned about her family, yet pleased with the results of her escapade with Belle and Scrooge.

At noon the following day, Scrooge returned to work in an even better mood than when he'd left. "Good af-ter-noon, Bob," he said in what bordered on a singing voice.

"Good afternoon to *you*, Mr. Scrooge. I trust you have some interesting tales to tell."

"Indeed I do, sir! To begin with, I owe that lovely wife of yours a big bouquet of flowers and my undying gratitude. I trust she told you Belle and I were engaged, once."

"Yes sir, I seem to remember her mentioning it." Robert couldn't help but smile in the presence of such radiant happiness on his business partner's face.

"Brilliant! Well, Belle and I talked all day and into the evening hours. A remarkable woman, I must say. Did you know she runs a home for women? I did not realize until she explained to me just how many women suffer from abuse or neglect. Without her, many of these women would not survive."

"No, sir. I mean, no sir, I did *not* know she operated a home. I have known her for years as a midwife. She was present at the birth of all of our children. If she had not been the extraordinary midwife she was at my son Peter's birth, he would not be here today. I'm certain of that."

"I tell you, Bob, I could scarcely sleep last night. I believe Belle and the work she does for women and children is a blessing to all humanity. I was a fool for leaving such a gentle creature when I last knew her. I am determined to use my resources to champion her cause and ease her many burdens."

"Burdens, sir?"

"Yes, Bob. It's time I start *giving* instead of *taking*. Long past time, really. This must be the reason I knew Belle once, and certainly the reason she has come back into my life-… thanks to your good wife."

Chapter 7

That evening, Robert inspected the mechanical brace that began below Tim's knee and ended beneath his heel, while Emily showed him the screws that would need weekly adjustments to slowly straighten their son's foot.

"Robert, I think we should discuss what happened during Tim's operation," Emily said, looking into Tim's eyes to reassure him of her concern.

Robert gently lowered Tim's leg and brace, so the three could gather comfortably around the table. "Tim, my boy, your mother told me about the fantastic dream you described to Dr. Cecil this morning. She also suggests we should listen to your story. So please, tell us what you remember from that day."

"I remember everything, Father, as though it was this morning when it happened."

"Go ahead, Tim. I'm listening."

"As am I, Timmy," Emily added. "Please, tell us everything you can. We aren't here to judge you."

"Like I told you before, I saw the doctors, I saw me on the table, and I saw both of you in a different room."

"He *did* describe a prayer to me, Em, exactly as I had prayed during the operation."

Tim continued, "What I *haven't* told you before now is that I entered Heaven. And I know it was Heaven because it's a place so wonderful I can't *begin* to describe it. There simply aren't words to explain, so *please* believe me when I say it is beauty beyond beautiful!

"Anyway, I was greeted there by a young woman who touched me deeply with her presence. But she told me I could not stay in Heaven, because I still have an important job to do on Earth."

"What did she look like?" Emily asked. "Have you seen her before?"

"No, never, but she was very pretty. She wore a shimmering white robe that seemed to float as if we were underwater. It wasn't a robe like any I have ever known."

"Was it silk?"

Tim thought for a moment and then said, "It glowed."

"You mean like the flame of a candle?"

Again, Tim hesitated to find the words. "The best explanation I have is it seemed to be formed from strands of light."

"What was her name?" Robert asked.

"Her name was Mary. She too had lived a life on Earth. We took a walk together through a meadow that was filled with thousands of colors I have never seen before. *Everything* was alive: the plants, the rocks, even a stream of water. And music was everywhere! Even the blades of grass were singing. What I remember most, though, is I felt so much love while I was there."

Looking from one parent to another, Tim said, "Mother, Father, please forgive me for this, but when Mary told me I had to go back to my life here on Earth, I begged her to let me stay. At that moment, I wanted to be with her more than anywhere else. There was no pain or sorrow where we were, nothing like that at all. But when she showed me how sad you would both be if I didn't return, I agreed."

Barely able to know what to say to her son, Emily asked, "Did she tell you what job you had to do still?"

"She did. She told me there is a battle growing over the fate of Christmas, and that it will be an incredible challenge to save it. But if Christmas is lost, she said, it will be the beginning of the end, and Heaven is very concerned."

"How can Christmas be lost?" Robert asked.

"I don't know, Father. She did not ask *me* to save Christmas, but to find the man who could. She told me to find the one who was her brother and that he would help me. I will know him when I see him, but I don't know his name or where he lives."

"But Tim," his father said, "it doesn't make sense. Why would she tell you to find her brother, but then leave out such an important detail as his name?"

Tim let out a big sigh, somewhat frustrated with his limitations at being able to describe his heavenly encounter. "When I say Mary *told* me something, I don't mean she talked to me like you and I are now. 'Talking' in Heaven is more like sharing a feeling or clear memory. She *showed* him to me by letting me see him through her eyes, as she took her last breaths on Earth. And I could feel the love between them, as well as the fear she felt while dying. I know he was her brother because she called him that as she lay in his arms, but she never spoke his name. I remember her name was Mary because, in that experience, he said her name over and over."

"So she showed you the man who was her brother?" Robert said.

"I *experienced* the man, Father. Through Mary, I met his soul. She showed me that the journey to finding her brother would reveal the true meaning of Christmas for us *all*. I don't know his name or where he lives, but when I find him, I will *know* him."

"Robert," Emily said, "I have not told you or Tim this, but today in the doctor's office after Tim shared some of this with Dr. Cecil, I spoke privately with the doctor. He explained to me that near the end of Tim's operation, he stopped breathing and his heart stopped beating. He said Tim was, by all reckoning, dead to the world. But several minutes later, his heart was beating once more, and Tim woke up."

"But how can that be?" Robert asked, astonished by Emily's revelation. "People don't wake up after they're dead. There must be some other explanation."

"Timmy," his mother asked, "do you remember when you first woke in your hospital bed, and we were by your side, you asked us if Mary was there? Do you remember that?"

"Did I? I don't recall." After a few moments, he asked, "Father, do you believe in spirits? Do you believe our souls will travel to Heaven after we die?"

Robert looked at his son, then to Emily and back to Tim, all the while tapping his finger on the table. "I do, Tim. I-… um, I never told anyone, not even you Emily, for fear of upsetting you."

"What, Robert? What is it?"

"You remember Jacob Marley, Scrooge's old business partner. After he died, more than seven years ago, his spirit found me and stayed by my side. He talked to me, and I to him. His presence was of a warm nature, though, as he continued challenging me to perform good deeds to help him redeem his past transgressions. It lasted up until this past Christmas when he told me he was finally ready to move on."

Tim was not shocked by his father's admission but suddenly felt vindicated for his own recent experience. "So you believe me then, Father?"

"Yes, I suppose I do, Tim, though I dare say your story sounds as unbelievable as my own."

Looking at his wife, he begged her pardon, "Please forgive me, Emily. I held my secret close to spare you from ridicule."

"I must say," Emily replied, "I never knew ours was such a *supernatural* family. I don't know if I should run screaming for my life or praise the days you were both born."

"One more thing, Father."

"What's that?"

"To this day, I do not understand the reason, but Mary showed me a vision of her brother and Uncle Ebenezer standing next to one another, as though they are connected in some way. I believe Uncle Ebenezer holds within him a key to help unlock this mystery of how to save Christmas."

"Uncle Ebenezer!" Tim called out, as he entered the office of Scrooge and Cratchit.

"Timothy, my boy!" Scrooge replied with equal enthusiasm. "Come, let me take a look at your leg brace."

Tim lifted his leg and rested it on a chair next to where Scrooge sat, while still balancing on his crutch.

"I'm happy to report," Robert said, "Tim is walking better every day, Mr. Scrooge, thanks to you."

"And eating like a horse, right, Father?"

"Yes, like a horse in the greenest of pastures, my boy."

"And to what do we owe the honor of this most special visit?" Scrooge inquired.

"I have another favor to ask of you, Uncle."

"Name it, Timothy."

"I'm looking for a man who I have never met, and I don't know his name."

Scrooge chuckled. "That should be easy, then. London is *filled* with men you've never met."

"But I know what this man looks like, and no other man in London shares his face."

"And why are you seeking this man who has a face and no name?"

"Perhaps, Tim, you should tell Mr. Scrooge your story from the beginning."

Tim looked at his father, who nodded reassuringly. "I will explain why I need your help, Uncle, but first I must ask you something rather personal."

"Ask me what you wish, and I will do my best to answer."

"This past Christmas, did you encounter a spirit, one not of this world?"

Scrooge froze when he heard Tim's question. He had told no one of his ghostly encounters from that night. "How did you-…"

"Was it more than one spirit?"

"Tim, I've told no one about-… How do you know this?"

Hearing the conversation between Scrooge and his son came as a shock to Robert, as well, but he respectfully listened without interjecting at that moment. Tim proceeded to share with his "uncle" the heavenly experience he'd had during the operation. At one point, Robert confirmed Tim's brief death, as Emily had explained it, per Doctor Cecil.

But Tim surprised his father by adding information *beyond* the revelations he'd shared with his parents the previous night. "Mary told me three spirits visited you, Uncle Ebenezer, and that those spirits were ghosts of Christmas, who lit the candle in your heart that had long ago been snuffed out. She said Heaven rejoiced in your change."

Scrooge looked at Robert, then nodded hesitantly before replying, "Yes, Timothy, I can confirm what Mary told you, though I must say I haven't the faintest idea who Mary *was*, or who her brother *is*. What I can tell you is this: on Christmas Eve, I *was* visited by the spirit of my old business partner, Jacob Marley. He came to warn me to change my ways or risk suffering a horrible fate, one such as his. To convince me, his plea was followed up by what I came to find out were three ghosts of Christmas. Each in their own turn and in their own way showed me how my life had affected the lives of those around me."

"Ah, the ripples," Robert said.

"Yes, the ripples I created of my own free will were devastating and heart-wrenching to witness, to say the least. From that moment forward, I have sworn to live every minute a changed man."

"Mr. Scrooge," Robert interjected, "On this past Christmas morning, we received a large turkey from an anonymous donor. By any chance, was that you, sir?"

Scrooge grinned and winked at Robert, "He would not be an anonymous donor if you knew his name, Bob."

"Between Mr. Marley's death and this last Christmas," Robert added, "I too was visited by Marley's ghost. So it seems we all have surreal experiences to share."

Scrooge stared at Robert. "You knew Marley's spirit, as well?"

"Indeed, sir. To me, he was neither frightening nor threatening. Looking back now, it was a very comforting encounter."

"One day, I would like to hear more, Bob." Returning his attention to Tim, he asked, "But Timothy, you say Mary told you a battle for Christmas is looming. What has this to do with me?"

"Mary showed me two men who are kindred spirits, standing next to one another. One of the men was you, Uncle Ebenezer. The other I do not yet know, who was her brother."

"If I may," Robert said, "from what you just explained, Mr. Scrooge, I can only imagine she is telling us that Christmas saved you-… and now you must help save Christmas."

"But how, Timothy? How can I save Christmas when I am not privy to the situation?"

"Mary couldn't reveal his identity to me directly. I believe it's the journey to finding him that will answer our questions."

Robert said, "My father explained apparitions to me once, when I was just a child who was frightened by shadows and sounds. According to what he'd said, the Christmas ghosts and Jacob Marley's ghost were spirit guides who help us navigate this life. They're earthbound souls concerned with earthly matters. Tim's Mary is not of this world, at least not anymore. She's a heavenly messenger concerned with Heaven's desires, and she planted a seed in Tim while he was with her. But she hasn't the power to intervene after he returned to this life."

Scrooge nodded and asked Tim, "Did she leave you with any clues that would help you find him?"

"Her brother loves to talk to the animals, exotic animals in particular. She showed me a memory of hers, in which her brother was echoing the sounds of monkeys."

"That could be anyone, anywhere," Scrooge laughed. "A man talking to a dog, a horse, even a bird."

"What about a zoo?" Robert suggested.

"Certainly a zoo or even a circus," said Scrooge. "But where? Zoo or stable, the world is filled with animals, both wild and tame."

"I don't think she would ask the impossible of Tim," Robert said. "No, she sought Tim because he will find her brother nearby." After a moment of thought, he lit up. "The largest variety of animals near us is at the zoo in Regent's Park. *That* is where I would start searching, Tim."

Reverend Potts seemed determined to sacrifice the entire Cratchit family as a means to bring the other parishioners in line with what he *knew* he needed: the entire congregation's allegiance and obedience. "It has come to my attention," he declared from the pulpit the following Sunday morning, "that some sheep have *strayed* from the flock. A family in our midst has succumbed to the temptation and false promises of Lucifer himself. I speak of a family who we all once loved, embraced and held in the highest regard. But this is a family who has only recently fallen from grace. My brothers and sisters, in the third row of this most sacred sanctuary, sits a family who has lost their faith and eaten the fruit of temptation."

Emily grabbed Robert's arm, as she felt the eyes of everyone seated behind them focused on her.

"When you are sick, when you are heavy laden, when you are cold or hunger or thirst, turn to the Lord, *thy God! He* will heal you. *He* will give you rest. *He* will give you shelter and food and clean water." Pointing now directly to the Cratchits, he said, "Yet sadly, the family Cratchit has turned away from God and run into the arms of a medicine man who works as the devil's faithful servant. This so-called 'doctor' cut open the belly of the youngest Cratchit and held the boy's guts in his hands, while his heart was still beating. Brothers and sisters, this man of medicine, this servant of Satan, beheld a realm of God's Kingdom that only God Himself should see."

"Mr. and Mrs. Cratchit, will you stand before this congregation and denounce your wicked ways? Will you confess your sin of turning from God to worship of the Devil's handiwork?"

The congregation was silent in anticipation of Robert's reaction to the reverend's accusations. Slowly Robert stood and turned to face the majority of the audience seated beside and behind him, while Emily reached to steady his trembling hand. "I-... *we* have done nothing wrong. Medical science has-..."

"Science!" Reverend Potts forcefully interrupted him with a thunderous scream. "You heard him with your own ears! You see him with your own eyes! He chooses *science* and *medical trickery* over our beloved faith! Now, do you see what becomes of a man who practices paganism, singing and dancing in the name of *Christmas*? Behold the man who has condemned himself and his entire family to burn in the depths of Hell!"

"Not true," a young voice cried out in protest. Robert turned to see Tiny Tim stand from his seat next to his sister Belinda, addressing the reverend directly.

"Tim, no," Emily whispered, but her plea was ignored.

"My father is a great man who will one day go to Heaven, just as I have been to Heaven."

The congregation suddenly broke its silence with a collective gasp. In every pew throughout the church, members began whispering with one another in hushed tones about the inconceivable nature of Tim's outlandish claim.

In an uncharacteristically subdued tone, Reverend Potts leaned as far over the podium as he could to look directly down to Tim and asked, "Boy, are you telling us that you have been to Heaven? You do realize that the only way to get to Heaven is to first die, don't you?"

"Yes, Reverend, I died and went to Heaven. Then I was brought back to life."

Reverend Potts slowly erected himself and took the deepest breath he could hold before pointing his long, boney finger toward the young boy and shouting, "Blasphemy! All of you heard him, as did I! This young Cratchit claims to have entered the Kingdom of Heaven! How *dare* he utter such claims in this, the Lord's house!? Does anyone here presume to offer their defense on behalf of these apostles of Satan?"

The congregation sat motionless, afraid to side with the Cratchits for fear of suffering the same ridicule. "Cratchits," Reverend Potts said with a rather guttural sound to his voice as if every letter of the name left a bitter taste in his mouth. "Arise and do now leave this congregation."

All seven Cratchits stood and walked to the center aisle, turned away from the pulpit and walked past their neighbors and friends. "Know that you are hereby excommunicated from this church!" Reverend Potts shouted as they approached the outer door. "You will never again darken these doors until you are willing to stand before us to confess your sins and denounce your wicked ways!"

The Cratchits walked out of the church in silence and remained quiet while leaving, each stunned by the morning's event. When they entered Regent's Park, Robert sat on a bench along the walkway, followed by Emily who sat at his side.

Martha eventually spoke up, asking, "Father, what does this mean?"

Robert turned his glassy-eyed stare to look at his eldest. "I don't know, my dear. I suppose we will find a new church. One that will be more welcoming."

"But where, Father?" Peter asked.

"Don't worry, my boy. We will find a church or a church will find us. Of this, I am quite certain."

With a defeated tone, Richard asked, "Are we evil, like Reverend Potts said?"

Emily quickly responded, "Oh, dear me no, Richard! Please remember, children, Reverend Potts is a man like any other man. He is entitled to his beliefs, just as we are entitled to agree or disagree, for that matter."

"This is all my fault, isn't it, Mother?" Tim asked.

Robert swiftly exonerated his son, saying, "No, Tim, not at all."

"But if I hadn't had an operation, we would still have a church."

"Oh, dear," Robert said, "if you hadn't had an operation, none of us would still have our Tiny Tim. Reverend Potts couldn't be more wrong about this. We all must understand that God used Dr. Cecil as His instrument to save a life worth saving. We couldn't be happier with the outcome, Tim. We didn't turn away from God to save you. We ran *toward* Him."

Tim's father leaned over and hugged his son, rubbing his hair playfully.

"Robert-... children," Emily said, a pleasant smile coming over her face. "I believe I have found our new church."

"Where, Mother?" Martha asked.

"We are already in it. Remember from the book of Matthew: *For where two or more are gathered together in My name, there am I in the midst of them*. I say, every Sunday we gather at this very park, at this very bench or one like it. Then, each Sunday, one of us will choose Bible verses to read, and we will all reflect upon and discuss their meaning in our lives."

"What a splendid idea," Robert said. "Our church is not a building where people go to be judged, like what happened today. Our church is wherever and whenever we gather to worship. And if it is cold or rainy, our home will serve nicely."

"Oh yes, Father!" Belinda gleefully agreed. "And we'll call it the First Cratchit Church of Camden Town."

"The First Cratchit Church of Camden Town. Say, I like the way that sounds," Robert said while opening his Bible. "And for this first service at First Cratchit, I present you with this. Please sit, children. Gather around. As your mother has already taken us to the Book of Matthew, so shall I read to you from Matthew seven, verses one through five."

"Judge not, that ye not be judged. For with what judgment ye judge, ye shall be judged: and with what measure ye mete, it shall be measured to you again. And why beholdest thou the speck in thy brother's eye, but considerest not the beam that is in thine own eye? Or how wilt thou say to thy brother, 'Let me pull out the speck out of thine eye,' and behold, a beam is in thine own eye? Thou hypocrite, first cast out the beam out of thine own eye; and then shalt thou see clearly to cast out the speck out of thy brother's eye."

As Robert closed his Bible, Emily asked, "So, my children, is it possible we were judged by a man who could not see clearly that it was God who worked through Mr. Scrooge, Dr. Cecil, Dr. Martin and all of the wonderful people who worked so selflessly to save our Tim?"

"Yes, indeed!" came the response from the entire congregation of The First Cratchit Church of Camden Town, all seated in the grass in Regent's Park on a sunny Sunday morning.

Chapter 8

Tim quickly became a standard fixture in the Regent's Park Zoological Gardens. Where most visitors watched the animals, Tim instead watched the visitors. Though he studied the faces of hundreds, if not thousands of people in and around the park on a daily basis, none appeared to be the man for whom he searched.

"I see you here quite often, do I not?" an older man said, approaching the young boy from behind.

Tim turned to see the stranger was bearded and wore dirty, tattered coveralls. His hair was red and curly with silver streaks, as was his beard. But to Tim, his most noticeable characteristic was his heavy Irish accent.

"Yes, sir, I come here almost every day, weather permitting."

"I'm Nathaniel Cook, but everyone calls me Cookie, at least around these parts." With that, he stuck his hand out to shake Tim's.

The boy reached out, shook his outstretched hand and replied, "My name is Timothy Cratchit, but everyone calls me Tiny Tim because I'm so small."

"Well, Tiny Tim Cratchit, since you appear to have made this place your second home, how would you like to work for me mucking pens and cages?"

"Are you joshing me, sir?"

"Not at all. It's my job to keep the cages and pens clean. I regularly take on young boys such as you to help out around here, if they're so inclined. You'd start out earning a penny an hour. You could earn half a shilling a day or more as my new mucker, if you put your back into it, as it were."

"Yes sir, Mr. Cookie, I would like that very much. I can't run very fast because of my leg, but I'm getting stronger every day."

Cookie chuckled and said, "Stay out of the lion's den, and maybe you won't have to run very often! Your chores will be cleaning cages and mucking stalls. I pay you when you work, however many hours you put in is up to you. It's as simple as that. Makes no difference to me if you work one day a week or seven. I keep five or six boys such as you on the payroll, so there's always someone working."

That evening, Tim was ecstatic when he explained his first job to his parents. "And the best part is, I'll be able to look for Mary's brother all the while!"

Emily spoke openly to Robert, "This sounds like dangerous work to me. Don't you think it's too soon after the operations for him to take on such a strenuous job?"

"Not at all, Em. I believe hard work and fresh air are the best resources for a growing body."

Pleased to hear his father's approval, Tim asked, "Father, is mucking honorable work?"

Robert took both of Tim's hands in his and said, "Son, it doesn't matter how you choose to serve, as long as it is honest work. What matters is that you do your best and stay faithful to your employer. Later in his life, my father worked in a stable for a blacksmith, and I couldn't have been more proud of him or to be his son. So yes, my boy, caring and cleaning for God's creatures is an honorable position, and I say you will be the best mucker the zoo has ever known."

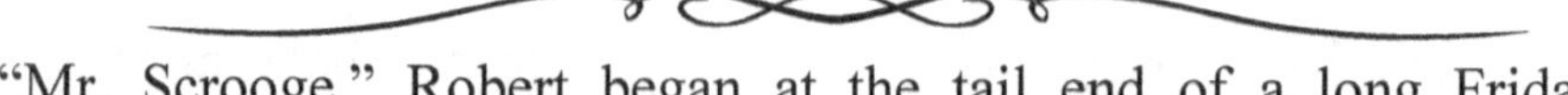

"Mr. Scrooge," Robert began at the tail end of a long Friday afternoon, "this Sunday, I plan to take my family on a picnic outing, and we would be honored if you and Chancy would join us."

"Oh, Bob, I'm too old to be doing such things! Besides, that should be a day for your *family* to enjoy together."

"But Mr. Scrooge, we are *your* family now, as well as you are *ours*. Please, sir, it would mean the world to Emily and the children if you and Chancy would join us. I've already arranged to rent a horse and cart. We'll ride out of the city until we find the perfect spot to enjoy the day. Besides, Belle has also agreed to join us, and after Tim's operations, I *did* promise him a day of fishing."

"Belle? Well, I suppose a day in the countryside *would* do me good." After a moment of looking out the window to the same street he'd watched every day for decades, Scrooge heartily agreed. "Why not? Chancy and I accept your offer, Bob, *if* you will allow me to bring some freshly baked bread and a bottle of wine."

"Splendid, Mr. Scrooge! I know I speak for all the Cratchits in welcoming your delightful company."

At precisely ten o'clock that Sunday morning, Robert stopped in front of Scrooge's house with a horse and cart, which was bedded down with straw and all five Cratchit children in the back. Emily climbed down from her seat on the bench next to Belle and Robert to greet Scrooge and Chancy, as they walked from his porch to the street carrying a sack of bread from their neighborhood bakery and a jug of gooseberry wine.

"Good morning, Mr. Scrooge. Good morning, Chancy," Emily sang out, leaning forward to hug her husband's business partner, who seemed dressed more appropriately for a board meeting than a casual outing. "Here, let me take those for you," she offered, before setting what he'd brought next to her bags of prepared food.

"Now," she said, "you just climb right up there on the bench to sit next to Belle."

"But where will you sit, my dear?"

"Don't you worry about me, Mr. Scrooge. Chancy and I will be perfectly content back here with the children, I assure you. I have been looking forward to a hayride all week!"

Chancy held one of Emily's hands, as Peter helped her up to the wagon, where she found a spot along the side rail to ride comfortably.

As the horse meandered through the London streets, Scrooge found himself relaxing with the rhythmic movement of the cart. By the time they left the city, clean country air filled their lungs, and the Cratchits sang songs to pass the time. Before long, every Cratchit realized what Scrooge had hidden for years from those who knew him: Ebenezer Scrooge had a genuinely melodious singing voice.

As the road turned from stone to dirt, they saw fewer and fewer travelers pass by. When the dirt road became two parallel ruts for the cart's wheels, they knew they were nearing their destination. Finally, Robert pulled the horse and wagon off the narrow path and under a majestic maple tree so the horse would be resting in the cool shade. Standing up from his seat on the bench, he looked around. "We're here, I think, wherever *here* is."

Through the trees, they all spied a nearby stream, and in the opposite direction, an open meadow surrounded by black poplars and crack willows.

"Yes, this will do nicely," Emily agreed, stepping down from the cart and brushing the straw from her dress.

Peter and Chancy jumped down next, to help the children who followed. When it came time for Tim to come down, Peter lifted him from the back of the cart and eased him to the ground, "There you go, Tim."

At the same time, Chancy positioned himself to help Martha. When he bowed at the waist and lifted his hand for her to hold as she stepped down, Martha blushed at the attention.

Meanwhile, Robert unhitched the horse from the cart and led her to the stream for a drink. After she'd had her fill, he took her to the nearby meadow, where she could graze. Fortunately, the tree line around the pasture and the thick foliage between the trees served as a natural fence, making it unnecessary to tie her.

Scrooge walked with Belle and Emily to a shady spot beneath a willow tree near the center of the meadow. There, the three spread two quilts, sat themselves down and commenced to relaxing. Martha and Peter began fetching food from the bags and picnic basket, along with enough cups for everyone. Chancy carried a ceramic pitcher to the stream and filled it with fresh water.

"What a lovely place to be on a picturesque Sunday morning!" Robert declared as he approached the tree where everyone had found a comfortable spot to sit.

"Martha, this is *your* Sunday, I believe," Emily said. "Gather around, everyone, while Martha reads."

Opening her Bible, Martha began, "For this Sunday's lesson, I'll read from John fifteen, verses twelve through fifteen. Since we're accompanied by our dearest friends, this seems most appropriate."

"My command is this: Love each other as I have loved you. Greater love has no one than this: to lay down one's life for one's friends. You are my friends if you do what I command. I no longer call you servants, because a servant does not know his master's business. Instead, I have called you friends, for everything that I learn from my Father I have made known to you."

While everyone heard the message in the lesson in their own particular way, for Chancy, it was like listening to the voice of an angel. Martha's straw bonnet protected her face from the sun while concealing her features from the side. The sleeves on her dress were ruffled, and her petticoat provided a moderate amount of fullness below the waist. He watched intently as she pushed a wavy clump of brown hair from her face to tuck it under the rim of her bonnet, only to repeat the process moments later after it fell in front of her eye. To Chancy, she had an attractive, almost childlike manner of widening her brown eyes when she smiled. *You are indeed precious*, he thought, clearly smitten by this eldest of the Cratchit siblings.

After resting for a few minutes and enjoying a refreshing drink, Scrooge asked, "Belle, might I interest you in a stroll with a gentleman who possesses only honorable intentions?"

Responding just as formally, she said, "Why, Mr. Scrooge, I would be delighted."

"Bob!" Scrooge barked. "Take Miss Belle on a stroll, would you my fine fellow?"

Silence fell over the group momentarily, until Scrooge could no longer bear it. When he burst into laughter, so too did everyone else!

Scrooge then stood, bowed to Belle, and unfurled his hand to offer her assistance in standing. "Since my fine young gentleman with honorable intentions seems otherwise preoccupied with his lovely wife, perhaps you would do *me* the honor of your company on a morning stroll."

Tickled by his antics, Belle placed her hand in his and stood, staring into his eyes a moment before turning back to Emily and saying, "Oh my, he's quite the gentleman."

"And such a handsome one at that."

As the couple wandered off into the meadow, Tiny Tim slowly approached his father from behind. "Are the fish biting yet, Father?"

Robert turned to see his son standing behind him holding a cane pole and bucket. For a moment, he saw himself as a young child, holding a pole and asking his father the very same question. "We won't know until we give them something to bite now, will we, Tim?"

With that said, Robert stood and raised Tim to his shoulder, along with his cane pole and bucket. "Anyone else care to join us on a fishing expedition?" Robert asked, loudly enough so all his children could hear.

Richard and Belinda, who were already halfway up a tree, yelled they'd like to do so, but a little later. Peter and Chancy were in the meadow tossing a ball to each other, while Martha chose to stay in the shade near the tree to continue reading from her Bible for a while.

"What about Uncle Ebenezer?" Tim asked. "Do you think he and Miss Belle want to fish with us?"

"They probably want to wait and see if we catch some really *big* fish before they try their luck."

The two fishermen found a shady spot along the stream, with a large boulder nearby. Robert situated Tim upon it, such that he could sit without difficulty, and so the brace on his leg would not get wet or dirty. Below the rock was a deep pool of still water, so when Tim lowered his line, it did not drift with the current from the stream.

Tim intently watched the cork floating at the end of his line, waiting for the sign of a hungry fish nibbling at the worm on his hook. As father and son watched a leaf ride the current, Robert broke the silence. "Tim? Where do you think this stream begins?"

Looking upstream, Tim contemplated the question. "I don't know, Father. Maybe it begins as a spring from underground, or maybe it comes from way up in the hills."

Turning to look downstream, Robert asked, "And where do you think this stream ends?"

"Well, I suppose it goes forever until it meets the sea."

"Tell me then, what this stream means to us?"

Tim looked upstream and then downstream again, before focusing on the cork tied to his fishing line. Moments of silent reflection passed before he said, "So really, this stream has no beginning and no end. Right, Father?"

"Outstanding, Tim," Robert said, proud of his son's perceptiveness. "Truer words were never spoken. It brings us fish to eat and water to drink. This stream is *life*. Just as God's grace is endless and nourishes our souls."

Robert hugged his son and said, "I could not be more proud of anything in this world than I am of you, my boy."

Suddenly, the bobber on the end of Tim's line disappeared underwater, pulling on the line at the end of his pole and nearly yanking it from his grasp. "Father! I think I have a fish!"

Robert shouted, "Pull it in, Tim!"

The line remained taut for a few moments, but Tim kept at it and eventually lifted a small, struggling bass out of the water, landing it on the rock right next to him. "I did it, Father! I caught a fish!"

"You most certainly did, Tim. And what a marvelous fish, indeed."

After briefly staring at the flopping fish, Tim agreed with his father's suggestion to return it to the water, where it could grow freely. As the fish darted off back into the water's depths, Tim sat breathlessly upon the rock, amazed at all that had just transpired.

Robert, too, found no words were necessary, and so stood silently by for a while, watching his smiling son, a newly made fisherman.

Scrooge and Belle were already back, sitting under the tree with Emily and Martha when Robert and Tiny Tim returned. Everyone enjoyed Tim's reenactment of the fish-catching he did, especially when he pulled it from the stream. For Robert, the parallel between the fishing trip with Tim and the fishing trips he'd had with his own father was beyond compare.

As others began sharing stories of their Sunday outing, the group commenced with their feast in the meadow. Robert sliced pork sausage and thin slivers of cheese. Portions of bread and pieces of fruit were handed around to all, as were cloth napkins. While Scrooge uncorked the bottle of wine, Emily asked Belle, "Would you tell us how you became such an amazing midwife?"

Although typically a shy woman and content to enjoy the stories of others, with all eyes suddenly on her, Belle agreed to share a bit of her life with the family she'd known for years. Taking Scrooge's hand in hers, she began. "After Ebenezer and I broke off our engagement, I fell in love with a man named Malcolm Owens. We married but never had any children of our own. My Malcolm passed away about five years ago."

Looking back at Emily, she said, "When we were first married, we had a large home that was passed down from his parents. More rooms than we needed, really, so it was not difficult for us to take in a young pregnant girl, whom I'd met one day. She was homeless and hungry, and as an unwed mother, had been disowned by her parents."

Except for the sounds of insects and the slight rustle of the wind through the leaves, the atmosphere was silent, as all listened intently to Belle's story. "Malcolm and I gave her a room in our home and the food she needed. This girl, even though not much younger than me, became like a daughter to me. When it came time for her baby to be delivered, I was the only one willing to help. So, I did what I needed to, and learned from it. Since then, in all, I have delivered over one hundred and fifty babies across

London, twenty-four of which were in my own home. Every birth is a gift, a blessing for which I can find no words."

A look of wonder spread across the faces of each person in the group. No one was eating or passing the picnic food, as Belle's story had everyone fully engaged. She continued, "I told the girl she could stay with us until she could provide for herself and her baby. Word spread, I suppose, and before I knew it there were three, then four, then *five* young women in our home at any given time, often for different reasons. Some were abused in their marriages. Others were homeless with nowhere to turn. I can't even remember a time now when there wasn't at least one pregnant woman living with me."

Belle's gaze went up to the sky for a moment, and she smiled quietly. "Sure, there have been difficult times, especially after Malcolm died, when I didn't know how I was going to feed so many mouths-… but somehow, we always find a way."

Still holding Scrooge's hand, she gazed into his eyes with a girlish look of affection and began, "And, now-…"

Scrooge took his lead from Belle's gesture, wrapping his fingers around hers, adding, "Yes, and now, I want you all to know what is in my heart." The Cratchits turned their attention to Scrooge, as he continued while looking into the face of the woman he'd once lost. "Tomorrow, I will establish an endowment to provide the necessary resources for Miss Belle to operate her home for unwed mothers as she sees fit. Never again will she lose a wink of sleep over concern for providing care for those in need."

All of the Cratchits and Chancy broke into cheers and a round of applause, praising the humbly smiling Scrooge for his generosity.

The hayride back to London was just as peaceful as the ride out. Their first stop was Belle's home, a modest, yet rather large dwelling not far from Bedford Square. After Scrooge helped her down from the wagon, she thanked each person individually for giving her such a lovely Sunday adventure. Scrooge walked Belle to the door, where they embraced, before walking back to the wagon and waving goodbye to her.

The next stop was Scrooge's house. Before stepping down from the wagon seat, he turned to Robert and said, "I am eternally grateful to you, Bob, for this day. There was a time in my life when I pitied you for your poverty. Now I can see that *I* was the one who was poor in spirit and alone in my greed." Looking back at the Cratchit children, all resting comfortably on the straw, he concluded. "You, Bob Cratchit, are the wealthiest man I know."

The next day, after his morning lessons at the Cratchit's home, Chancy entered the office of Scrooge and Cratchit, as he did most afternoons, but on this day he did not tend to his work assignments, which Robert kept current on a piece of slate, written in chalk. Instead, he approached his employers and stood in a spot just between their desks. "Mr. Scrooge, Mr. Cratchit, may I beg a moment of your time?"

"Yes, Chancy," Robert said, returning his quill to its holder. A moment later, Scrooge did the same, offering Chancy his complete attention.

"Mr. Scrooge, you have been most kind to me these last few months, by the way you took me into both your home and your confidence. And Mr. Cratchit, by the way you and your family have devoted so much of your precious time and effort toward my education. I can never repay the generosity each of you, *all* of you, have bestowed upon me."

Chancy bowed his head to hide the tears he felt welling up in his eyes.

"What ails you, my boy?" Scrooge finally asked, seeking to break the silence.

Wiping his eyes and raising his head, he said, "I-… I regret that I must leave you fine gentlemen."

Scrooge looked at Robert and back to Chancy. "But why, Chancy? Aren't you happy here?"

"Oh! Very happy, indeed, Mr. Scrooge. But please, don't ask me to explain why I cannot complete my apprenticeship. I pray you will accept my deep gratitude, along with my heartfelt apology for leaving you in this manner."

"Well, if you insist, I suppose I-…"

"No, sir," Robert said abruptly, interrupting Scrooge.

"Sir?" Chancy asked.

"I said, 'No sir,' I do not accept your apology. Not without a better explanation than you have offered."

Scrooge looked at his partner, astonished by the sharp response from one who he'd always known to be so gracious in his manners.

"Chancy, something obviously has you very distressed," Robert continued, "but please remember, sir, we are more than your employer. Friends do not end friendships in this sudden manner without talking with one another. So pull up a chair, dear fellow, and let us know what is in your heart."

Scrooge nodded in agreement, stood and pulled a chair close to their desks for him to use.

"My past haunts me," Chancy began. "When I lived on the street, I was one of the older boys and took it upon myself to look after the younger ones. Sometimes I could find a day's work here or there, but most days I was penniless."

Robert leaned forward, as Chancy continued. "I am not proud to say that I stole from time to time when food scraps and handouts could not be found. And I am not ashamed to admit that I did what I had to do for my sake, as well as that of my friends. I truly knew no other way until I met you, Mr. Scrooge."

"And now?"

"Well, a couple of days ago, I saw some of my old mates. They started tugging at my clothes, remarking how I'd obviously struck it rich. When I explained that I was apprenticed at Scrooge and Cratchit, they demanded I share my newfound wealth. I tried to explain that I was cared for, but not paid. Still, they insisted I steal from you or face the consequences."

"And what might those consequences be?" asked Robert.

"If I don't start paying them off every Friday, they have sworn to give my name to the authorities, to report me for past crimes I've committed. So you see, Mr. Scrooge, Mr. Cratchit, I must leave to spare you the embarrassment of hiring a thief."

"Tell me the names of the boys," Scrooge said, his face turning red with protective anger, "and I'll-…"

"No-… no, sir," Robert said, again interrupting. "Pardon me, Mr. Scrooge, but street life is more my area of expertise if you will permit me, sir."

Scrooge nodded, gladly handing the situation over to his partner.

"First and foremost, Chancy, you do not need to resign your position to protect us, dear fellow. As much as we appreciate your consideration, it is *not* necessary. Secondly, believe me when I tell you I speak from experience. You *can* erase your past transgressions by making amends."

"Amends, Mr. Cratchit?"

"Yes, sir. You begin by making a list of everyone, be it business, man or woman, from whom you wronged. Next to each name, make an honest estimate of the scale of your offense. Then you write a promissory note and deliver it to the holder of your debt."

"And most importantly," Scrooge added, "you must make good on your promises, henceforth."

"But how can I make good on a debt when I have no money, no resources of my own?"

"In your note," Robert replied, "simply explain that you will satisfy your debt as you earn your way."

"You're suggesting I confess to the crimes? But won't that merely implicate me? What will prevent someone from using my confession against me-… or worse, against you?"

Scrooge smiled. "Chancy, no businessman in his right mind would convict a boy who humbly and honestly confesses to a crime and offers to make it right. What Mr. Cratchit has laid out for you takes the stinger away from the bees who threatened to do you harm. Once you've delivered your confessions and your terms have been accepted, your mates will no longer have any power over you."

Robert added, "When I was but a lad, about your age, I found myself in a very similar situation. I can tell you that confessions are difficult and often painful, but the rewards, especially one's gaining freedom from guilt and shame, far outweigh any embarrassment."

Chancy sat silent for a moment, then smiled at both men. "This must be what it feels like to have parents."

Pulling his chair up against Robert's desk, he took quill and paper in hand and began writing. After blotting the ink and blowing it dry, he handed the paper to Scrooge.

Scrooge read the note, and then declared, "Your promissory note tells me two things, Chancy. First, you are a man of honor and integrity. And second, you have learned much from your lessons with the Cratchits, at lightning speed, I might add."

Handing the note to Robert, he said, "I accept your apology and your terms."

Dear Mr. Scrooge,

With heartfelt sorrow and regret, I confess to stealing five shillings from your home for the purpose of paying bees who would otherwise sting me. I promise this will not happen again, and that I will make good the debt once I earn an honest day's wage.

Please forgive me,

Chancy

Chapter 9

Word had begun to spread throughout London's commercial community of the remarkable differences between the business of Scrooge and Cratchit and that of Scrooge and Marley. Whereas Scrooge and Marley were known as the partners who never missed an opportunity to make a profit on the suffering of others, Scrooge and Cratchit gained a reputation as morally just businessmen who accepted only those opportunities that undoubtedly caused no harm, and moreover, benefited the community.

Where once he was ashamed to be known as an employee of Scrooge and Marley—for the name alone understandably left a bitter taste in the mouth of anyone who spoke it—Robert now took pride in the business. More and more, he enjoyed introducing Scrooge to *his* portion of the business community, those he had come to know over the years, back when he was Scrooge and Marley's clerk. News regarding the excellence of their current practice spread to other reputable businesses, as well—adding to the considerable upsurge of new clients—and it was not long before the firm of Scrooge and Cratchit was boasting larger profit margins than Scrooge and Marley ever attained.

However, Robert saw to it that the firm's resources remained small. Instead of stockpiling large sums of cash, he kept the money moving. One of his favorite projects, with Scrooge's heartfelt blessing, was to renovate and conserve in good repair the buildings held by the company, including his own. To Scrooge's delight,

Robert showed him that by maintaining the homes of their renters, profits increased, because occupancy increased. Without raising anyone's rent, income flourished, thanks in kind to the sterling reputation of the landlords.

Their wish for continually maintaining the buildings they rented out also provided a constant source of employment for able-bodied men willing to work. Further, for those without a home to call their own, Robert occasionally arranged for a workman and his family to live in one of the buildings still under renovation.

Indeed, Robert could be said to have had it all and then some, both as a respected businessman at work and as one who enjoyed the love of a good family at home. On one unusually warm summer evening, he returned home looking forward to one of his wife's piping hot, home-cooked meals. Upon entering, Robert found Emily, Martha, and Belle sitting around the table. "Why, what a lovely surprise," he said, hanging up his hat. "Three of my favorite women, all gathered together in one place."

"Please sit with us, Robert," Emily said, as a distinct chill swept through the room.

Robert looked at each woman's expression as he sat down, noting the rest of his children were not about. "Here now, is something wrong?"

"Robert, I have invited Belle to be with us, because I believe we may be in need of her help. Something has happened at Martha's work."

Looking at his daughter, who would not look at him, he turned back to Emily and said, "Please, go on."

"I don't know any way to tell you other than to say it outright," Emily said. "Robert, Martha is pregnant."

With a shocked look in his eyes, Robert sprang to his feet, tipping the chair to the floor. "No! This can't be! Is it true?"

Emily started to leave the table to comfort her husband, but Belle grabbed her hand to stop her, shaking her head *no*.

In a solemn, controlled voice, he asked, "Who is he?"

Emily began to answer, "It isn't a simple-…"

Interrupting his wife, "Please, Em, I want to hear it from Martha—*who is he?*"

The room fell into silence until Martha found the strength to speak. "Mr. Gains, my foreman at work."

"And is Mr. Gains your foreman at work going to do the honorable thing and marry you?"

The uneasy silence persisted, before Martha responded with a faint, "No."

Belle intervened, "Robert, please listen. Martha needs you right now."

"Needs *me*? Apparently, she needs this *Mr. Gains* more than she needs *me*!"

His knees trembled as he made his way to the washbowl and splashed some fresh water on his face, staying at the basin for a moment, contemplating the impact of his daughter's distressing news. "I'll be right back. I need some air," he said, not looking at any one of them, as he walked out the back door and proceeded down the alley. Robert felt the damp, sticky evening air on his neck and face while plodding past dimly lit houses for several blocks. Perhaps ten minutes later, after clearing his mind, he reentered through the front door.

The three women stopped talking amongst themselves when Robert came into the room and took a seat at the table. In a defeated voice, he asked, "So what happens now? She's an unwed mother. No man will have her for his wife."

Martha began crying, hearing both her father's bleak conclusion and sense of humiliation. "Robert!" Emily snapped back. "She is our *daughter* carrying our *grandchild*!"

"Robert, there's more than you realize," Belle said in a calming voice. "I want you to hear the whole story from Martha. Will you let her explain?"

Robert shifted around in his chair and looked at his shoes before responding, "I'm not sure I can take much more. What is it?"

Belle turned to Martha and said, "Go ahead, my dear."

Wiping the tears from her face, she quietly began, "A few months ago, Mr. Gains offered me advancement by becoming his assistant. It meant more money and less sewing, as I would be ordering supplies and doing some of the office work."

Still looking at his shoes, Robert replied, "I remember."

"Well, it wasn't long before I noticed he was flirting with me, even complimenting my work and telling me how pretty I was. He seemed to genuinely like me and even started bringing me little gifts. One thing led to another, and he began finding reasons to touch me. Nothing bad at first; just a hug or a hand on my back. Things that seemed innocent enough, or so I thought."

She paused and lowered her eyes. "Then a day came when I was working in his office, and I could smell the stench of alcohol on his breath. I tried to leave, but he closed the door, told me I had been *teasing* him long enough and-… and-…"

"He *took* her, Robert," Belle interrupted, saying the words Martha could not. "He took her against her will and had his way."

Martha sniffled, trying to hold back the tears, and continued, "He said if I told anyone, anyone at *all*, I would lose my job and he would see to it I never worked again."

Looking up from his shoes, Robert said, "You should have *told* me. You should have come to me and *told* me."

"And what would you have done, Father? What happened, *happened*. You couldn't *fix* that. *What?* Would you have *killed* the man, only to die on the gallows?"

Returning his eyes back to his shoes, he muttered, "I don't want you working there anymore."

"Done and done, Father. When I went to him this afternoon to tell him I was pregnant, he denied it was his and dismissed me from my position. He said a *tramp* like me could be carrying the bastard child of a hundred different men."

"It's her word against his, Robert," Belle said. "I've had run-ins with this man before. At least two or three unwed mothers have delivered his children in my home. Every time I have confronted him, he denies it. Had I known before today that Martha worked for such a man, I would have warned you before this happened."

"And now, it's Martha's turn," he concluded.

"Robert, I can help. If you don't think Martha should stay with you, she can come with me to my home. I will care for her during the pregnancy and be there to deliver her baby. If we're lucky, we may even find a childless couple willing to adopt it. I've seen it happen *many* times."

Robert looked over at Emily, who had remained mostly silent, and said, "Maybe that would be best."

Challenging his callous acceptance of Belle's proposal, she snapped, "Oh no, Robert! We can't send her away now, not when she needs us the most. I won't hear of it! She is our *daughter*, not some piece of moldy bread."

"Emily, I have worked hard my whole life to get to where I am now. I have developed a reputation in this town that serves us well. If word gets out that my daughter is an unwed mother, the stigma could ruin me."

"Mother!" Martha interrupted. "I would prefer to go with Belle myself. He's *right*. This is the best thing for all of us. Besides, I would be around other girls like me. Right, Belle?"

"Yes, I have three girls living with me now."

Robert, visibly shaken, said, "This is a very difficult conversation to have. I need some time alone." He promptly stood and left their home through the front door. Outside, he paced the walkway in front of the building and eventually sat on a bench across the street.

Looking up into the dark, starless night sky, he spoke to anyone in the heavens willing to listen, "And when I need help, when I am the one hurting, where are you?"

Across the street from the bench where he sat, Robert saw the front door to his flat open slowly, and the silhouette of Tiny Tim stepping outside. After a moment, Tim's eyes adjusted to the dimly lit street lamps, and he saw his father on the bench. Walking without a crutch, the boy labored with each step, the brace on his leg clanking at his side. Slowly, one step after another, he worked his way across the street and sat down by his father.

After a few silent moments together, Robert said, "I think Martha will be leaving us for a while, Tim."

"I heard."

"Then you know your sister is going to have a baby?"

"Yes, I heard that, too. But why does that mean Martha can't live in our home?"

"You see, Tim, a woman who gets pregnant and is not married is shunned by society. Not only her but the family from which she comes. Neighbors, businesses, churchgoers, they'll turn against us. Having a child out of wedlock is a mark of shame that can follow us for years. It gives people something to talk about, and people can be cruel."

He gazed uncomfortably into his young son's eyes. "So the way we handle this is to let Martha live in Miss Belle's home for a while. Eventually, she can come back to us, and people will assume she is widowed and moved back home with her family. Do you understand, my boy?"

"Yes, Father, I understand."

Tim sat quietly, considering his father's words. "Miss Belle is nice for letting Martha live with her, isn't she, Father?"

"Yes, Tim, we are fortunate to have her as a friend."

"Would you do the same?"

"Do what, Tim?"

"If you met a girl who was going to have a baby and needed a place to live, would you let her stay at our house?"

Robert thought for a moment before answering, "Yes, I suppose if she were desperate with no family and nowhere to turn, we would take her in, as well."

A few minutes passed, as the two watched a man walk his horse down the street in front of them. As the slow clopping from the horse's hooves faded, Tim asked, "Father, why would you bring a pregnant stranger into our home, yet send Martha away?"

Robert laughed uneasily and replied, "It's just not that simple, Tim. You see-... I mean, people don't just-..."

Robert wondered at his son, who he knew was wiser than his years. "I'll see you inside, my boy," he finally said, standing up and walking briskly across the street. By the time he reached the top step, his mind and heart were clear. He threw open the door and headed directly to Martha, who was still seated at the table with Emily and Belle. Without a word, he lifted his firstborn to her feet and hugged her tighter than ever before. "You're not going *anywhere*, my dear! Do you hear me? *This* is your home, and *we* are your family."

Martha burst into tears, still locked in her father's embrace. When he released her, she wiped her eyes and asked, "But Father, what about the people? What about the things they're bound to say?"

"I've never in my life cared what people say about me. Why should I start now?"

Robert turned to see tears streaming down Emily's cheeks, as well. Belle reached over and squeezed Emily's hand.

Martha stood before Robert and, looking him squarely in the eyes, whispered, "I love you, Father."

Suddenly, they all heard the step and clank of Tim's walk, as he came through the open door, closing it behind himself. Looking around the room at the emotional adults, he cheerfully said, "Welcome home, Martha."

Chapter 10

Chancy stayed busy most every day. *No time for tomfoolery*, he thought. *I've got much to do.* On any given day, he could be found cleaning or making repairs to Scrooge's home or the office building. Besides the chores were his studies. Five days a week, Chancy was at the Cratchit's family table practicing penmanship with Emily, math with Peter, and reading with Martha. Scrooge drilled him at night after dinner in whatever subject suited the youth, until it was time to retire for the evening.

By far though, reading with Martha had become his favorite subject. Not so much for a love of reading, but for his growing affection toward his teacher. For two consecutive days, though, Chancy's disappointment flourished, since Martha was nowhere to be found when the time came to practice his lesson. While at the office organizing books, he asked Robert matter-of-factly, "Excuse me, Mr. Cratchit, I was wondering if all is well with Martha? She's not been in your home for our normal reading sessions and, well, I'm concerned, sir. Is it maybe something I've done to offend her?"

Robert stopped his work and looked up at the young man who was less than clever when he tried to hide his obvious affection for his eldest daughter. Clearing his throat, he said, "Chancy, come here and sit, my boy."

Scrooge leaned back in his chair and asked, "Bob, should I excuse myself?"

"Thank you, no, Mr. Scrooge. What I have to say affects us all."

Chancy pulled a chair next to Robert's desk and sat attentively.

"I believe Martha is avoiding you because she is quite vulnerable at the moment. She feels ashamed, you see, because-… well, she's pregnant, Chancy."

"Oh, Bob," Scrooge sighed at a loss for words.

Chancy's eyes widened as the words sank in. "Martha is married?"

"No, it was not of Martha's choosing. A man forced himself on her a few months ago, and now she carries his child. He denies the baby is his and refuses to accept responsibility."

"Poor Martha," Chancy said, shocked by the revelation. "Poor, sweet Martha."

Though he returned to his office chores, Chancy's mind was somewhere else. Over the course of the afternoon, his thoughts went from pity and sympathy for Martha into a fit of smoldering anger toward her assailant.

The following afternoon, Chancy found Martha at her favorite place in Regent's Park and sat on the bench next to her, near the bird cages in the zoo. "How did you find me?" she asked without much surprise.

"Your mother told me you've been coming to the zoo every day with Tim. And I know how much you love birds. The rest was easy."

"So you know?"

"Yes, I know. I also understand why you're so upset. What I don't understand is why you avoid me. I'm not the one who hurt you."

Martha paused to consider her reply. "I suppose I'm rather fond of you and was ashamed of what you would think of me."

"But you didn't do anything to cause this, did you?"

"I've thought through this a million times, Chancy. When I relive the events in my mind, I see no warning signs I may have missed. I was not aware of the other girls he hurt, nor was I ever warned. I realize, now that it is too late, how naïve I was. I wish I had fought harder to escape, but I was frightened at that moment, so terrified that I couldn't even scream. I just kept crying and begging for him to stop, pleading for it to end."

"What will you do now? This certainly changes your life."

"Indeed it does. My dreams of finding a man as kind and loving as my father are gone now. No man would take a wife with a bastard child. However, I am one of the lucky ones. My family will take me in and love my child. Most women would be cast out to a shelter or worse, forced to live on the street."

"And some women would abandon their son on the street with nothing more than a first name so that they could find acceptance in another man's arms."

Martha stared at Chancy, realizing he was now talking about himself. "Oh Chancy, I'm so sorry. I didn't mean *you* when I said 'bastard child.'"

Gazing into her tearing eyes, he said, "Don't worry, Martha. If anything, it makes me feel closer to you. And perhaps even a little more able to understand what my mother must have been going through. Maybe it's time I stop hating her and try to forgive her."

"Well, Chancy, maybe that *would* be something good to come from all of this."

"I am by no means a perfect man myself. Living on the streets of London, I stole what I needed, as well as to provide for others like me. We did what we had to do to survive."

"And now?"

"It was your father and Mr. Scrooge who set me on the right path. I've accounted for my crimes and have promised retribution to those I've wronged."

Martha laid her hand on Chancy's. "Then to me, you *are* the perfect man."

The pair sat together watching the brightly colored parrots flying about in the tall aviary. Chancy finally broke the silence. "What's the man's name?"

Martha hesitated. "His name is not important. He's nobody to me."

"I would like to know so that if I ever meet this man on the street, I will surely avoid him."

Instead of responding, Martha continued to observe the birds flying overhead. After several minutes, though, she quietly said, "Mr. Gains, the foreman where I worked."

Chancy nodded his head and leaned forward, resting his elbows on the tops of his legs, staring up at the same birds Martha was watching. Changing the subject, he asked, "Will you be home for my reading lessons tomorrow?"

"If you think you still want to study with-… with someone-…"

Chancy interrupted her by quickly standing up and saying, "Good, right. Well, I best be off. Mr. Scrooge gets quite worried when I'm not home at the end of the day. Good-bye, Martha."

"Good-bye, Chancy. I'll see you tomorrow."

The frantic knocking on his front door gave Scrooge an impression of urgency. "Martha, my dear," he said after opening the door. "What has you so-…"

"Mr. Scrooge, is Chancy here?" she asked, nearly breathless from running.

"Why, no he isn't. I expected him home hours ago."

Without waiting to be invited in, she walked past him and closed the door herself. "I may be wrong, but I'm afraid Chancy is going to do something horrible tonight, and it's my fault!"

"Come and sit, Martha. Tell me what has you so distraught."

Martha sat down and recounted for Scrooge her conversation with Chancy at Regence Park. "Suddenly, just as he stood up and left, I felt a cold chill and thought about the tone of his *Good-bye*. There was a sense of permanence to it that frightened me. And I recognized he had talked me into divulging the name of the man who attacked me several months ago. My sense is Chancy intends to hurt Mr. Gains *tonight*, perhaps even kill him. I don't know if it's because he believes he needs to protect my honor or because he associates Mr. Gains with the man who was his *own* father. The reason isn't important. If he follows through, we will eventually find him swinging from the end of a rope!"

"My lord, Martha, I pray it's not too late to intervene in Chancy's plan! That is if your hunch is indeed correct. I'll go now and do all I can to find him, trust me. What time does Mr. Gains normally leave his office?"

Martha looked at the clock on the wall and said, "About an hour from now."

"You go home before your parents begin worrying about you and I'll start searching for our Chancy. You did the right thing in coming here, my dear."

Scrooge hurried through the darkening London streets and alleys, moving faster than he had in many years. Rounding a particularly busy corner, he stopped in his tracks when he saw the black wrought iron front gate of the textile factory across the street from him. Casting his gaze up and down the block, Scrooge finally spied Chancy crouched in a shadow, himself watching each factory worker and pedestrian who passed before him. Not wanting to frighten him, Scrooge cautiously moved forward, eventually coming up behind him.

"You're late for dinner, you know."

Hearing Scrooge's voice, Chancy sprang to his feet, dropping the metal pipe he'd been holding, which clanked when it hit the stone walkway. "Mr. Scrooge, how did you-…"

"Martha is very worried, as am I. When you find this man, what will you do, Chancy?"

"Nothing, sir. I mean-… he *hurt* Martha. This man does not deserve to live!"

"Maybe not, Chancy, but neither do you deserve to die. If you attack an unarmed man from behind, you will spend the rest of your days in prison, or *worse*. What this man did to Martha was undoubtedly wrong, but hurting him and losing your freedom won't help Martha. It will only make things worse."

In his anguish, tears began running down Chancy's cheeks. Then, the words he'd held tightly within him since he'd first laid eyes on her burst through his lips: "But I love her!"

Chancy fell against Scrooge's chest, and he began sobbing uncontrollably, as the only man who had ever cared for him wrapped his arms around his back. Years of pent-up fear, anger, and sadness spilled from him in a river of emotion. The pair stood there in that healing embrace until at last Chancy had purged his thirst for revenge.

While comforting his young friend, Scrooge watched as a stream of women, from the very young to the very old, passed through the factory gate. Near the end, a single man followed the crowd of workers, a man Scrooge knew would live to see another day and defile another innocent girl along the way.

After Chancy regained his composure, he backed away and said, "I'm sorry, Mr. Scrooge. I don't know what came over me."

"It's quite alright, my boy. This has been a long time coming, I'm sure. But always remember, lad, to think before you act. Is it better to show your love for Martha with a kiss and a hug, or by losing your life to the executioner?"

"You're right, Mr. Scrooge. I wasn't thinking. I was just so *angry*. Can we go home now? I'm truly exhausted."

As the two walked side-by-side through the narrow streets, past shops that had locked their doors for the evening and the lamplighters hard at work, scurrying from pole to pole, Scrooge finally said, "I didn't realize you had such strong feelings for Martha."

"Mr. Scrooge, do you think a girl like Martha could ever be interested in the likes of me? I would never be able to provide for her the way other men could. You know well that I'm uneducated and undeserving."

"Don't tell me what Martha deserves," Scrooge replied. "*No* man can ever provide for a woman who wants more than they have to offer. No, tell me instead what sort of man Martha needs."

"Well, I suppose she needs a man who will love her. She needs a man who will look forward to coming home to her every night. She needs a warm place to lay her head and nourishing food on the table."

"Good, Chancy. But I tell you, Martha needs more than these things. There is only one man in a million who can satisfy her needs, and you have to decide if you are that man before you take another step."

"What else? Tell me so I can be that man."

"Martha needs a man who can love her, despite the fact that she carries another man's child. Not many men can find it within themselves to be that benevolent. But even more, Martha needs a man who can love her child as his own, to be the child's father. If you can be all of these things to Martha, then my answer is *yes*, Martha *can* find favor in a man, the likes of you."

Chapter 11

After dinner, Robert sat on the steps outside the front door and lit his pipe, having received a gift of tobacco from his friend, Mr. Knight, that very afternoon. Soon, Peter, who was now maturing as a young man in his own right, came out front and sat beside him. "Father, can I talk to you about something?"

"By all means, my boy. What's on your mind?"

"When I was making a delivery for Mr. Holloway today, I went to a man's home and found a little girl out front crying. When I questioned her, she said her father was hitting her mother again. At the same time, I could hear a man yelling inside, along with a woman's screams."

"My *Lord*, Peter."

"Yes, and when I knocked on the door, a man who seemed no older than me, really, answered very harshly and demanded I get off his doorsteps. Behind him, I saw this woman sitting on a chair crying, with blood on her face."

"What did you do, son?"

"I turned and ran, Father. I feel like such a coward, now, because I ran away."

Robert sat his pipe down and said, "You're no coward, Peter. It was not your fight. But I tell you, son, I think you should talk with a constable and report what you saw. Maybe they can go there and check on the situation."

"Is that what you would do?"

Robert thought back to a similar situation at the Miller's farm, many years earlier, where he'd met a young woman who'd been beaten by her husband, only to discover later she'd been murdered that very evening at the hands of her aggressor. There had been an opportunity to tell a constable what he'd seen, but he'd chosen not to act. "No, I suppose I wouldn't. The constable would not intervene in a man's home. A man has a right to discipline his wife and children as he sees fit."

"So, what should I do?"

Robert hesitated before telling Peter to do what he himself would do since Peter was a man now and needed to make his own decisions. "Well, if it were me, Peter, I would watch for an opportunity to speak to the woman alone, without her husband around. Tell her what you saw and ask if she would like your help. Do whatever you can to talk her into going to Belle's home. If you can convince her, then I know Belle will protect her."

After weighing his father's suggestion, Peter began walking several streets out of his way after work each day to pass by the home where he'd seen the battered woman. On the third day, he watched as she left her house with her young daughter. Peter noticed the woman wore a scarf around her head, apparently an attempt to conceal the bruising.

Following from a safe distance, he eventually approached them on the street, after they were out of view from where she lived. "Pardon me, Miss."

The woman did not stop walking but responded without looking at him. "Yes, sir, do I know you?"

"No, Miss, I don't believe so, but I was at your home a few days ago making a delivery, and I could tell your husband was hurting you, and-… well-… I thought you might need some help."

"No, sir, thank you for your concern, but I'm fine. Please leave me be. I should not be seen talking to you."

"If you're afraid, I know a woman who can help. She can offer you and your daughter safe haven, to protect you from any further harm."

"No!" she responded, startling Peter with her firm tone. "Thank you just the same, sir, but you don't know my situation. If he saw us talking now, he'd-…"

Before finishing the sentence, her husband yelled, "So *this* is the bastard you've been sneaking off to see!"

Peter leapt in front of the woman and her child, upon seeing a burly young man, whose face showed a history of fighting, emerging from behind the corner of a side street shop.

"No, James, No! Not again!"

Pointing to Peter and stepping out of the shadows, he yelled, "I remember you! You were at my house the other day. Probably thought I wasn't home and came to see her, eh?"

Peter turned quickly to confront the man, who was not about to listen to reason. Within seconds, her husband's loud accusations caught the attention of other pedestrians, one of whom spotted and called out to a constable walking not far down the street. As the constable ran to the scene, his blowing whistle caught Peter's attention. But when he turned, James stepped in close and swiftly thrust a knife blade low and deep into Peter's back.

The constable's whistle and screams from the woman and her child faded away quickly, as Peter dropped to his knees and fell forward into darkness.

"I think he's waking up," Emily told Robert, both of them sitting next to the hospital bed in which Peter was lying.

"Father?"

"Hush now," Emily responded. "You need your rest."

But Robert responded to his son's confused look, "You're in the hospital, son. A man stabbed you in the back, and you lost a lot of blood. Thank God, the doctor thinks you'll pull through. However, you were fortunate, my boy. He said a fraction of an inch in any direction and the blade would have punctured a vital organ. Your mother is right. You need to rest now."

With that, Peter closed his eyes and returned to a deep sleep.

It seemed like only a moment to Peter, but a full day passed before he opened his eyes again. Thin white sheers waved in front of the tall, open windows of the hospital ward, filling the large room with fresh summer air. His mother was by his side, but in his father's place was the young mother who he'd approached on the street. "Peter?" Emily began, "How are you feeling, love?"

Instead of answering, he looked into the face of the woman who said, "Peter, I'm Rose. I just had to come see you. I've been here with your mother for several hours. We need you to get better so your mother can whack you over the head with a rolling pin!"

Peter managed a faint smile before asking, "Where's Father? Is he alright?"

"Other than a severe case of the *guilt's*, he's fine, dear. He's home helping the children and writing a thousand times, 'I will never tell my son to save a damsel in distress again.'"

Rose giggled at Emily's subtle way of chastising her son, yet was charmed by their close relationship. Peter asked Rose, "Did you get away? Did you make it to Miss Belle's home?"

"No need. A constable saw my husband attack you. I believe he'll be locked away for a good while. I still cannot imagine why you came to my aid. We've never even met!"

Peter smiled and said, "Because you needed me."

A nurse in the ward walked in, noticing Peter was awake and talking to the two women, one on either side of his bed. "I'm Nurse Gable," she said, standing next to Rose and grabbing Peter's wrist. "What's your name, young man?"

"I'm Peter Cratchit."

"Cratchit-… Cratchit, I remember another-…" Stopping her sentence short, she looked across the bed at Emily and suddenly recognized her. "Oh, Mrs. Cratchit. Aren't you Tim Cratchit's mother?"

"I am, indeed. I'd say you have quite a memory."

"Not so special a memory, I dare say. Dr. Cecil talks almost every day to anyone who'll listen about his all-time favorite patient. So, how is Master Tim doing? He was quite the young fighter, as I recall."

"Oh, he's doing very well, thank you for asking. I'll be sure to let him know you were asking about him. He eats well and walks with his brace, *but* without the crutch, I'm proud to say. He's a bit single-minded these days, though."

"My dear?" she asked, lowering Peter's arm and resting it by his side.

"Silly, really, but he's got it in his head that he *must* find a man whose sister recently passed. Her name was Mary. I don't suppose you knew of a girl named Mary who passed away here at the hospital recently?"

"No, I can't say I remember anyone named Mary, and I know pretty much anyone who leaves this hospital, whether through the front door or out the back with the mortician."

Turning back to Peter, she said, "Your pulse feels a little weak to me. I want you to start eating some broth, my dear. I'll have some sent over, and I'm quite certain one of these lovely ladies will help feed you."

Chapter 12

Peter's recovery proceeded slowly, but surely. Two weeks passed before he was able to begin walking the streets near his home for exercise. A week later, he managed without the use of a walking cane. One morning, his mother said, "Peter, I want you to take these clothes to Miss Belle's home. They were Tim's things, but I'm pleased to say, he's outgrown them. You know, the walk will do you good."

Agreeing with his mother to take the trip to Belle's, Peter stopped briefly on his way to pay a visit to his employer. "Pardon me, Mr. Holloway, sir," he said, stepping through the office doorway.

Though engaged in discussion with his foreman, Mr. Holloway broke off the conversation immediately when he heard Peter. "Mr. Cratchit, God bless my soul! How in the world are you, my boy?" he exclaimed, moving quickly to shake Peter's hand.

"Much better now, sir, thank you for asking."

"You gave us quite a fright," the foreman said, taking his turn to shake Peter's hand. "I'm sure your parents must have been worried as much as anyone, eh?"

"Yes, sir. I dare say they're quite relieved by now. I should be well enough to come back to work in a day or so, Mr. Holloway, if you'll still have me, sir."

Looking to his foremen, then back to Peter, he said, "I don't know-... what do you say, John? Do we have a position for a young scrapper who would step in front of a knife to protect a mother and her child?"

"I don't know-… if we *do* take him back, I think I may need to teach him which end of a knife is the sharp one!"

Both men burst out laughing. "Of *course* you can come back to work, the day you're ready and not a moment sooner-… *or* later, for that matter. The place just hasn't been the same without you."

"Thank you, sir," Peter said, as they shook hands once again. Lifting the bag of clothes he was to deliver, he said, "I best be off, then. I'm delivering these children's clothes to Miss Belle."

"Oh, if she needs children's clothes, I'd be glad to add some of Adam's and Allie's clothes they can no longer wear."

"I'm quite sure she's always in need of such, sir."

"Good! Then please come by here again tomorrow, and I'll have twice as much as you have now."

"Thank you, sir, I will indeed."

Peter knocked on the front door of Belle's home and waited. Hearing a lot of movement inside, he noticed the curtains near the front entrance move several times, as various children looked at the stranger standing on the front porch. Finally, the door opened just a fraction, wide enough for a single eye to peer onto the front stoop. A second later, the door swung open, and Belle exclaimed, "Peter Cratchit, what a pleasant surprise!"

"Miss Belle, the pleasure is all mine. My mother asked me to deliver these clothes to you."

"Oh, do come in," she said, pulling him by his arm. "I'm sorry about the way you were received just now. I must confess, I can't be too careful these days. For every woman or child in my home, there's a man out there who would do them harm."

"I quite understand," Peter said, realizing there were women and children looking at him cautiously from behind various doorways. "Right. Well, I should be going then."

Belle stopped Peter before he could make his way back to the door, saying, "Just a moment, Peter. I have someone here I'd like you to meet."

Putting her hands on his shoulders, Belle turned him around to see an attractive young woman who had just stepped into an adjoining alcove. Her hair was unusually blonde and neatly brushed, forming a picturesque frame around a face of clean, pastel white skin. From Peter's perspective, however, what stood out the most was her ocean blue eyes. "Rose," he finally muttered, realizing he'd only seen her in the past with a face covered with cuts and bruises. The heart-struck way Peter froze at the sight of Rose, whose radical transformation caught him entirely off guard, elicited instant giggles from the girls who were watching from the doorways.

"Good afternoon, Mr. Cratchit," Rose said, her young daughter easing her way around from behind her mother. Pulling her daughter squarely in front of her, she said, "I don't believe you've met my daughter. This is Cassandra."

Peter could barely bring himself to lower his eyes from Rose to that of her child. Eventually, he managed a slight bow to her, saying, "I'm very pleased to meet you, Cassandra."

From behind him, Belle nodded to one of the other young ladies standing nearby, who promptly leaned over to take the child's hand and whispered, "Cassandra, come with me, and you can help me bake some bread in the kitchen."

As she ran off, Belle spoke up, suggesting, "Peter, perhaps you'd like to take Rose for a walk to get better acquainted?"

Though still mesmerized by her beauty, Peter gathered himself and replied, "It would be my pleasure, if Rose would allow me to escort her on a stroll."

Rose nodded and stepped past Peter toward the front door, already being held open by Belle. As he passed by Belle, he paused to thank her. With a finger to her lips, though, she acknowledged his gratitude and silently ushered him out.

What seemed like five minutes to Peter was actually over an hour, by the time the two returned to the front steps leading up to Belle's home. "I will be bringing more clothes for Miss Belle tomorrow, from my employer. I wonder if I might call on you again," Peter asked from the bottom of the stairs.

The curtains in the front windows, once again, seemed to move continually, with both children and young women taking turns spying on the pair as they finished their conversation.

Standing two steps higher than Peter, Rose looked at the young man who had been nothing but charming to her. "I would like that very much, Peter."

His walk home seemed more magical than any he could ever recall.

That evening, after dinner, Peter asked, "Father, could we talk, in private?"

After gesturing to the front door with a nod of his head, Robert followed his son outside and sat down next to him, the two taking their usual places on the steps. Peter said, "I went to Miss Belle's home and saw Rose today."

"Who?"

"Rose, the girl I was talking to when her husband stabbed me."

"Ah, yes. Your mother took her to Belle's house after they met, while you were in the hospital. But Rose is married, is she not?"

"She is, but Belle has already helped her fill out the paperwork for a divorce. Belle told her that because her husband is incarcerated, and a number of witnesses have signed affidavits attesting to the physical abuse, it will be just a matter of days before her divorce is finalized. The courts will intervene so that her husband's agreement is not required."

"Good, excellent. The sooner Rose is rid of the brute, the better. Does she have family around to help care for her?"

"Her mother died when she was young, and she hasn't seen her father since she was fifteen. I think that's why she married the first man who showed any interest in her."

"She has a child, doesn't she?"

"Yes, a daughter who seems to be about six years old. My question is, do you think it's appropriate for me to be calling on her?"

"That depends. Are you attracted to Rose the victim, or Rose the woman?"

"What do you mean?"

Striking a match to light his pipe, Robert said, "Right now, you still see a girl who was abused by her husband. She, on the other hand, sees a knight in shining armor who nobly saved her. These are great stories to tell your grandchildren someday, but it's quite likely they aren't enough to lay a foundation for a good marriage."

"So, what should I do?"

"My advice would be to spend time with each other, looking deeper. It may be that you discover you *are* meant for each other, brought together by the most amazing circumstances. But on the other hand, once you get to know each other, you *may* find the spark is not enough to produce a flame."

"How did you know Mother was the right woman for you?"

Robert thought back to the infatuation he'd first experienced when he began courting Emily. "I believe I felt about her just as you do now about Rose, but the feeling never left. Our love may have changed over the years, but always for the better. We don't always agree on everything, but I honestly can't imagine being with a different person. I have been blessed."

"Well, I hope I can find that person in my life." Then he turned to look at his father squarely in the eyes, peering deeply into them with an earnest sense of gratitude. "Father, I think the greatest gift you have *ever* given me was the love you have for my mother."

Peter continued to call on Rose cordially and respectfully. He took comfort in knowing she was safe under the watchful eye of his mother's dearest and most trusted friend.

Even though Belle was duly protective of all her girls, she knew this particular young gentleman caller as well as anyone, having been the midwife at his birth. Therefore, she felt both content and quietly pleased each time he'd appear at her door.

One Sunday, while Peter was waiting in the foyer for Rose to come downstairs, he recalled a bit of his father's advice: *Remember son, it's easy to discover the things you have in common when falling in love, but much more difficult to realize your differences.*

Once they'd left the house and began their stroll through a nearby park, Peter said, "My religion continues to mold me into being the man I want to become."

"Hmm-… I've never had much call for religion or church of any sort."

"You can't mean that!"

"I do indeed. I was not raised in the church, nor have I come to know the Bible as your family has. I would say I'm guided by my wits. Now that I'm free from a hateful marriage, Cassandra and I will take care of each other."

"But what you describe is a very lonely life."

"Which is what I have always had. After my mother died, I learned to keep to myself. If I vied for my father's attention, I was rewarded with abuse and despair. No church ever came to my rescue. God never eased my suffering. If there is a God, He doesn't know the likes of me."

"Oh, I most strongly disagree, Rose! You must look at each situation with an open mind. Look at us, for instance. You could say God was not with me when your husband stabbed me. But I know in my heart, it was by the grace of God the knife was directed to enter my back in the only place, and at the perfect angle, to avoid causing serious organ damage or my death! Though it is true I was attacked, it is *just* as true I was saved."

"I respect your beliefs, Peter. They just don't fit my life or who I am."

The pair walked in silence until they came to a park bench facing the sun. Sitting down, they each quietly appreciated the natural beauty surrounding them and the feeling of warmth on their faces. Peter eventually said, "My youngest brother, Tim, had an operation earlier this year, during which he died."

"Oh, Peter, I'm so sorry for your loss."

Peter smiled. "It was no loss, actually, because as it turned out, he came back to this life."

"Is that some sort of joke?"

"No, I'm sincere. The doctor confirmed to my mother that Tim had indeed stopped breathing. His heart stopped beating and blood no longer pulsed through his veins. After he came back, he told an amazing story of having been in Heaven during his short death."

"Oh, Peter, surely you don't believe such nonsense!"

"I *do,* Rose. And you would, too, if you knew Tim. He said he met a woman while in Heaven, who gave him a mission to fulfill while he's still on Earth."

Rose laughed, although certainly not to ridicule him. "Peter, do you hear yourself? Everything you've told me is hearsay. You offer no evidence, other than your own desire to believe the things your brother claims. You're being *deceived,* my friend. I've seen people swindled with far less imaginative tales my whole life."

"And now you can't believe anyone, is that it?"

"Oh, Peter, don't be cross! I apologize if I've offended you. I think we're just coming from two different worlds. You want to see the good in people, yet I see wickedness in humanity, filled with hatred and misery. I wish I could believe you, but I'm the sort who can only believe what she sees."

"And *that* is the difference in a nutshell. I believe in things I cannot see, which is my faith. Without it, we're limited by what our senses can perceive."

"Alright, tell me. What *is* the mission Tim was given?"

"Many of the churches are coming together to forbid any sort of Christmas celebration. Tim is convinced this will spell an end to Christmas as we know it. His heaven-sent mission is to find the man who he believes can save it."

"But would it be so terrible, a world without Christmas? I have never taken any real pleasure from it, I must say."

"Christmas is a time for people to put their differences aside and understand we are all kindred spirits who share the same domain on a common journey. Rich or poor, we are all the same under Heaven. It serves us well to remember this, and we should treat one another as such."

"I agree, but why do we need Christmas to remind us to be fair-minded? Shouldn't we be kind to others all the days of the year, not just the one?"

"We should, indeed, but men tend to go about their business through the year, self-absorbed in their fears and desires, until they lose touch with the true meaning of peace and goodwill. Christmas serves to pull us back to the fundamental reason we're all here."

"And why *are* we all here, Mr. Cratchit?"

Peter looked into the eyes of the striking young woman who he was now coming to realize, as his father had warned, did not share his core beliefs. "We are here to love and respect one another, and to serve those who are less fortunate."

Chapter 13

Chancy grew in favor with all of the Cratchits, as well as with Scrooge. His schooling at the Cratchit table accelerated, where he found genuine pleasure in learning. No lesson was more alluring or intriguing to him than literature, during which he cherished the hours spent in Martha's company.

With his finger moving from word to word, Chancy read aloud from the chronicles of *Oliver Twist*, serialized in Martha's treasured collection of *Bentley's Miscellany* magazines. To support him, Martha followed along, skillfully, yet graciously correcting his mistakes and pronunciation.

"You're bored, I can tell," Martha said, noting Chancy's voice had begun to drift while reading.

"No, Martha, I'm not. I swear it. I'm just a little tired, I suppose."

Looking about the dimly lit room, over to her mother who was quietly mending Belinda's dress, she declared, "Mother, we're going to the park."

Emily looked up only briefly. "It *is* a nice day out."

Closing the magazine, Martha gingerly asked her student, "Would you please grab the quilt from the drawer?"

Chancy did as instructed and followed her out the door. As the two walked along, she explained, "Sometimes it's just as important *where* you read as *what* you read. For instance, if you were reading about a brave knight in a castle, it would seem so much more alive to you while reading in a *real* castle than on the back stoop of a bakery. Do you understand?"

"Yes, of course, that makes sense. But I would add, sometimes it is just as important *who* you're reading with."

Martha stopped walking, as did Chancy, realizing he had just made a flirtatious suggestion. She struggled for a moment to find the words, "You mean-... with *whom* you are reading."

"Either way. As long as *you* are the person-... with *whom* I am reading *with*."

Martha laughed out loud at Chancy's intentional grammatical error while blushing at the compliment. When they'd found a secluded spot under a large oak, he spread the quilt, and they both sat with their backs against the tree's trunk. "Now, Chancy, you relax and close your eyes. I will read to you. I want you to hear how the inflections in my voice can make the story seem more real than just reciting words."

Martha chose a short story about a squirrel and a rabbit, which seemed quite fitting, for a warm afternoon in the park. Chancy crossed his hands behind his head, closed his eyes and let the sound of her voice take him on an imaginary journey. In his whole life, he had never known such a feeling of peace and tranquility.

"You seem very distracted tonight," Scrooge said. "You've hardly touched your dinner, and I don't think you've said ten words."

Looking at his plate, Chancy realized he had done little more than stirring his corn into his potatoes. Lifting his head off his hand and sitting up straighter, he said, "Mr. Scrooge, do you think I will marry one day?"

"Ah, I should have known. A girl has captured your attention. Her name wouldn't by any chance be 'Martha,' would it?"

Chancy grinned, realizing he must be more transparent than he'd intended. "I don't think she looks upon me as more than just another household chore. But when I'm with her, it's as if we are the only two people in the world. If I thought for one minute she considered me more than an illiterate wretch, I'd climb the highest mountain just to bring her a flower from the top of the world."

"You seem to have quite an elegant way of expressing yourself, sir. I wonder, though, why you're telling *me* these things, instead of the person for whom they're intended."

"Oh, I could *never* say such things to Martha. She would laugh and ridicule me for being a silly boy with a childish crush. Martha is *so* much more refined and polished than me."

"You concern yourself too much with the things you're not. Consider, instead, the things you *do* have to offer. You are devoted, light-hearted and fun-loving, my boy. All good qualities when it comes to the desires of the opposite sex."

"But I must also be of a mind to provide security and comfort to such a delicate creature."

Scrooge turned sternly serious, pointing his finger at Chancy. "Now, you listen to me, young fellow. I had those same words on my lips when I was barely older than you are now. Look at what it got me. I missed my *only* opportunity for the love of a good woman, and I've been alone my whole life because of it! If I had someone in my life tell me what I am about to tell you, I would be a better man today: *Don't let love pass you by!*"

"But what have I to offer that would let her know of my sincerity? I have no job, other than the odd jobs I do for you. I live entirely off of your generosity, Mr. Scrooge. I don't have a single resource to my name, other than the clothes I wear, and even *those* were a gift from you. Martha needs a man who can provide for her if even the most basic of necessities."

Scrooge backed down and looked at his plate, as they both contemplated the conversation. "You're right in a way, Chancy. You *do* need to have the means to provide. I have been thinking about this for a while now, and I believe the time is right to hire you as an apprentice clerk at my business if you're willing."

Chancy looked straight into Scrooge's eyes, to determine if he was sincere in his proposal. "Oh, Mr. Scrooge, yes! Of course, I accept!"

"This will only be part-time, for now, as I expect you to continue your studies with the Cratchits for half of every day. As our apprentice, Mr. Cratchit and I will pay you a shilling a day, plus continued room and board in my home."

"Bless my soul, Mr. Scrooge. I don't know what to say other than thank you! Thank you from the bottom of my heart!"

"Promise me you will not wait to work your way up to being an officer of the company before you tell Martha how you feel about her."

"I promise, sir."

"All the things you need to provide for a wife and family will come to you, if you will let them, Chancy-… save one."

"What one thing is that, Mr. Scrooge?"

"With hard work and perseverance, you can achieve anything your heart desires, except a name."

"A name? But I have a name."

"You have a Christian name, but you need a sir name if you want to make it in this world. You cannot *earn* a sir name. It must be passed to you by your father."

"But I never knew my father *or* his name."

Scrooge smiled at the boy's innocence. Reaching his hand across the table, he took Chancy's hand in his. "I'm offering to adopt you, my boy, and to share my name. I'm asking you, Chancy, if you will be my son."

Neither Scrooge nor Chancy showed up to work the following morning at their usual time, and it wasn't until the afternoon before they made their first appearance. "Bob, I have someone I want you to meet!" Scrooge shouted, bursting into their office.

Robert stood up immediately, expecting to meet a new client, and was confused when he saw only Scrooge and Chancy. "Sir?"

"Yes, Bob, I'd like you to meet my son, Chancy."

Chancy smiled as he accepted Robert's handshake, while Robert asked with a puzzled tone, "Your-… your son, Mr. Scrooge?"

"You're going to have to be more specific than that, Bob. There are *two* Mr. Scrooges in this office now."

Robert steadied himself against the top of his desk. "Pardon me, sir?"

"That's right, Bob. We just came from the Hall of Records and filed all of the proper paperwork. I have adopted Chancy. He is now my son."

"And you are my father," Chancy added with a glowing smile.

Taking a moment to absorb the announcement, Robert stood up straight and enthusiastically shook Scrooge's hand, saying, "God save you, sir! You're a father. Congratulations, Mr. Scrooge. This is the most wonderful news."

Reaching for Chancy's hand once again, Robert shook it and said, "I pray I am the first to address you as such, and may I say, God save you as well, Master Scrooge."

"Cups, Bob. We must have a toast," Scrooge exclaimed, producing a bottle of amber ale from his desk drawer.

"A toast indeed," Robert replied, retrieving three mugs from a shelf.

After pouring the bottle three ways, Scrooge raised his cup to join theirs, while Robert delivered a brief, yet heartfelt toast. "To Ebenezer Scrooge and Chancy Scrooge! May God bless this happy family!"

"Thank you, Mr. Cratchit," Chancy replied. "I dare say this is still as much of a shock to me as it must be for you, sir. I'm sure I will have to be corrected often when, out of habit, I address my father as, *Mr. Scrooge.*"

"Oh, one other thing, Bob," Scrooge interjected. "I hope you don't mind, as we have discussed this between us on multiple occasions, but I have hired Chancy as our new clerk. Part-time, mind you because he still needs to progress in his studies under Emily's leadership. You take care of paying him, Bob. After very tough negotiations, we have agreed upon a single shilling for every day he works."

"Oh my, yes-… yes indeed," Robert said. "We can certainly use the help around here. Welcome aboard, Chancy Scrooge," he added with another hearty handshake.

"Brilliant!" Scrooge declared. "And Bob, I trust you'll train Chancy in the duties necessary for him to be our clerk. God knows you know more about it than I ever did."

"Of course. It will be my pleasure, sir."

"Good. And Chancy, this is your opportunity to learn from the very best. Take heed or I'll-… I'll send you to your *room*, son."

All three burst into laughter at Scrooge's witty remark, then hugged each other in a warm embrace.

Chapter 14

Tim scoured the bottom of the drained pool, while two other boys scrubbed the walls with long-handled push brooms. After a few hours of work, the three boys stood off to the side, as water was diverted into the pool and the caretaker led both hippopotamuses into the pen. During his brief rest spent sitting on the stone fence surrounding the enclosure, Tim saw a man mimicking the sounds a hippo makes when it yawns.

Tim's heart began racing, and his soul rejoiced when he realized he knew the man's face, which earlier had been etched in his memory. "Hallo!" he called out from inside the animal pen.

The man turned to the sound of the greeting to see a small boy in a leg brace, waving in his direction. And even though the man shrugged his shoulders and walked away, Tim knew he had just seen Mary's brother.

The moment he stepped into his home at the end of the day, Tim shouted, "I found him! I found him!"

Robert stood next to the hearth, surveying the fire he'd just tended, glowing brightly under a pot of stew. "You found who, Tim? Mary's brother?"

"I did for certain!"

"Well, tell us, Timmy," Emily said. "What did he say? What's his name?"

"I didn't actually get a chance to talk to him yet, but I saw him, nonetheless. I'll go back tomorrow, and the next day, and the day after that, if need be. Now that I know him, he'll eventually know me."

Tim stood near the hippopotamus pen, looking around for the man he'd seen the previous day. After some time, he noticed from a distance a man who was waving his arms and walking in small circles with his legs purposely bowed, gesturing in front of the monkeys' cage. Tim hurried over to the man, who he could see was trying to "speak" the monkeys' language.

"Hallo, sir!" Tim called out.

Turning to face him, the man reached into his pocket and pulled out a few pence. "Here you go, boy."

"No sir, I don't want your money. I want to ask you a question."

"Oh? What is it then?"

"Did you have a sister named Mary, who passed away recently?"

The man looked around somewhat cautiously, to see if others were watching. "What business is that of yours?"

"She asked me to find you so that you could help me."

Noticeably irritated, the man scolded Tim. "Now see here, young man. I don't know what sort of prank you're pulling, but I do *not* appreciate your outlandish claims."

"She told me her name was Mary-… Mary Christmas."

"Bah! Off with you, before I call the constable!"

His face reddened with anger, the man turned his back on Tim and scurried down the walkway, until he rounded a corner and disappeared from sight.

With a frustrated sigh, Tim turned toward the caged monkeys, some of which jumped up and down, seemingly laughing at him. "It's not funny at all, you know!" Feeling rejected, he stood alone in silence and reflected on what to do next.

A full week and a day passed before their next encounter. Tim stopped his mucking of the Arabian antelopes' stall and walked over to the monkey cages, in hopes of spotting the same fellow he'd now seen twice. Soon, much to his delight, Tim saw the man with the familiar face approaching with a book in his hand. As the gentleman got nearer, though, his face tightened with a look of distress.

"You again!" he exclaimed. "I thought I told you to leave me alone!"

"Was that her name?" Tim asked, as though little time had transpired since their last meeting. "Was her name Mary Christmas?"

"Why do you haunt me, young fellow?! Have I done something to offend you? Is it money you want?"

"No, sir. I only want to talk to you."

"Well, I do not wish to talk to you, sir. Mary is dead, and nothing you have to say to me can change that fact."

As he turned his back on Tim once more to walk away, Tim began reciting something from his memory:

"The pure, the bright, the beautiful
That stirred our hearts in youth,
The impulses to wordless prayer,
The streams of love and truth."

"Where is it, where is it, where is it?"

Mary's brother frantically searched through stack after stack of papers and notes, piled upon his desk. Pulling drawers, one after the other, he let the contents spill to the floor. Like a child scrambling blocks this way and that, he searched through dozens, if not hundreds, of random writings and notes until he found it.

"Who has been in my office?!" he bellowed, entering the drawing room where his wife and four children were sitting together. Holding the paper above his head, he demanded, "Who took this from my office or copied it to share with someone?"

One by one, he asked, "Catherine, was it you?"

"No my dear. Please love, you're frightening the children."

Ignoring his wife's plea, he continued. "Boz, have you been in my office?"

"No, Father," his six-year-old son cautiously replied.

"Mary? I promise I will not punish you. Just tell me if you were in my office."

"No, Father, I have not," his five-year-old daughter said, her shaking voice just above a whisper.

Looking around the room at four-year-old Kate and two-year-old Walter, he realized his line of questioning was bordering on insanity. Again waving the paper in the air, he ranted, "*Someone* from this household has taken this piece of paper from my office and shared it with a young boy I met this morning! He recited it word for word, yet it has never been printed or published, at least not to *my* knowledge!"

The next morning, Tim stood, as he usually did, at the entrance to Regent's Park, waiting for the horse-drawn cart to arrive. On this particular morning, his typical gratitude for the carriage ride to the zoo was overshadowed by his being filled with anticipation, bordering on impatience. When she finally arrived, Sandy, the old chestnut mare, slowed as she approached Tim. Most riders of the six-bench wagon she pulled stepped up or down without breaking her stride. For the crippled youth, though, the moving target was more than he could manage. When she was just a short distance away from him, Tim stepped directly in her path and held out a carrot, which easily brought her to a full stop. While Sandy munched on the treat, he briefly stroked her neck and then stood on the first side-step, before lifting his leg and brace up to the same step. After repeating the process for the second step, he took a seat on the first bench behind the driver. "Good morning, Willy."

"And to you, Master Tim," the elderly black man replied with a tip of his hat. "Sandy says 'Good morning' too, and thanks you for the carrot."

Feeling a slight wiggle of the reigns, the gentle mare resumed her slow and steady pace with her nose drooped just above the height of her knees. As she clip-clopped her way along the route around the park, Tim eagerly kept an eye out for the man he knew only as Mary's brother. When Sandy passed the southern entrance,

Tim glimpsed a familiar face among the people strolling in the park. "Stop, Willy-… please. I need to get off!"

"Already? But we're nowhere *near* the zoo."

"I know, but I must get off here!"

After dropping his usual hay penny in the jar set next to the old driver, Tim let himself down to the street level and watched as the cart moved slowly away. Just as it passed from between them, he found himself facing Mary's brother.

"What's your name, young fellow?" the man asked, seemingly not the least bit surprised to, once again, be staring down at the young boy with the leg brace.

"Tim Cratchit, sir."

"Well, Tim, yesterday I heard you recite a poem drawn directly from some writing I did six years ago. Would you please tell me how you came upon those words?"

"*Mary* told me, sir. Mary Christmas showed me your words."

"That's not possible, young man! I wrote those words in my grief after her death."

"I know, sir. She stayed with you because you were so distraught. She wants to know why you never finished it."

"Tell me, how is it that you come to know the thoughts and desires of the dead?"

"Just Mary's, sir." Tim looked at the man's right hand, nervously twitching by his side. "I see you still wear it. You still wear Mary's ring."

Lifting his hand, he looked at the ring on the smallest finger of his right hand. "Many of my family and friends know this ring belonged to Mary."

"I watched as you removed it and swore to wear it until your dying day. I saw you kiss her on her forehead."

The man stood bewildered and silent, towering over Tim, staring at the boy who he sensed was speaking sincerely. "I believe we should go somewhere to talk."

"Yes, sir. Is your name Mr. Christmas?"

"No, Tim, my name is Charles Dickens."

Dickens walked patiently alongside Tim, the two moving along a pathway through Regent's Park until they found a bench he felt suited his purpose. There, he asked Tim to describe what led him to know what he'd shared. Tim explained his two operations and the time he'd spent in Heaven. Listening intently, Dickens seemed fascinated by the seemingly earnest boy's account, yet also leery, searching for flaws in his story.

When the young Cratchit had finished, Dickens said, "Mary Christmas was not her real name. It was her nickname, but one she cherished over her given name."

"So her real name was Mary Dickens?"

"No. Although we were very much like brother and sister; by birth, she was my wife's sister. Her real name was Mary Hogarth. I met Mary when she was just fourteen while I was courting her sister, Catherine. She came to live with us two years later to care for Catherine, who was pregnant by then with our first child. I trusted her opinion above any other, to help me develop the characters in my stories."

"I loved her as dearly as any brother has ever loved a sister." With a deep, mournful sigh, he looked at the young boy sitting next to him and said, "She died in my arms six years ago, when she was only seventeen. We named our first daughter after her."

The two sat without saying a word for what seemed to be a long time to Tim, but he felt respectful of what his newfound confidant had shared with him.

Finally, he broke the silence. "Why did you call her Mary Christmas?"

"Mary loved Christmas like no one I have ever known. No sooner had Christmas passed than she was preparing for the next. To her, Christmas was a time for goodwill and generosity, which is how she lived every day of her brief life. I called her 'Mary Christmas' one day, and she loved the name, so that is how I always knew her."

Tim nodded and agreed. "I cannot think of her with any other name, either, from what I know of her. She was truly full of joy and laughter. The love that radiated from her was certainly of Heaven."

"I appreciate how well you describe her, Tim. It certainly lends to my believing you have, indeed, met her. You've said she asked you to find me, and find me you did. But to what end?"

"Mary showed me a world without Christmas, sir. Without it, a dark shadow will overtake the souls of mankind. Heaven is worried and has called upon you to preserve Christmas and all that is holy about it."

"That's quite an outrageous demand, Tim. I am a mere mortal. What can I do that Heaven cannot?"

"I don't know, Mr. Dickens. Mary did not explain or show me the solution. Instead, she showed me a vision of you standing next to Mr. Ebenezer Scrooge, my father's business partner."

"I don't know anyone by that name."

"Yes, sir, I know. But if you'll permit me, I'll introduce you."

Chapter 15

When Tim entered his home, the Cratchit family was already sharing their evening meal. "Come and take your place, Timmy," his mother said. "I've kept your dinner nice and warm for you."

By now, Emily had become accustomed to Tim's late arrival, although she wondered how many more days he would remain in pursuit of the nameless stranger he only referred to as *Mary's brother*.

Sitting down with his family, Tim promptly said, "I have good news!"

"What is it, Tim?" his father asked.

"I finally met the man I've been searching for! I met him, and I *talked* to him. Everything Mary told me about him is true. He's a very kind and considerate soul, once you get to know him. At first, I had my doubts, because she was not actually *his* sister, but his *wife's* sister, instead. Still, he is the man she showed me, and he told me himself he thought of Mary as his own sister."

"Well, tell us, Tim," Peter asked, "what's his name?"

"His name is Mr. Charles Dickens."

"Charles Dickens, the writer?" Martha asked.

"I don't know. He never told me how he made a living."

"Charles Dickens, the writer?" Martha repeated, only more loudly. "Are you telling us you met Charles Dickens, the author? My stars, Tim, don't you know who he is?"

Shaking his head to indicate he did not, Tim felt confused by his eldest sister's enthusiasm.

"Tim, he is only the most famous author in all of *London*. No, he's the most famous author in the entire British Empire! You met him and talked to him, just the way you and I are talking now?"

Tim nodded.

"I have read and reread the chronicles of *Oliver Twist* for years, *dreaming* of the day I could simply catch a glimpse of Mr. Dickens, and here you are telling me the two of you just now had a conversation!"

Martha leaned back in her chair, processing the fantastic revelation made by her youngest brother, while Tim tried to steer the conversation back to the subject at hand. "Yes, right. Well, Father, Mr. Dickens would like to meet with you and Uncle Ebenezer."

"Me-... and Mr. Scrooge? But why, Tim? What have we to do with all of this, I wonder?"

"I'm not certain, really. But I *do* know it was vitally important to Mary that Mr. Scrooge and her brother should come together."

Just then, Emily scooted her chair back and ran to the coal-burning stove in the kitchen. There she stayed with her back to the family. Robert looked around the room, trying to determine what had frightened her. Befuddled, he stood himself and approached her. "Emily, what's wrong, my dear?" Placing a hand on her back, he felt her quietly crying.

Shaking her head, she waved him off, "I'll be alright, Robert. Please, go back and finish your dinner."

"But why are you crying?"

Emily turned to her husband, her red swollen eyes and tears on her cheeks confirming his hunch. "It's all just a bit much for me, Robert. You're used to this, I suppose, but a son who died, and then *didn't* die. Messages from a dead woman, which lead to a living soul, and apparently a famous one, at that. It's just too much for the likes of me."

Robert pulled Emily to his chest. "I understand, my love. And I promise you, no harm will come to any of us. But Em, I feel something truly wonderful is about to happen. Somehow Tim has seen beyond this mortal veil and gazed upon something extraordinary, perhaps even divine. I'm inclined to believe we owe it to him to do everything in our power to help him through this journey."

Emily nodded her agreement against her husband's chest, and then slowly pulled away. "I'm sorry, Robert. I just got frightened and overwhelmed. I'm alright now. Let's go finish our dinner before it gets cold."

Midafternoon the next day, Tim opened the door to the business of Scrooge and Cratchit and was followed inside by Charles Dickens, who promptly removed his top hat. "Uncle Ebenezer!" Tim called out.

"Timothy Cratchit!" Scrooge replied, using the same exuberant tone as his partner's young son.

"Father, Uncle, I'd like you to meet my new friend."

Robert and Scrooge rose from behind their desks, as a rather tall, well-dressed man accompanied Tim into the inner office. Tim pointed first to Robert. "My father, Robert Cratchit."

Robert and Charles shook hands, "Your servant, Mr. Dickens."

"Your servant, Mr. Cratchit."

Next, Tim introduced the eldest of them all with a slight bow of his head. "Mr. Ebenezer Scrooge."

The two gentlemen gazed at each other and firmly shook hands. "Your servant, Mr. Dickens."

"Your servant, Mr. Scrooge."

Scrooge then gestured to Chancy, who was working at the clerk's table, to join them. "And may I introduce our clerk, my-..." Scrooge hesitated, a lump in his throat arising upon his realizing this was the first time he was able to say these words of introduction. "My son, Chancy Scrooge."

"I didn't realize you had a son," Dickens said.

"Before a month ago, I didn't. He only recently adopted me."

"Marvelous! Congratulations to you both," Dickens said, as he reached out and shook Chancy's hand.

"The pleasure is mine, Mr. Dickens."

"Please, have a seat, sir," Robert suggested.

The three men sat in chairs, while Tim sat on a taller stool so his leg brace could stay straight, and Chancy returned to his clerk duties.

"I must say, Mr. Cratchit, this is a very convincing son you have," Dickens began.

"Thank you. Tim is, indeed, a unique light in this world. And may I add this is an honor for Mr. Scrooge and me to meet such a truly outstanding author as yourself, sir."

"Indeed so," Scrooge added. "Though I must confess I am not much of a reader of literature, which leaves me at a disadvantage to knowing your work, sir."

Dickens laughed and said, "Gentlemen, you flatter me, but I am no better than any other man you meet in the course of your lives. I merely take words, of which we are all familiar, and put them in a different order. If the structure is pleasing to a reader, they publish it and call it *literature*. What has truly captured my attention is Master Tim's account of my wife's sister, Mary—a young woman I'm quite satisfied he never met, at least in this life."

Tim listened intently and respectfully, as the three men talked well past dark, together trying to make sense of Mary's desires. Much to Tim's delight, the question of doubt never surfaced. All three men sincerely believed him, and seemingly even more so, Mary.

"Mary foretells life as we know it without Christmas," Dickens cautioned them. "Christmas is a holiday, a season, a state of mind and heart. How can it be, I dare ask, taken from us? It would be just as arduous to forbid a man from falling in love."

"Earlier this year," Robert said, "the minister of our church, Reverend Potts, adamantly declared the church would no longer sanction Christmas as a religious holiday. He referred to it as a pagan celebration that had no place in modern day Christianity. Accordingly, Christmas carols are now banned, and the bells in the church tower will remain silent on December twenty-fifth."

"But this is just one church, one congregation," Dickens said.

"I'm afraid it's more than that," Scrooge replied. "I go to the London exchange weekly and have heard men speak of similar referendums in their own churches, as well. Many plan to keep their businesses open on December twenty-fifth and to give their employees a day off on January the first, instead, to celebrate the New Year."

"How then, do we stop this wave of close-minded dissent?" Dickens asked. "We are but three. How do we stand against a unified church proclamation?"

Tim, who'd been sitting quietly across the room, spoke up. "Mary said to me, 'My brother holds the answer.' It was the reason I searched for you these past months."

"Why would she not tell you what she *expects* of us, or how to achieve her certainly daunting goals?" Dickens asked.

"When I was with her," Tim explained, "Mary showed me a path. It was clear to me at the time she was showing me the journey, not the answers. There were many branches in the path, but only one of them led to you."

"And find me you did, Tim. But to what means?"

"My sister Martha tells me you are a well-known writer, not just in London, but around the world, as well. Perhaps Mary believes you can use your talents as a writer."

"Yes, well said, Timothy!" Scrooge exclaimed. "It may be a well-drafted 'opinion' piece written by Mr. Charles Dickens and published in *The London Times* would do the trick. If it is well read in *The Times*, it may be syndicated to other newspaper publications."

"Perhaps so," Charles agreed. "But I think *more* is needed. A newspaper is read once and then used to start the fire in a stove. No, gentlemen, we need something more. We need a story that will be published time and time again, worldwide-... one that will fill the hearts and souls of every man, woman, and child who reads it. I believe-… hmm-… I could conceivably turn Tim's fantastic story of going to Heaven to learn of Heaven's desire for mankind to preserve and celebrate Christmas into-… into a book that, upon publishing, would capture the imagination of any soul who read it."

"I'm afraid, Mr. Dickens," Robert said, "that approach might not work. When our church learned of Tim's claim to have had a heavenly visit, we were immediately cast out for heresy and blasphemy—excommunicated, to be precise. I'm afraid Tim's story would bite us like a two-headed snake and only make matters worse."

When Tim abruptly stepped down from his stool, the three men watched and listened in silence, as every other step he took was followed by a clank from his leg brace. Eventually, he stopped at the desk around which they all sat. "What if Mary wants Uncle Ebenezer's experience from last Christmas told?"

"Why, Tim?" Dickens asked. "What happened last Christmas?"

"Uncle Ebenezer was visited by three Christmas ghosts."

Robert suddenly blurted out, "My Lord! At first, I thought those visitations were to change him from the man he was. But what if Tim is right? What if they were the sparks that will inevitably light the fire to save Christmas itself?! It's not merely the *day*, Mr. Dickens. We are being tasked with upholding the *spirit* of Christmas."

Dickens stared openly at Robert and then Scrooge. "Perhaps, Ebenezer, you should tell me about last Christmas."

Chapter 16

The following morning, Dickens entered the business of Scrooge and Cratchit at eleven-thirty to begin taking notes. "Top of the morning to you, Mr. Dickens," Scrooge cheerfully said, standing up to greet the much-heralded writer.

"And to you, sir," Dickens replied, reaching out and shaking his hand.

Following a similar greeting with Robert, he took a seat. "Right, well, first allow me to beg your pardon for being two hours later than we'd agreed last night. I must confess that, as a writer, I live in a state of constant doubt. So I paid Dr. Cecil an impromptu visit this morning and am pleased to report he confirmed for me the series of events concerning Tim's brief departure from this existence, as the lad had declared. Please don't take offense, gentlemen, but I regularly seek second and third-hand confirmation when writing about true life events."

"Dear me, no offense taken, sir," Robert replied. "It's quite understandable, indeed."

"And by the way," Dickens continued, "I have not discussed these matters with my dear wife, Catherine. The death of her sister still weighs heavily on her heart, and any talk of a miraculous encounter such as Tim's would surely derail her delicate sense of sanity. So I would ask, if ever you meet my Catherine, either by chance or circumstance, please do not discuss Tim's revelations in her presence."

"Oh, certainly not, sir," Scrooge agreed.

"By the by," Dickens asked, looking around the office, "where *is* Master Timothy?"

"His job at the zoo, I'm sure, sir," Robert said. "As today's discussion was to focus on Mr. Scrooge, I did not see the need to include Tim. I would be more than happy to send for him if you would prefer he be here."

"No, Bob, no need. I'm sure the three of us will fare well on our own."

"As you wish, sir."

"Right. So last night, Tim mentioned an encounter with three spirits, Mr. Scrooge. Please start from the beginning and tell me everything you remember, but please speak slowly so that I may transcribe your thoughts into notes."

"Well, to begin with, there were *four* spirits that night. The first to contact me, in a most startling manner, was my previous business partner, Jacob Marley. I must say, Mr. Dickens, what we're speaking of was the most terrifying night of my life."

"Great wisdom often begins with fear, Mr. Scrooge. Please continue."

"To truly comprehend what I am about to tell you, one must first understand I had allowed myself to become the most selfish, stingiest, greediest person ever to walk the face of the earth! At least, that is the way, looking back now, I see myself. And I dare say no one knew better than Bob Cratchit, poor fellow." Turning to his partner, he patted him on the shoulder. "This man suffered perhaps more than anyone under my oppressive demeanor."

Dickens looked up from his writing to the lack of expression on Robert's face. Having heard no rebuttal, he muttered, "Fascinating."

Scrooge proceeded to describe to Dickens the ghostly encounters as he remembered them, sparing no small detail. For hours, the celebrated author scribbled notes in his own form of shorthand. Robert replaced the quill for Dickens frequently, whenever the tips broke or failed to hold ink. Long through the afternoon and into the evening, Scrooge described the ghost of

Christmas past, the ghost of Christmas present, and most frighteningly, the ghost of Christmas yet to come.

As well, Scrooge told Dickens of his youth and his apprenticeship at Fezziwig's, his courtship with Belle and his partnership with Marley. He also spoke of the foreshadowing of Tim's death and his own. No stone was left unturned. Scrooge was as honest and forthcoming as possible, with no regard to the ugliness of his self-portrait.

After seven hours of talking, Scrooge said, "Gentlemen, I am exhausted. Last Christmas drained me to the core, and I have just relived the entire experience. Though I have devoted what little time remains for me in this world to erase my past, I still bear these chains forged by my life of greed and contempt." Raising his arms from his sides, the elderly businessman gestured to the invisible iron links he still felt tethered to his body. "I seek now only those opportunities that will allow me to ease the burdens of my fellow man."

As he lowered his arms, he implored, "I pray, Bob, you can forgive me for the man I was."

"Mr. Scrooge, last December twenty-sixth, all was forgiven and forgotten. You have since been a finer friend, and a finer master, I dare say, than any man in London has ever known. And may I add, sir, this day has been *most* enlightening. I have known you for much of my life, longer actually than anyone, I believe, but I have learned more about you in just this one day than I have known in the sum of these years. I see now why both Mary and Tim believe your story must be told. Christmas saved you, sir, and now I truly believe Mary calls upon you and Mr. Dickens to save Christmas."

Two days passed and neither Scrooge nor Cratchit had received word from Dickens. Finally, on the third day, as dinner approached at the Cratchits' home, Robert heard a knock on their door. Standing outside with his hat in hand, Dickens asked, "Pardon me, Bob. I wonder if I might have a word with you concerning our-… project?"

"Mr. Dickens sir, as I live and breathe. Please come in! Come in and meet my family."

Dickens briefly looked inside before begging off. "Oh no, sir. I see I'm intruding on your dinner and do not wish to disturb your family. It's with *you* I wish to discuss-…"

"Oh, *please* do come in, Mr. Dickens," Robert said, pulling the hat from his guest's hands. "You cannot *imagine* the heartache I would incur if my daughter discovered you were on our doorstep, yet missed the opportunity to meet you, sir."

Dickens blushed at the compliment, nodded in agreement and stepped through the doorway, Robert closing the door behind him. As they approached the dinner table, Robert began, "Children, Emily, I'd like to intro-…"

"Mr. Dickens!" Tim cried out when he saw the visitor standing next to his father.

Robert smiled and finished his introduction. "Yes, I'd like to introduce Mr. Dickens." Then pointing to each Cratchit in turn, he said, "You already know Tim, and this is Richard and Belinda. On the other side is my eldest son Peter, who is currently employed by Mr. Scrooge's nephew, Fred Holloway. Beside Peter is your biggest fan in London, my first born, Martha."

Unaware of the awe-struck tremble in her hand, Martha failed to recognize her spoon had begun a steady clanking on the side of her soup bowl. Reaching over quickly, Peter grabbed her hand to steady the spoon, an act of seeming kindness that everyone but Martha found humorous.

"And next to my happily surprised daughter is my beloved wife, Emily."

Although Emily stood to shake the handsome visitor's hand, she instead received a gentlemanly kiss on her knuckles. Nervously pulling her fingers through her hair, she managed a whispered, "Oh my."

"I'm very pleased to meet all of you," Dickens said. "I feel as though I already know a little about each and every one of you from the stories Mr. Cratchit and Mr. Scrooge have shared with me."

Abruptly, Martha stood and ran straight to her room. Robert looked at Emily with a confused expression. Moments later, though, she returned with five *Bentley's Miscellany* magazines.

"Mr. Dickens, sir, I have the first five installments of *Oliver Twist*-... and of course, I'm saving up to buy the sixth. I wonder if I might-... could I ask you to-... would you consider autographing one of these for me?"

Dickens looked kindly at Martha, still trembling as she clutched the treasured magazines tightly in her hands. "Ah, I'm sorry my dear, I cannot sign *one* of your magazines. But if you would be so kind as to fetch me a quill and ink, it would be my great pleasure to sign all *five*."

Martha released the breath she didn't realize she had been holding, and with a relieved giggle, led him to a writing table near the fireplace.

After the excitement of such a famous visitor had relaxed, Robert and Dickens excused themselves from the others and settled by the stone fireplace, both lighting their pipes and pausing to watch the red embers encircle the glowing pieces of coal. To the left of the fire, Tim sat in a child-size chair. Behind him, Dickens noticed a very short crutch hanging from a peg. "You don't need the crutch anymore, Tim?"

"Sometimes I use it if I have a long way to walk, or need to stand for a period of time."

"That's right, you were using it when I first met you at the monkey cages."

"Yes, sir, but with my brace, I walk better every day without the crutch, don't I, Father?"

"You certainly do, my boy."

"Bob, the reason I came here unannounced this evening is to pick your brain concerning Mr. Scrooge. The man I met the other day does not at all fit the profile he shares of himself."

"Yes, sir, I certainly understand your confusion. The man I knew for years as my employer was nothing like the man I know today. I suppose he is living proof that it is never too late to change."

Emily interrupted the conversation with her own opinion, "Well, I hated him."

"Emily, my dear!"

"Well, I'm sorry, Robert. But no one knows it better than you do, poor fellow,"

"No, no, please, Mrs. Cratchit," Dickens said. "No apologies are necessary. This is exactly what I wanted to hear. Please, go on."

"I hated everything about the man. The only thing good about him was that he treated everyone the same-… *mean*. I never met the man before this year, but I knew him well enough, I can assure you of that. Poor Robert came home every day, drained and exhausted from the mean-spirited nature of both Scrooge *and* Marley. Each of them was mean for meanness' sake. Then after Mr. Marley died, Scrooge became *twice* as wicked, merely to pick up the slack. No, I *hated* the man, indeed."

"And now?"

"Now, he's the most generous, kindhearted gentleman you could ever meet. I don't believe he has had a cross word for anyone since I have come to know him. Pardon me for being so bold, but I truly love the man."

"Fascinating, Mrs. Cratchit. And what do *you* believe happened to change him from being the worst London has to offer, into London's finest?"

"Well, you can talk about ghosts and goblins all you want, but if you ask me, I say it was simply Christmas. Somewhere between Christmas Eve and the day itself, *something* or *someone* reached into that man's chest and pulled out a heart that was black as coal, then replaced it with one of pure gold."

"And you believe it is possible for a man to change so dramatically, overnight?"

"Believe it? I have seen it with my own eyes! And you don't have to take *my* word for it. There are plenty of others who knew Mr. Scrooge before and after. Just ask Mrs. Dilber, his charlady, or Fred Holloway, his nephew. They'll tell you just as I have. But you've come to the right place, because no man, living or otherwise, knows Mr. Scrooge better than my Robert."

After rubbing her hands on Robert's back, and sensing a lull in the conversation, Emily stepped away, pleased she was able to speak her mind after holding her tongue all evening. Dickens took a puff on his pipe, blew the smoke toward the fireplace and watched it go up the chimney, along with the smoke from the burning coals. "I think I have enough to go on, Bob. I think I can make this work."

"That's wonderful news, Mr. Dickens! When do you think you can get started?"

"Started? We've already begun, my good man! With a lot of hard work and a publisher at the ready, I believe we could be in print within a year."

Tim, who had been silent for most of the evening, stirred in his seat. "A year? That will be too late, Mr. Dickens!"

Smiling at the young boy's innocence, he replied, "Tim, these things take time. Most books are *years* in the making. For us to have this book-..."

"It doesn't matter! If we miss this Christmas, there won't be any Christmas worth saving. Father, *surely* you understand."

"But Tim," Dickens said, attempting to reason with the boy's single-mindedness. "Please try to understand. Here we are in the middle of October. For us to have a book published before Christmas, it would have to be in print by the first of December. That's not humanly possible."

"No sir, Mr. Dickens. Returning from Heaven to this life with a message from your sister who has been dead these six years, *that* is not humanly possible. It's been said, 'Time and tide wait for no man,' Mr. Dickens. And in this case, Heaven won't wait, either. *I'm* not worried, though. I believe in you, sir."

With that, Tim stood up and said, "I'm tired, Father. I'm going to bed. Good night all. Good night, Mr. Dickens."

The two men watched in silence, as Tim walked into the bedroom he shared with his brothers. With a dumbfounded expression, Dickens turned to Robert and said, "But I can't-... he *must* understand-... there's-..."

"Tim has a way of getting the most out of the best of us, Mr. Dickens. It's almost as though he has lost his concept of the passage of time. As a cripple, he does not see himself as handicapped. Do you remember Mr. Scrooge describing the chains he saw wrapped around Jacob Marley's ghost?"

"Yes, of course, but-..."

"Tim is the only person I've ever known who bears no chain, not even a single link. The metal leg brace he wears is on the outside. It makes him amble, while still enabling him to walk. But on the inside, he is *untethered*."

Over the months of Tim's employment at the zoo, Cookie, the caretaker, had grown fond of "the cripple boy." Certainly, he knew the other boys were stronger and faster at mucking the animals' stalls, but Cookie recognized Tim had a remarkable work ethic, as well as an extraordinary rapport with the animals. "I don't know if the animals sense you're lame, or if you just have no fear," he told him one day. "But they listen to you better than anyone I've ever seen with my own eyes. It's clear you have a way of calming them, soothing their spirits."

It was Tim's lack of fear, however, occasionally bordering on recklessness that gave Cookie cause for concern over his young protégé's safety. Time and time again, he instructed Tim to stay away from the fiercest animals and to wait for a handler before entering their pen. But the seemingly fearless boy consistently failed to heed the warnings. On one cloudy afternoon, Cookie found Tim in the aviary sitting on the ground beneath a golden eagle's nest. As he drew closer to the cage, he could see the female eagle-... *in Tim's lap*. Cookie asked in a loud whisper, so as not to frighten the bird, "Tim, what are you doing?"

When Tim didn't answer, Cookie insisted, raising his tone to a hissing whisper. "Tim, get *out* of there! Those birds can tear you to shreds!"

Hurrying around to the aviary door to enter the cage, Cookie could see the bird was lying listlessly atop Tim's outstretched legs.

Looking up to see Cookie standing next to him, the young Cratchit whispered, "She's dying, Cookie."

Kneeling next to Tim, he explained, as a father would to his son, "Y'know, lad, I can't have you being so reckless around these animals. Every time I turn my back, you're breaking the rules and risking your own life."

Tim looked past Cookie, up at the male eagle perched on a branch overhead—the distinguished bird keenly watching the two of them with his mate—and quietly said, "He knows why we're in here. He knows she's dying. No one, not even an animal, should die alone if it can be helped. So I told him I'd stay with her. In a few minutes, I think, she'll be free and flying higher than we can imagine."

Cookie sat down on the ground next to Tim, joining him in gently stroking the bird's feathers. "Do you really believe it-… that animals go to Heaven?"

"I more than believe it, Cookie. I know it for *sure*. I saw them there."

With the eagle resting peacefully in his lap, Tim told Cookie about his own death and visit to Heaven. Fascinated by his young friend's account, Cookie replied, "I consider all of these animals my family, y'know. And every time I lose one, I say a prayer that God will let it into Heaven so I can be with 'em when I get there."

"That's a nice prayer. And somehow, I believe it will happen, just as you wish."

Cookie left Tim's side and soon came back with a burlap bag for the bird that had silently passed as they were talking.

"Let's put her in here."

"What will you do with her?" Tim asked, while Cookie gently wrapped the carcass.

"Come with me, and I'll show you."

Carrying the bagged eagle under his arm, Cookie and Tim slowly made their way to the outskirts of the zoo grounds, through a gate that displayed the sign: *Restricted Area -- Zoo Personnel Only*.

In the field beyond the gate stood a small shed, barely large enough to hold a pushcart and a few gardening tools. Cookie opened the rickety door and came out with a wood-handled shovel. "This is it, Tim. This is where I bury all of the dead animals. We can't use them as food for the other animals, because we don't know what disease they may have died from. So, I give them a proper burial."

After digging a hole, placing the burlap-wrapped eagle within it and covering the animal with dirt, Cookie stood over the grave and closed his eyes to offer up a silent prayer.

A few silent moments later, he said, "Tim?"

"Yes, sir?"

"I have something I want to show you."

Together they walked to the back of the field, where they came upon a boulder that protruded from the grass-covered ground. "I want you to promise me something, Tim."

Nodding his head, Tim gazed at the large rock, while Cookie continued, "I've never been much of one for people. The animals are my friends. *They're* my family. When the time comes to put me in the ground, don't let them bury me in some pauper's grave next to people I don't know. I want to be buried right here, in front of this rock, surrounded by my family. Will you promise me that, Tim?"

"Yes, sir, Cookie. I promise."

The following evening, as the day came to an end, Dickens entered the business of Scrooge and Cratchit. "Good evening, Charles," Scrooge said, warmly greeting their visitor.

"What's so good about it, I wonder?" Dickens replied with a disgruntled response. Pointing to Robert, who was finishing some notes in a ledger, he explained, "This man's son has *refused* my olive branch. That's right, Mr. Cratchit! I was at your home this morning and have suffered a *miserable* failure in trying to convince Tim to be patient for a year. That young schoolboy dared to tell me I may have to work harder!"

"Oh my, Mr. Dickens! I *do* apologize for anything Tim may have said that offended you."

"I'm not *finished*, Mr. Cratchit. When I explained to him that it would take me six weeks to write the first draft, and another six weeks for editing, and still another six weeks for publication, do you know what your son said? He suggested I write, edit and print *at the same time* to make the best use of each hour!"

"Mr. Dickens, Tim is just a boy. He doesn't-..."

"*So*, Mr. Cratchit," Dickens said, interrupting Robert, "I called upon my *editor*, who has agreed to review and edit every page as I write it. I called upon Mr. Leech, who has agreed to illustrate as I write. I have also called upon my publisher, who has agreed to promote the book for December sales. And I've called upon the printer, who has agreed to typeset the pages as they are approved, even before the book knows an ending. All of this will be funded from my private resources and credit with the bank. In short, gentlemen, if we wish to be in print by December of this year, we must all continue working together to bring this story to fruition!"

"Bravo!" Robert cheered, openly clapping and applauding the author's progress and commitment.

"You certainly have our complete support," Scrooge added. "Just let us know what you need, and we *will* make it happen."

"Yes, right," Dickens replied. "First and foremost, Bob, when this is over, I want it clearly understood that I will never again work for that boy of yours! He challenges me beyond my abilities!"

Sensing the lighthearted jest, Robert said, "I promise, Mr. Dickens; this will be Tim Cratchit's farewell publication."

Turning to Scrooge, Dickens said, "Ebenezer, I want you to take me home with you tonight. You must walk me through every detail of the last Christmas Eve. Show me the door knocker that became Jacob Marley, the doorway where Marley entered your chambers, the window through which you saw the wandering spirits, the place where the ghost of Christmas present sat. I want to see it *all* and experience it just as you remember."

"Certainly, sir."

"Oh, and I have already sent word to my wife that I will not be home this evening. Do you have a guest room?"

"I do, indeed. You are more than welcome to the bed and all of the accommodations I have to offer."

"The guest room is not for *me*, Mr. Scrooge, it is for *you*. I will be sleeping in *your* bed. I need to be as *you* were that very evening. I want to see every shadow and hear every sound of the house as it breathes. I want to hear the clock strike each and every hour, just as you did before the ghosts manifest before you."

"As you wish, sir!"

"Now, gentlemen, the first thing we must do is list the names of your characters."

"What's wrong with the names we already have?" Scrooge asked.

"Mr. Scrooge, if by some miracle we pull this off and create a manuscript people want to read, the last thing you would want is to be the subject of ridicule and mockery."

"Charles, my past is of my own making, but my friends and family weave the path to my future, whatever that may be. I am more than proud to be known as Tiny Tim's uncle. I say, let the chips fall where they may."

"And I second that, Mr. Dickens," Robert added.

"Bob, you as well? And so say you for your wife and children?"

"And so say I, Mr. Dickens."

Chapter 17

“You read, now, as well as any man I know,” Martha said, as Chancy closed the book from which he’d been reciting aloud to her.

“A testament to your teaching skills, I’m sure.”

Fall was in full control of the season, majestically displaying its seasonal colors, as the young couple left the Cratchit’s home for a stroll. For Chancy, entering Regent’s Park was like stepping into a painting, with countless yellow, gold and red leaves dotting the walkway. “You should hold my arm,” he tenderly suggested.

“Is this some elaborate scheme to hold me close as we walk?”

Chancy blushed, but quickly altered his course, “Well, remember you’re eight months pregnant, Martha. If you lose your balance, you should cast me beneath you to soften your fall.”

Slipping her hand around his elbow, she replied, “How could I possibly refuse such a chivalrous offer from a gentleman *and* a scholar such as yourself, Mr. Scrooge?”

Chancy smiled at both her gesture and words. “I still find it so remarkable to be referred to by that name.” They continued walking in silence, until he found the courage to ask, “Martha, do you think we will-…”

“Listen, Chancy, do you hear the birds?”

Chancy sighed, before saying, “Martha, you can’t keep changing the conversation every time I want to talk about it.”

Martha lowered her head and dropped her smile. "Why can't we just enjoy the day?"

"Because after today, there will be a tomorrow, and after that, another tomorrow. You always want to live only for the day, my love, but tomorrow is bound to replace today."

"Am I? Am I 'your love'?"

"Yes, of *course* you are. I love you more than life itself! How can I convince you of my sincere devotion?"

"You are such a good boy, Chancy. Excuse me, I mean you're such a gentle-*man*, Chancy. You could do so much better than me! Your father is raising you quickly in his business, and soon the fairest ladies of this city will be throwing themselves at your feet. It would be cruel and unfair of me to tie you down."

"But it is *you* I love, Martha, not one of the silly girls who can be swept away with a pretty dress. Marry me, Martha, and I will make you happy every day of your life. I swear my love and devotion to you."

A moment after falling deeply into the tender, dark brown eyes of her suitor, Martha winced as her eyes suddenly filled with tears. "Oh, Chancy, *you* are the silly one. How can you be so blind?"

"Because of your baby?"

"Yes, you precious fool! I am an unwed mother carrying a bastard child! How can I be certain I would love you when I don't even know if I can love this *thing* inside of me? It is simply not fair to ask you to become a husband and a father at the same time." Reaching up and laying her hand on his cheek, she added, "You have such a good heart. *Please*, I beg you, give it to someone more deserving than me. The love you profess is-... it's your kindhearted pity."

"No, Martha, I'm not-..."

"Let me go!" she demanded, putting both hands against his chest and pushing him back. "I don't want to see you anymore-... not like this."

In tears, she turned and hurried down the pathway toward her home.

Heartbroken and dejected, Chancy could only watch as she turned past a great oak and faded from sight. With his hands pushed deep into both pockets of his trousers, he slowly began the long walk back to Scrooge and Cratchit's office.

As Chancy made his lonely way past the Keystone Church of Camden Town, he suddenly recognized two of his old mates standing with sledgehammers in the adjacent cemetery. Entering through the cemetery gate, he hollered to his friends. "Billy, Sammy, how're you fellas doing?"

Both boys were shocked to see their old friend, especially dressed as spiffily as he was. "David!" said Billy, grabbing Chancy's shirt. "Good Lord! Where did you score such fancy clothes?"

"I have a lot to tell you, mates, but what are you doing here in Camden Town? Have they got you digging graves now?"

"Nah'," Sammy said, gesturing to the pile of gravel in front of him and holding up his sledgehammer. "The preacher here hired us to bust up a gravestone. I guess he didn't want it anymore."

"Yeah," Billy added, "or maybe the dead fellah' here forgot to pay his rent."

Both Billy and Sammy laughed like jackals at the witty response. Chancy asked, "Well, whose grave was it?"

Both boys shrugged their shoulders. Billy said, "I don't know. We can't read, y'know."

Sammy said. "I think the first letter was a C, followed by an R. Oh, and the last letter was a T. I remember because T looks like a cross."

Immediately, Chancy's fists clenched with rage. "Pardon me, mates," he said, turning and sprinting from the graveyard up the steps and into the church.

"Potts, where are you?!" he shouted into the empty sanctuary. "Where are you, preacher?! I want to see you right now!"

From a side office, an elderly man appeared and asked, "Here, what's all the shouting? We are in a house of worship, and I would mind you to respect it as such."

"Are you Potts?" Chancy demanded.

"I am Reverend Potts. What matter has you so riled up, young sir?"

"Did you just pay those boys outside to smash a tombstone of the Cratchits?"

"I may have," he replied with a smirk. "And what business is that of yours, Mister-…"

"Scrooge. My name is Mr. Scrooge, and the Cratchits are my friends. You've gone too far now, Potts, desecrating the grave that belongs to my most trusted friend and employer!"

"Now see here, boy," Reverend Potts responded angrily. "You are standing on *private* property. I am the curator of this church and cemetery, and it is my responsibility to preserve these holy grounds. The grave you refer to belonged to the mother of a man who has been excommunicated, along with all of his relatives. By my orders, the stone has been removed, and just as the Romans did to the city of Carthage, the earth will be heavily salted, so that nothing will ever grow there again!"

As two brawny men approached Reverend Potts from behind, he did not turn to greet them. Instead, he merely instructed, "Show this 'friend' of the Cratchits how our door swings only one way for him."

The Reverend turned and passed between the two men, who stepped forward and took Chancy by his arms, dragging him backward toward the doors. "You'll answer for this, Potts!" the young man shouted.

Outside, the two muscular lackeys viciously tossed Chancy on his back, such that he tumbled roughly down the stairs and landed on the last step. Subsequently picking him up, each man began pounding him in the face, one then the other, taking turns pummeling Chancy hard, bloodying his nose and badly bruising his eyes and cheeks. After severely beating him to the edge of unconsciousness, one of the men gave him a final warning, "Next time, we won't be letting you crawl away."

Billy and Sammy, who had watched the tail-end of the one-sided fight from the cemetery, dropped their hammers in fear and ran in the opposite direction.

After several minutes spent lying in his own blood and throbbing pain, Chancy finally managed to muster the strength to pull himself up and begin the long walk to his closest refuge, the Cratchit's home. His nose continued bleeding profusely and his aching jaw's swelling increased by the minute, but still, he hobbled on.

Hearing a faint knock on the front door, Emily left Martha's side, who was still crying at the dining table, after her having abruptly left Chancy in the park. Opening the door, she screamed, seeing Chancy beaten and bloodied, barely able to stand against the door frame. "Oh, my stars! Chancy! Get in here!"

Holding his arm around her shoulder, Emily helped him step into the house. Martha ran to his other side, and together, they moved him to a chair where he was able to lower himself down. Martha asked, "Chancy, what in the world happened?! Who did this to you?!"

Emily snapped, "Never mind that now! We have to see how badly he's hurt!"

Fetching a bowl of water with a cloth towel, Martha handed both to her mother, who quickly soaked the towel and gingerly began cleaning his wounds. "Here, Martha, see if you can stop the bleeding." Emily gave her a clean cloth from her apron pocket and motioned to his nose. Though she knew she could clean the cuts and bruises on her own, after listening to her daughter cry for over an hour about how she had rejected Chancy, Emily sensed it would serve the highest good to involve her daughter directly in Chancy's healing.

Moments later, Richard came home from school. Emily took the books from him and said, "Son, run as quickly as you can to your father's office. Tell him and Mr. Scrooge that Chancy is here and he's been hurt very badly. Tell them they should both come at once. Now hurry!"

As Martha gently wiped the blood from Chancy's face and applied pressure to the oozing cuts, she quietly asked him to tell of the events that occurred after she'd left him in the park.

"Well, my old chums Billy and Sammy were smashing a headstone with the Cratchit name there in the church cemetery-…"

"Mother? Could that have been Grandmother's?"

"Yes, I'm afraid she *is* the only Cratchit in the cemetery. It was her stone, I'm quite sure."

"That preacher was proud of what he had done, I could tell," Chancy bitterly said. "It was malicious and spiteful."

"Chancy, I know you never had the pleasure of meeting her," Emily said, as a sense of anger boiled inside her, "but I am here to tell you that Rebecca Cratchit was the kindest, most loving woman who ever lived." She burst into tears while imagining the cruelty of someone doing such a thing.

Martha continued cleaning Chancy's face. The left side of his jaw was severely swollen, and already showing discoloration, so she had him hold a wet towel against it. Through the pain, he went on and explained his altercation with the Reverend Potts.

Martha asked, "You confronted him when you found out it was my grandmother's stone?"

"I couldn't stand by for one moment, knowing someone would do such a thing, Martha. But it wasn't directed at your grandmother. Potts did this to punish your *father*."

"You love my father that much?"

Chancy lowered the towel from his face and said, "Martha, I would die for that man."

Martha lifted the towel she was holding to put pressure against a cut under his eye. "Chancy, ask me again."

He turned to face her.

"Ask me again, Chancy, before I change my mind."

Chancy looked over at Emily, who was sitting quietly on his other side. She smiled and nodded at him. "Martha Cratchit, will you marry me?"

"Yes!" she exclaimed, throwing her arms around his neck, which immediately made him wince. Seeing his pain, Emily sprang up and stood behind his chair. "Chancy, lean forward," she instructed, as she lifted his shirt carefully to his shoulders. Her head twitched when she saw his back. Martha stood as well, cupping her hands over her mouth to hold back from screaming.

"Chancy-…" Emily began, "you have one solid bruise from the bottom of your ribs to the top of your shoulders. Good Lord! It looks like you're going to be sleeping in a chair for a few weeks."

Chancy didn't even notice what Emily said. His attention was entirely on his beloved. Taking her hand, he asked. "You said 'yes'?"

Martha smiled, nodded her head and grasped his hand tightly in hers. "Yes, Chancy, I would love to be your wife."

The three sat silently at the table, as the women continued tending to Chancy's wounds. The battered victim, on the other hand, could not take his eyes away from his fiancée. Within a short time, Richard returned with Robert, who had sprinted ahead of Scrooge. When the door opened, and Robert rushed in, he immediately asked, "What happened to Chancy?"

Emily was the first to stand and lead him to the table. Nearly bursting with pride, she said, "Chancy asked Martha to marry him!"

Staring in astonishment at the blood-soaked towels and bowl of bloody water near the youth whose face was covered with deep cuts and awful bruises, he added, "Was all of this really necessary? She couldn't just say 'no'?"

Consumed by emotion, Robert dropped to his knees upon his mother's grave, atop a thick layer of salt, in the church cemetery. Pale moonlight illuminated the place where her upright marker had once stood. Gathering the rubble, piece by broken piece, into a pile where the headstone had been, he said under his breath, "Tell me, Mother, how do I control my anger? How do I find the strength to forgive the man who did this?"

Moving over to the grave adjacent to his mother's, he ran his fingers across the name, tracing the engraved letters that spelled "Elizabeth Madison." With a forced smile, he said, "Thank God he didn't know you were my sister, Lizzy, or I would be gathering two piles of rock tonight."

Standing up and stepping back, Robert vowed, "I swear this to you, Mother. By all that is holy, I will mark your resting place in a way that will stand the test of time. It will take more than one man's hate to erase you from this world or my memory. I love you always; please remember me."

Brushing the salt from his knees and hands, he walked back through the cemetery gate and solemnly homeward.

"Am I doing the right thing?" Martha asked, while slowly walking, arm in arm with her parents toward Regent's Park.

Emily looked behind them to see her other four children, not far behind. "Too late to get the jitters now, my dear."

"I remember our wedding day," Robert chimed in. "Along with the birth of you and our other children, it was one of the happiest days of my life."

Martha squeezed her father's arm, gladdened by his comforting words. "But Chancy and I have only courted for a couple of weeks. Is that long enough to know if we are meant for each other?"

Emily smiled at her daughter's innocence. "Maybe *you* have only been courting for two weeks, but Chancy has been courting you for six months. I could see it in his eyes, the first time he saw you."

"Oh, Mother," Martha said, blushing and giggling at Emily's observation.

"She's right," Robert added. "Chancy has been taken from the moment he first met you. I think he'll be a fine husband and a good provider for your family. He is kind, honest and loves you with all of his heart."

"And there's nothing more important than that," Emily said.

Martha looked back at her siblings, pleased by the sight of Belinda holding Tiny Tim's hand to help him keep pace with the family as they entered the park. "Mother, I don't know how to be a good wife any more than I know how to be a good mother. How did you learn these things?"

"Who taught you to be such a supportive, loving sister? Who taught you to be the daughter who brings joy into our home in so many ways?"

"Well-… no one. It's just who I am."

"Then that is your answer. You will be a good wife and a good mother because that is who you are."

As the two Scrooge's walked side by side into Regent's Park, the elder stopped, turned to the younger to face him, and then made some minor adjustments to the groom's high collar, "This has been a very short engagement, Chancy. Are you sure you're ready to take this next step?"

"I'm quite certain, Father."

"But we haven't had much time together, you and I. You know, as father and son."

"My marrying doesn't mean you'll see any less of me. I *promise* we'll be around and very likely underfoot until you can tolerate us no longer! You see, it's important to me that Martha's baby has a last name-… *my* last name. But in the meantime, won't it be nice to have a woman around who can cook better than *me*? You and I will *both* be benefitting. Mrs. Dilber is not getting any younger, I dare say."

Scrooge laughed. "So you think we'll be enjoying something more than boiled potatoes?"

"Most *certainly*. But you know it'll not be long before there's a baby in the house, which will be new to all of us, but mostly you. Promise me, you'll let me know if the noise is too much. We will be more than welcome to stay with Martha's family, where crying babies have lived off and on for many years."

"Nonsense! My grandchild will always be welcome in our home. A growing family is exactly what the old house needs to make it come alive again. I'm proud of the man you've become in the short time we've known each other, and I feel blessed to have Martha for a daughter."

"Thank you, Father, but it is *I* who feel blessed. You, sir, are the kindest man I have ever known, and it is a privilege to be your son."

Entering the park's botanical garden from the east, Scrooge asked, "Is this the place?"

"Yes, the large oak next to the duck pond. Martha named this tree Goliath. She says it is a mighty tree, of which all other trees are jealous. This is where I've been attending Sunday service with the Cratchits, and this is the place Martha chose for our sanctuary."

Moments later, the Cratchits approached the same oak tree. Chancy and Martha locked eyes. "You look very dashing, Mr. Scrooge," Martha said to her fiancé.

"And you are the most beautiful vision God ever placed in this world."

"Gather around, everyone," Emily said, identifying the correct place for each person to stand. First, she positioned Martha on Chancy's left. On the other side of Chancy stood Scrooge. To Martha's left was Belinda. As Emily was moving her children into place, Belle found them and approached Martha.

"For you, my dear," she said, handing a bouquet of white rosebuds to Martha and kissing her on the cheek.

"How nice of you!" Emily said.

Stepping back and walking behind the small crowd, she replied, "The second greatest moment in a midwife's life is when she gets to see one of her children marry."

At about the same moment, Fred Holloway approached with his wife, Alice, and their children, all taking their places behind the Cratchit children.

Finally, Robert took his position directly in front of Chancy and Martha, facing the bride and groom. "I found out, only recently," he began, projecting loudly enough for all to hear, "that because I have been conducting Sunday services for all of these months, it was a simple process for me to apply for a license to conduct a wedding. Yesterday, I received my license and today we gather here to marry Chancy Scrooge and Martha Cratchit in holy matrimony."

As the reality of his words sank in, Emily and Belle both began crying into their handkerchiefs.

"All who've gathered here have come to bear witness to this marriage, held in the sight of God, in His garden of clover and flowers, serenaded by the wind and water, and bound in love until the end of time. Chancy, do you take this woman as your wife, to have and to hold, through sickness and health, until death do you part?"

"I do," the nervous young man responded.

In accordance with Chancy's wishes, unbeknownst to Martha or Emily, Robert added, "And Chancy, do you take Martha's *baby* as your own, and vow to be father and guardian, and love the child for as long as you shall live?"

"I do."

Martha squeezed her groom's hand tightly and stared with affectionate eyes into his.

"And Martha, do you take this man as your husband, to have and to hold, through sickness and health, until death do you part?"

"I do."

Hearing her daughter's response, Emily lost control of her emotions and burst loudly into tears-... but still, the ceremony continued.

"Then before these witnesses, and with God's blessing, I now pronounce you man and wife. Chancy, you may kiss your bride."

As the couple tenderly put their lips together and embraced, Robert proudly announced, "Friends and family, it is my privilege to present to you, Chancy and Martha Scrooge. Those whom God has joined, let no man put asunder."

Scrooge gazed at the young couple, suddenly overcome with a sense of familiarity. As Chancy and Martha clung to one another, he was reminded of the children beneath the robe of The Ghost of Christmas Present.

He knew he saw the face of the boy named *Ignorance* when he first met Chancy, but now he could clearly see the innocence of the girl named *Want*, in Martha's eyes. These children, 'man's children' as the ghost had reminded him, were now his.

I understand clearly, Scrooge thought to himself. *The girl named Want, was not a creature of greed, as I first thought. All she wanted, was to be loved. It was my greed and my ignorance of which the spirit forewarned. By all that is holy, these children before me will have refuge; they will have resource; I swear it!*

Once the applause died down, as quickly as it had begun, the wedding ceremony was over. After everyone had a chance to shake Chancy's hand and hug Martha, all those who had attended the wedding stood on the walkway. Robert held Emily's hand; Ebenezer held Belle's hand; Fred held Alice's hand, and all stood silently watching Chancy help Martha step into a horse-drawn coach, hired by Scrooge, which they would ride into the world to begin their lives together.

On the doorstep of the home where their married life was to commence, the house they now shared with Ebenezer Scrooge, a gift wrapped in brown paper and tied with string greeted them when they arrived. Martha squealed when she unwrapped the complete three-volume set of *Oliver Twist*. Inside the cover of each book, the inscription read, *To Chancy and Martha Scrooge, on the day of your wedding. Your friend, Charles Dickens.*

Chapter 18

Dickens meandered quietly amongst the cages and pens that populated the zoo in Regent's Park. Observing the animals and studying their behavior was a favorite pastime, one which he'd rarely enjoyed as of late, given the busy days and late nights required to meet his recently accepted deadline. "Timothy, my boy!" he called out, upon finding him in the aviary, scooping seed into a variety of bowls.

Tim returned the scoop to the seed bucket and walked to the edge of the cage, where Dickens stood. "Good day, Mr. Dickens. Tell me, sir, are you in the cage or am I?"

Both laughed at the humor.

Dickens replied, "From my perspective, I'm not sure I can tell the difference, but whereas I feel trapped most of my days, I would have to assume *you* are the one on the outside."

Tim smiled and replied, "Give me a minute, and I'll be right there with you."

Walking at a steady pace through a double set of cage doors designed so no bird could escape, Tim joined his friend on the walkway. "I wonder if we might talk for a few minutes," Dickens said as Tim approached.

"Yes, sir. Certainly."

The two walked toward a nearby bench, and after sitting down, Dickens looked around at the various animal habitats. The Fall season had taken its toll on the trees, spreading their leaves around the pathways and bushes. The pungent smell of the animal habitats and musty leaves was a pleasant change to the burnt coal ash that hung heavy over the city. "I enjoy this place more than any I have known in all my travels. The four-legged animals bring a sense of calm to my spirit, the likes of which no two-legged animal ever has."

"Yes, sir, I quite agree. Not one animal in this entire zoo has ever seen me as a cripple."

Dickens looked down at the brace on Tim's leg and realized he had never thought of Tim as being crippled, either. "Tell me more about Heaven, Tim. What else do you remember about the time you were with Mary?"

Tim paused before answering, recalling what he'd already spoken. "I realize now my time in Heaven was brief, but on that day I could not have told you if I had been with Mary for a minute or a year. In our world, sir, time moves in only one direction-… but in Heaven, it moves in many. When I think about it, I feel sad. Not because there was sadness in Heaven, but because I am not there, now. It's hard to explain because I simply don't have the words. What we know of our world, we learn through our five senses. Imagine how much better we could understand the universe if we had just one more sense! When I was in Heaven, I truly felt as though my senses were without limit."

"What did Mary look like when you saw her?"

"Very much as she appeared in her earthly life, I imagine. But I believe that was by her choice, so I would be able to describe her to you.

"With so much beauty and love to be experienced there, how did you manage to return to this life?"

"I was not forced or tricked. Mary even told me Heaven would understand if I chose *not* to return. But when she showed me how sad my family would be, and the darkness that would overtake a world without Christmas, I knew I had to come back."

"Fascinating. What else, Tim? Tell me more about what you saw."

"There was no sun or moon in the sky, but nonetheless the light was brighter and more perfect than any I have ever known. There were wisps of clouds above us, or so I thought. But when I looked closer, I could see it was actually groups of countless beings, moving together like a river in the sky."

"These beings, were they angels?"

"Yes, that is probably the best way to describe them. I learned so much in Heaven, but I also lost some things."

"Lost? It sounds to me as though you gained insight into the unseen workings of the universe. What could you have lost?"

"While I was there, I lost the ability to feel jealousy, or hate, or envy. None of the bad thoughts or feelings that help us choose between right or wrong were with me. Even now, I struggle to understand such feelings."

"That sounds like a good thing to lose."

"Well, those things are not with us in Heaven. Apparently, we leave them behind. But here, if I don't have any 'fear,' for instance, I may make a wrong decision that will get me, or someone else hurt. Cookie chastises me regularly for the way I behave with the animals. He tells me fear is healthy and shows respect in the animal kingdom."

Shifting their conversation's direction, Dickens asked, "When the book is published, will Mary be satisfied?"

"She showed me two futures. The first was a world *without* Christmas, shrouded in darkness and misery. In the second, I saw endless bells from countless churches ringing in Christmas morning, and people sharing in the glory, hope, and inspiration that represents. So I believe the bells will answer your question, Mr. Dickens. Come Christmas morning, they will ring for peace and goodwill to all, or remain silent in despair."

"How can a story about a man who was lost to the world make the bells ring on Christmas morning?"

"According to what Mary showed me, the tide is going out, Mr. Dickens. People are losing their faith. My prayer is, with the publication of your book, the bells will ring once again because people will know the peace Christmas brings to their lives."

"And I pray your faith in me will be justified. I could sit and listen to you talk about Heaven for a week, but this is not the reason I came here to see you today, Tim. My main purpose is to discuss the title of the book."

"You know the title?"

"What would you think about calling it, *The Three Christmas Ghosts*?

"But this isn't a ghost story. It's a Christmas story."

"Yes, a Christmas story with ghosts."

"But the story is not about the ghosts. It's about a man who finds Christmas in his heart, where it once was lost."

"Ah, well, then what about calling it *A Christmas Spirit*?"

Tim paused to reflect. "You asked me a lot about what I *saw* in Heaven, but you never asked me what I *heard*. Mr. Dickens, I cannot begin to describe how-... heavenly the sounds and music were. From the grains of sand beneath me to the skies overhead, and all the beings I saw, both near and far, everyone and everything made a sound that was perfectly harmonized and filled with such love and joy. What I heard were *carols*, more pure than any I had ever known."

Dickens sat quietly, thinking through the word combinations. "*A Christmas Carol*," he said emphatically.

Staring at the birds in the cage in front of him, Tim turned his sight to a flock of birds flying free overhead. "Yes"

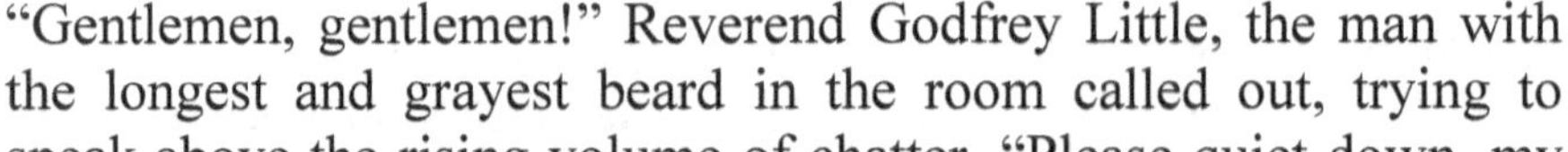

"Gentlemen, gentlemen!" Reverend Godfrey Little, the man with the longest and grayest beard in the room called out, trying to speak above the rising volume of chatter. "Please quiet down, my brothers! Let's call this meeting to order."

From his table at the front of the room, he looked around at the chairs scattered about, as though a child's marbles had been dropped on a wooden floor. Only the three men seated at the table seemed interested in waiting their turn to speak. "I-... will-... have-... order!" he shouted, slamming the palm of his hand to the table with each word.

Finally, the crowd of forty-three clergymen stopped their bantering and began taking their seats, adjusting their position as necessary, to face the trio at the front. The somber room's shades were drawn and smoke from a dozen or more pipes added to the mystique of the meeting.

"That's better. Thank you, gentlemen. Represented here today, we have Catholic priests and Protestant preachers, the Church of England, Church of Wales, Christian monks and various other denominational leaders. We have called this most unusual gathering to give one among us an opportunity to speak regarding a matter of concern to us all." Looking directly over to the man on his right, he said, "At this time, I would like to introduce the Reverend Potts from the Keystone Church of Camden Town. Please, my brothers, hold your tongues until he has had a chance to state his concerns. There will be plenty of time for discussion afterward."

All eyes were on Potts as he stood to take the floor. "My brothers," he began, spreading both arms wide in a welcoming gesture, "and we are all brethren of the same cause. We are entering into a holy war, a war that pits good against evil!"

"Which one are we?" a nameless voice called out from the back of the room.

"Who said that?" Potts shouted.

No one spoke, so Potts waited for the bits of snickering to subside. "In my congregation and yours, as well, pagan practices are spreading like a plague. In this modern age, we must cast out the demons that lure our flocks with false promises and tempt them with sins of the flesh. We must take a stand, starting here and now, and I propose to you our first target be the pagan practice of Christmas."

Heads in the crowd turned from side to side, while whispered opinions passed among many of the clergymen.

Potts referred to his notes and began reading, "Mario Righetti, a renowned Catholic liturgist, writes: *The Church of Rome, to facilitate the acceptance of the faith by the pagan masses, found it convenient to institute the twenty-fifth of December as the feast of the temporal birth of Christ, to divert them from the pagan feast, celebrated on the same day in honor of the 'Invincible Sun,' Mithras. The mixing of pagan Sun-worship and Christianity is exemplified by the testimony of a Syrian scholiast on Bar-Salibi, who said, 'It was a custom of the heathen to celebrate on the same twenty-fifth of December the birthday of the Sun, at which they kindled lights in token of festivity. In these solemnities and festivities, the Christians also took part.'"*

"In other words, my brothers, we must stand fast in our belief that Christmas is actually a day of celebration for pagan Sun worship and has *no* haven in modern Christianity!"

A murmur of disapproval stirred throughout the assembly.

"Practically *all* the known Sun-deities were born on the twenty-fifth of December," Potts continued. "First-century Christians did not know when Jesus was born. Early Christian leaders bemoaned this fact. When they *did* celebrate Christmas, they generally did so in April and May. Pope Julius I, in the fourth century commanded a committee of bishops to establish the date of the nativity of Jesus. December twenty-fifth, the day of 'the invincible sun' was decided upon. Not coincidentally, that is the day when the pagan world celebrated the birth of their Sun gods: the Egyptian Osiris, the Greek gods Apollo and Bacchus, the Chaldean Adonis and the Persian Mithra. Thus, the ancient festival of the Winter Solstice, the pagan celebration of the birth of the Sun, came to be adopted by the Christian Church as the nativity of Jesus, and was called Christmas."

The clergymen listened intently, as Potts paused, looked with urgency out over the crowd and continued. "In what is to be our final straw, my brethren, the pagans are promoting the practice of cutting down evergreen trees and nailing them to stands in their own homes and decorating them *to form false idols*. Now, to some, this may sound harmless, but consider Jeremiah ten, versus two through four:

Thus saith the Lord, learn not the way of the heathen, and be not dismayed at the signs of heaven; for the heathen are dismayed at them. For the customs of the people are vain: for one cutteth a tree out of the forest, the work of the hands of the workman, with the ax. They deck it with silver and with gold; they fasten it with nails and with hammers, that it move not."

The men in the room nodded at one another and began raising the level of chatter until Potts lifted his hands high to hush the crowd. In a softened tone, he implored them, "We *must* stand united to suppress the pagan influence on our society. Excommunicate those who will not renounce their sinful ways, as I have done in my own congregation. Keep the bells silent, do not let them ring in the pagan day of Sun worship on this or any other twenty-fifth of December. Write letters to your sister churches across this land, into Europe and the Americas. Beginning today, *we will take back our religion!*"

Chapter 19

"Close the damper on the stove, please, Chancy. I'm burning up!" Martha said, pushing the comforter down past her knees. Scrooge's house still seemed entirely foreign to her, despite their pleas for her to realize this was now *her* home, too.

"Five minutes ago you were freezing," Chancy replied. "Are you coming down with a cold or a fever?"

"No, I don't believe so. I feel flush, though. *Please,* sit with me. Belle said I need to stay in bed as much as possible before the birth."

Chancy did as he was asked, and immediately took his wife's hand in his.

"Chancy, I'm scared."

"What about, my dearest?"

"What if I can't love this baby? I'm terrified it will remind me of the man who attacked me. Oh Chancy, how could I look into that man's eyes every day, if they're in our child?"

Chancy smiled to reassure her while squeezing her hand. "Martha, this child you carry was made by God. Our child will be unique in all the world. Most importantly, it will call you *Mother* and me *Father*. It will walk in fields of clover and swim in crystal clear lakes. In the winter, the three of us will play in the snow. In the summer, we will lie in the park and guess the shapes of clouds. How lucky our child will be to have two parents *and* grandparents who will spoil it, and scores of aunts and uncles to teach it! Most importantly, our child will have a sir name and a Christian name. Our child will have everything *I never had.*"

Martha managed a smile. "Oh Chancy, I do love you! Please forgive me and my silly insecurities."

"You'll see. The moment you hold it in your arms, all of your fears will disappear."

"Breakfast, my dear Martha," Emily declared, entering the bedroom with a tray of food.

Martha sat up higher in the bed so her mother could place the tray of food next to her. Emily patted her son-in-law on the arm and said, "You had better get to work, Chancy. Your father is already there waiting for you, I'm quite sure. Don't you worry about Martha. I'll stay with her until you get home this evening. If anything changes, I'll send for you."

Chancy stood and kissed Emily on the cheek before kissing his wife's sweet lips. "You'll be fine, Martha. I leave you in better hands than mine."

Tim walked around the zoo habitats, looking for Cookie, but no one he asked had seen him recently. Standing at the barrier protecting the American Bison, he hollered to one of the other boys, "Hallo, Michael! Have you seen Cookie?"

"I saw him this morning in his shop!"

Waving to Michael, Tim headed toward the small shed where Cookie kept his tools, right alongside his bed. The cramped, dank quarters had been his home on the zoo grounds for more than thirty years. Making his way to the gate beyond the back lot, Tim eyed Cookie's shed, which stood among stacks of bent fences, broken tools, and various throw-away items, all of which Cookie had originally intended to fix-… someday.

"Hallo, Cookie! Are you home?"

Although receiving no answer to his call, he *did* hear the familiar hacking cough of his mentor. Respectfully, he slowly opened the door and stepped inside. "Cookie, how are you, sir?"

Peering through the darkness to the back of the shed, led by the wheezing sounds Cookie made with each breath, Tim approached him lying on his cramped, makeshift bed.

"Cookie, are you ill?"

"Aye, Tim," he said, before violently shaking with a fitful spell of coughing. "I won't be of much use to the zoo today, lad. You and the other boys will have to make it without me, sorry to say."

Tim hesitated. "Should-… should I start with the monkey cages again today?"

Cookie tried laughing but quickly fell into another coughing jag. Leaning toward his young assistant, he hoarsely whispered, "Aye, lad, *you* know what needs doing. Just go where you're needed the most."

As his eyes adjusted to the dim light in the room, Tim could see his friend's pained, pale face. Looking around, he found a rickety wooden chair and pulled it next to the bed. After sitting, he whispered back, "You're right Cookie, and I'm needed here."

Martha flinched as she grabbed her belly, "Mother, I think I just had a contraction. Is it time? Where's Belle?"

Emily set her knitting down on a small wooden table beside the rocker. "Hush, my dear, stay calm," she said in a soft, soothing voice. "There's plenty of time, I assure you. This is just the beginning."

Though frightened, Martha managed to nod and reposition herself in bed, hoping that would help her relax.

"I'll be right back, Martha," Emily said and went downstairs.

"Belinda, my dear, we're getting closer. Please go over to Belle's and tell her Martha's contractions have started. She'll know what to do."

"Yes, Mother. Should I find Chancy as well and tell him?"

"Not yet, we still have a long wait. It will be tonight at the earliest. There's no point in making Chancy worry about anything just yet."

An hour and a half later, Belle entered Scrooge's home and climbed the steps to the second-floor bedroom, where Emily had pulled a chair next to Martha.

"How's my new mother?" Belle serenely asked, as though she had been through this a hundred times before-... which of course she had.

"Good, but nervous," Martha replied.

"How often are the contractions?"

"About every five minutes," Emily answered. "But not very regular, at least not yet."

"Uh-huh," Belle acknowledged, approaching the bed on the opposite side from Emily.

Pulling the blanket down, she felt Martha's belly through her nightgown. "Lift your knees for me, Pet."

Belle moved two fingers inside to check her, but felt Martha's legs tense up and saw her face turn red.

"Now, Martha, you and I are going to become very familiar with one another over the next few hours, if you know what I mean. I need you to try to relax and let me do my job."

Suddenly Emily burst out laughing. "Dear me! Belle gave me the same exact speech just before you were born, Martha! And she's right, you know. Now is not the time for any sort of embarrassment. We ladies are all kindred spirits under our clothes, indeed."

Martha meekly smiled at the two women, who seemed as excited as she was scared. Relaxing her muscles, she let Belle spread her knees so she could get an idea of how the birth was progressing.

"Alright, you can relax now and let your knees down," Belle said in a motherly tone. She pulled the blanket back up to cover Martha's belly and keep her warm. "We still have quite a while to go before we meet your baby."

Emily nodded. "That's just what I've been telling her. The first one takes the longest."

When Belle noticed Belinda standing near the door, she waved her in and said, "Come here, Belinda, my dear. You should be a part of this too. Someday you'll be calling on old Belle to help bring *your* baby into this world, just like your mother did when *you* were born."

Belinda took three steps forward but looked terrified as she approached the scene, imagining her sister would soon be screaming in agony. Suddenly she stopped and retreated to the doorway, shaking her head. "No thank you, Miss. I can see fine from over here."

Emily laughed, then said, "Why don't you go make Belle and me a cup of tea? Oh, and bring your sister a cup of warm water to drink."

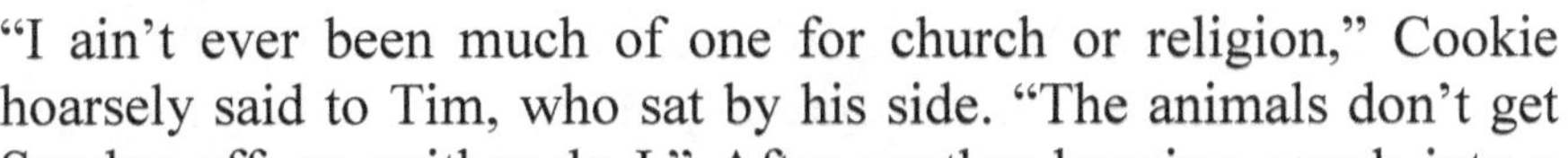

"I ain't ever been much of one for church or religion," Cookie hoarsely said to Tim, who sat by his side. "The animals don't get Sunday off, so neither do I." After another heaving cough into a rag, he said, "I suppose God ain't interested in the likes of me."

"You have spent your *whole* life caring for God's creatures, Cookie. How could He *not* love you for your devotion and service? When you tend the animals of His Kingdom, you are surely serving Him."

Cookie coughed so hard his whole body shook. "I'm dying, lad."

"I know."

"Do you remember the promise you made me?"

"Yes, sir, I do."

Tim stayed next to his friend's side throughout the afternoon, while Cookie tried to teach Tim everything he needed to know about animal care. Finally, satisfied he had said everything he could remember about the zoo, he shifted the conversation. "What's it like, Tim? What's it like to die and go to Heaven?"

Putting his small hand on top of Cookie's, he said, "More wonderful than wonderful can be. Love, peace, and joy surround you-… and also move *within* you."

"Aye. Do you think there will be animals there?"

"Animals, yes. Everything good about this world-… with none of the bad."

Hearing Tim's soothing words, Cookie relaxed somewhat. Tim wove his fingers between those of Cookie and felt his friend squeeze his hand. When the coughing subsided, a sense of stillness settled into the damp, quiet shed. Tim watched as Cookie's eyes widened and looked up toward the ceiling. At that moment, he knew Cookie could see the light he too once saw, illumining for him a realm beyond the confines of this world.

"Belinda, go get Chancy from the office, but make sure he stays outside this room until I call for him," Belle said, while Martha gritted her teeth through another contraction.

"Right away, Miss."

"Martha, you're about two minutes apart. I know you want to, but I don't want you to start pushing until I tell you. Remember, short quick breaths in and out of your mouth is all I need from you, for now."

Martha nodded and continued panting. "It won't be much longer," Emily said to her daughter. "Try to focus on Belle, and do exactly as she tells you." Slipping her hand in Martha's, she added, "Squeeze my hand whenever you feel the need."

About twenty minutes later, Belinda came back into the room and closed the door behind her. "They're all here," she announced. "Chancy ran faster than I did."

"Very good, my dear," Emily said while wiping Martha's forehead and neck with a washcloth soaked in fresh water.

"Belinda," Belle said, "There's hot water on the stove. Bring me a bowl of it along with more clean towels."

Turning around and heading back downstairs, Martha's sister opened up three separate cabinets to gather as many spare towels as she could find. Pouring hot water into a metal pot, she ran back up the wooden stairs and placed the supplies next to Belle.

"What else can I do?" she asked.

"Very important, Belinda. I want you to keep the father and grandfathers informed of Martha's progress. Can you do that for me?"

"Yes, Miss, I certainly can."

Turning to Emily, Belle said, "She's about two fingers dilated." Looking back at Belinda, who stood frozen at the end of the bed, she firmly told her, "Go!"

"Oh!" Belinda uttered, running out the door, closing it behind her. At the end of the hallway where the men nervously stood by, she said, "Martha's about two fingers dilated."

"What does that mean?" Chancy asked.

Belinda shrugged her shoulders and ran back into the room. Seconds later, she was again standing before the three men. "It means the baby is coming soon."

Fifteen agonizing minutes passed before Belle sent Belinda down the hall to further update the men. "Four fingers dilated, which means it won't be long now."

Belinda again hurried back inside and closed the door behind her.

Shifting her position between Martha's legs, Belle instructed her, "This time, Martha, when I tell you, push as hard as you can, alright?"

To maintain her rhythmic panting, Martha simply nodded her head.

Emily stood next to her daughter, while Martha, for the first time since her labor began, tightly squeezed her mother's fingers.

"*Now*, Martha!" Belle commanded. "Push! Push! Push!"

Belinda stayed close by, but at that point, she opened the door slightly and yelled down the hallway, "She's pushing!"

"I have the head!" Belle said.

"She has the head!" Belinda hollered through the cracked door.

Martha let out one last blood-curdling scream, just before the new life slipped into Belle's hands. Martha raised herself in the bed to see the small, wet, gray mass in Belle's hands.

"It's a girl!" Belle announced.

Belinda stuck her head out the door just long enough to yell, "It's a girl!"

Back inside the room, the women laughed at the cheering outburst from the three men in the hallway. "I believe they heard me," Belinda said.

Martha looked at her mother, standing by in joyful tears, and to the glistening baby in Belle's hands.

"What's wrong? Why isn't she crying? Is she breathing?"

Forcing her little finger into the baby's mouth, Belle pulled out a long strand of mucus. Then, while holding the infant upside down by her ankles, she slapped the baby's bottom, which was immediately followed by her first cry. "See, she just needed a little encouragement."

Martha laughed and let out a deep sigh of relief. "Thank you, Belle, a thousand times over!"

Placing a clean towel on Martha, Belle laid the baby on the cloth. Holding her daughter still, Martha watched as Belle tied the umbilical cord with a thread before cutting it. Next, she expertly wrapped the baby in a comforting bundle. "We have to keep her warm," Belle explained. "Poor dear hasn't even had her first meal."

Martha held her baby for the first time. Through tears of joy and relief, she looked at her mother and said, "I *love* her, Mother. I truly love her!"

Belle continued to clean Martha with warm water, while the mother and baby bonded for a few minutes. "Now, Martha," Belle explained. "You and I still have some work to do. Why don't you let your mother take the baby to meet her father and grandfathers, while you and I finish up?"

"What else *is* there? I'm not having twins, am I?"

As Emily lifted the bundled newborn from Martha's arms, Belle replied, "No, my dear, one baby is enough for today. This will not be pleasant, but I have to remove your afterbirth."

"Come along, Belinda," Emily said. "You don't want to be here for this part."

Belinda followed her mother from the room, continually looking at the tiny nose and mouth, barely visible in the wrap.

Ten very long minutes passed before Chancy was allowed to see his wife. After enjoying a long kiss from her husband, Martha wiped the tears from his eyes and asked, "Did you see her? Isn't she beautiful?"

"Every bit as beautiful as her mother, my love."

Soon, Emily entered the room, still holding the baby, followed by Belinda and both grandfathers. Chancy helped Martha sit up with her back against the wall. After lying the baby back in Martha's arms, Emily asked, "Well, you two? Have you a name for her yet?"

Martha looked at Chancy, who nodded with approval, before saying, "We've decided to name her Fanny, after Ebenezer's sister."

"Hoorah!" Robert said, clasping his hands together. "What a wonderful name!"

Scrooge stood speechless, then with a widening grin, slowly eased himself into a chair.

"We will call her Fan," Chancy added, "just as my father's sister was."

Scrooge pulled a handkerchief from his vest pocket to wipe his eyes, "What a *wonderful* gift, Chancy and Martha. My sister would be honored."

"Pardon me, sir," Tim said, as he stood at the zoo administrator's door.

"Yes, what is it, boy?"

"Tim Cratchit, sir. I work here."

"Eh? Well, what do you want?"

"It's Cookie, sir. He died about thirty minutes ago."

"Who?"

Tim searched his memory, back to the time he first met Cookie. "Sorry, sir, Nathaniel Cook was his name. He was the caretaker. I worked for him."

"Hm," he said, as a minor acknowledgment. "Well, I'll hire a new caretaker in a week or so. Where's the body?"

"He's in the back lot, sir, in the maintenance shed."

"Alright, I'll send word for the undertaker to pick him up."

"That's just it, sir. Cookie asked to be buried in the animal cemetery."

"What?! Now see here, boy. I'm not running a pauper's cemetery here! Everything has a place and time. His place is where the undertaker plants him and the time is now. Do I make myself clear?"

"Very clear, sir," Tim said, lowering his head.

"Now you go wrap the man's body in a blanket, and I'll send for the undertaker.

Tim returned to the zoo grounds, where he spread the word to the other boys who worked for Cookie. A couple of the boys cried when they heard the news, while others stood in silence for a few moments and then toasted him with imaginary cups held high in the air. Tim led four of the boys to Cookie's "home," where they each took a turn wishing their friend the best on his new journey.

The boys spent the next couple of hours sitting just outside the shed door, telling each other stories about their exchanges with Cookie and insights they learned from him: sometimes about animals and sometimes about themselves. One boy had just finished describing one such encounter when they finally saw the undertaker slowly approaching. His old grey mare walked with the tip of her nose nearly touching the ground, her sway back giving the illusion of an invisible saddle weighed down heavily with bricks. The undertaker himself sat tall and erect on the wagon's bench. His dusty black top hat and coattails seemed nearly as old and tattered as the man himself.

"Crikey!" one of the boys said, while they all stared at the ancient, pasty-faced man. "If that old stiff lies still too long, they'll put *him* in a box."

When the undertaker's wagon pulled up to the shed door, the boys carried the body, wrapped tightly in a blanket and lashed securely with rope, to the waiting casket.

Suddenly, the undertaker said, "I'll need to inspect the body.

Michael, who was the oldest and had worked for Cookie the longest, said, "I wouldn't, guv'nor. We found him this morning in the lion's den. Half of him is in the lion's stomach. There just ain't much left, and what's there really ain't worth looking at, if you get my meaning, sir."

The boys, in unison, verbalized their agreement: "Terrible, it was-… Very gruesome, sir-… Ending up a lion's dinner-… No sir, I wouldn't."

The undertaker asked, "No funeral then? No family to speak of?"

"None, sir," Michael said. "I dare say we're all there is."

Curling his upper lip, the undertaker looked at the neatly wrapped remains already lying in the casket. "Help me nail the lid on this poor beggar, and I'll put him to rest, or at least what's left."

The boys steadied the lid, while Michael drove six nails into the casket, using the undertaker's hammer. Moments later, they watched him climb onto the cart and ride off.

Under cover of darkness, well after the zoo was closed for the day, Tim, Michael, and the other three boys lifted Cookie's body, wrapped in burlap, into a pushcart and wheeled it into the animal cemetery, where a hole in front of the large rock had been freshly dug to receive it. Before they began filling it in with dirt, Michael pulled a chain from his neck and laid it on the burlap. He placed it face-up, displaying the pewter medal pendant of Francis of Assisi, the patron saint of animals.

"This here was his final wish," Michael said to the boys. "We've done nothing wrong in my opinion, but still we must agree to keep this a secret, for Cookie's sake."

Michael spit in the palm of his hand, stretched it out toward the others with his palm up and said, "Come on, mates, swear it with me. We'll each take this secret to our graves, or die a painful death if we don't."

One-by-one, each boy spit in his own palm, laid his hand above Michael's and earnestly said, "I swear it."

Chapter 20

Stepping through the office door, Dickens lifted his hat from his head and set it on the shelf above the coat rack. Before he could remove his overcoat, he felt some helping hands from behind him. "Thank you kindly, Chancy. How have you been?"

"I'm very well, sir. May I announce you to Mr. Scrooge or Mr. Cratchit?"

"No need, my fine fellow. They know me all too well, I'm sure. And how does married life suit you?"

"Couldn't be happier, sir! And if I may, thank you once again for the wedding gift. Martha reads from your books to me every night, but will *not* allow me to touch them until I have properly washed my hands."

Dickens laughed heartily and patted Chancy on the back. "You speak music to my ears, Chancy. The greatest gift a writer can receive is for his words to be enjoyed. Please excuse me while I greet your father."

As the author proceeded into the inner office, Robert rose from behind his desk. "What a pleasant surprise," he said.

Scrooge also stood to shake hands and welcome their visitor, asking, "What brings you out on a day with such a chilly rain as this?"

"I wish to discuss the progress of the book, gentlemen."

Seeing Chancy standing next to the clerk's table from the corner of his eye, Scrooge interrupted, "Ah, first may I share some exciting news of our own?"

"By all means."

"Chancy, come in here if you would."

As the courteous young man entered the room, Scrooge put his hand on his shoulder and said, "Since we last talked, sir, my son has become a father, and as well, Bob and I both became grandfathers, all on the very same day."

"Gentlemen, I don't know what to say. A hearty congratulations to each and every one of you. Mother and baby are all well and good, I pray?"

"All well and good," Scrooge confirmed. "And much to my delight, they named their daughter after my beloved sister."

"Fan."

"Yes, Fan. That was a most unexpected gesture on their part. I must tell you, Charles, I have been bursting with pride these last couple of weeks."

"This is such an amazing turn of events," Dickens said. "Let me see if I can take this in. Over the course of these last few months, Ebenezer became a father, Chancy a son. Chancy became a husband, Bob gained a son-in-law and Ebenezer a daughter-in-law. Then, Chancy became a father, which makes Bob and Ebenezer both grandfathers. My Lord, things do move fast in your world, gentlemen!"

Scrooge could barely stop smiling. "My apologies, sir. You came to discuss the *book*, and here I distracted you."

"Quite alright, Ebenezer. I only wish there was enough time to add the recent events of this year to the story, as well."

Chancy returned to his duties, while the other three sat near the stove, each with a cup of tea. "We have but one chance to get this right," Dickens began. "It will take a miracle, even if the book is well received, to fulfill Mary's wish. My thought is to have a reading before an audience from all walks, so we can see how it will be taken. I fear the events of this story may frighten some, while others will be skeptical."

"A reading does sound like a fine idea," Robert agreed.

"To me, as well," Scrooge added. "What can we do to help?"

"I realize this is short notice," Dickens said, "but I would like for you gentlemen to make the arrangements. This means renting a venue, creating a guest list, preparing food and so on."

"When would you like to have the reading?" Robert asked.

"On or near the first of December."

"Aren't we expecting to be in publication on the first?" Scrooge asked.

"We're slipping, but not by much," Dickens explained. "We're looking toward the middle of the month, but we will accept pre-publication orders after the reading. That will be our best indicator of success or failure."

"What if-…" Scrooge thought aloud for a moment. "What if we hold the reading at my house? Yes, you could read different chapters drawn from different rooms so the guests could get a feel for where this or that event occurred."

"A capital idea, Mr. Scrooge!" Dickens exclaimed. "I would assist you with the details of this myself, but frankly, gentlemen, I have been writing and re-writing day and night for a month at lightning speed, and it has begun to take a toll on my health, so I beg your pardon and ask for your support."

"By all means, Mr. Dickens!" Robert said. "We'll handle the details, in order to give you as much time as possible to prepare."

"*Excellent*, gentlemen," Dickens said. "I'll invite publishers, editors, clergymen, bookstore owners, shopkeepers and the like. Please extend your own invitations to friends and clients as well. In particular, I would like anyone who is named or plays a part in the story to be included. If someone takes offense or wishes their character's name be changed, better to find out now than in a court of law. My attorney will be at the reading with a release form for any of the aforementioned to sign, yourselves included."

"Here-here," Scrooge said. "We'll fill the streets with Christmas carolers, for certain!"

"And I can already smell the Christmas goose from a thousand kitchens," Robert added.

As he stood to leave, Dickens said, "Oh, and Bob, I leave it in your good hands to tell Timothy we're slipping a couple of weeks. I dare say I don't have it in me to face him with such news."

Robert chuckled and said, "I'll break it to him gently, sir."

"Martha, my dear," Scrooge said, as she joined him and Chancy for the evening meal after laying Fan down for a nap. "I have a favor to ask of you."

"Yes?"

"Mr. Dickens came by the office today. He has asked us to host a reading of his Christmas book."

"Host-… you mean here? In this house? When?"

"Yes, my dear, in this house around the first day of December. Can it be done?"

Martha's eyes widened, and she looked at Chancy. "How many people?"

"As many as this drafty old house can hold," Scrooge said. "I would plan for a hundred."

Martha dropped her fork on her plate and raised her voice, "You want to host a hundred people in less than two weeks? Are you *mad*?"

"It does sound overwhelming I must agree," Scrooge replied, "but everything we have asked of Mr. Dickens has been just as impossible. Remember, this is what *Timothy* asks of us. This is what Mary demands of us."

"I know, but-…"

"My dear," Chancy interrupted. "We were discussing this after Mr. Dickens left earlier today. Obviously, there's no way you can do everything on your own with a baby in one arm. Father is suggesting you plan the event and hire the work done."

"Yes, Martha," Scrooge said. "Hire some cleaning women to scrub this house from top to bottom. Hire cooks to prepare hors-d'oeuvres, and by all means, let's get a competent staff to clean up afterward."

"And bring in a nanny to stay in our room with Fan," Chancy added.

"A nanny, for a baby who isn't even a month old?" Martha replied, dumbfounded by the gravity of the request.

"It will be fine," Chancy said, laying his hand on hers for comfort. "We'll be here in the house with her. You, your mother and Belle can take turns checking in on Fan as often as you like."

"My mother will be here?"

"Your entire family, I pray, will be here," Scrooge said. "I insist."

Martha rested against the back of her chair and blew until her lungs were empty, watching the flame on the candle dance, while the mere thought of going through with such an undertaking already had her feeling exhausted. However, she saw the look of enthusiasm on everyone's faces and finally said, "Alright, I'll do it, but I'm going to need plenty of help!"

Chancy leaned over and kissed her on her cheek, "All the help you need, my love."

Martha had been working in the house for days, preparing the great room for the guests. The center of the room was cleared, and long tables framed the walls. She'd hired an excellent cook since she'd been provided with a sizable budget for food and drinks. The space, having been decorated in a festive manner, was bright and cheery, with lamps burning along the walls and large candles on every table. With the help of Emily, Richard, Belinda, and Tim, everything was in place by the afternoon of December the first.

As the sun set, an accomplished string quartet began playing a collection of Christmas favorites. Within the hour, the halls of Scrooge's home were filled with a warm, friendly spirit and abundant Christmas cheer. While Scrooge floated about, socializing with all who'd come, Fred introduced his wife, Alice, and his children, Allie and Adam, to a wide range of guests in attendance. Belle spent a good deal of time with two young women from her home, Kate and Chloe, who seemed nervous in the crowd. But all around, local businessmen and clients, friends and strangers alike, talked and laughed, sang and danced.

At one point, Belle found Peter by the food. "I haven't seen you in quite some time, Peter. I think Rose misses your company."

"Yes, ma'am. Rose is a lovely girl, and Cassandra is an absolute delight. But I struggle to find enough common between us upon which to build a relationship."

"You know, Peter, people grow on the inside as well as out. Over time, you may find you are not as different as you once thought."

Blushing in response, he replied, "I'm sure it's too late now, Miss Belle. She would certainly have found a more fitting suitor than me, I'm sure."

"Oh, I think there may be another who feels as I do."

Belle took Peter's arm and turned him around to see a pretty blonde girl in a yellow dress standing across the room, glowing like a sunny Sunday.

Belle walked past Emily with a wink to her friend and spoke through the corner of her mouth, "Midwife and now matchmaker. I believe my work here is done."

Peter approached Rose and smiled. "You came. I didn't think you would want-…"

Rose touched her fingers against his lips and said, "Every night, Belle tells me about a miracle she experiences each time she delivers a baby. Last night, she told me about the miracle of your birth, Peter. I broke down crying on her lap, and my eyes were finally opened. I believe in miracles. I believe in Heaven. I believe in love, and I believe in Christmas."

To the delight of his mother, Peter embraced Rose. Cherishing this romantic moment, Emily stood silently by, saying nothing.

Scrooge approached Belle and said, "My dearest, it has been a long time since we have danced together. But if I may beg your pardon, I believe I owe my hostess the first."

With a smile and nod of approval from Belle, Scrooge found Martha seated with her back in a corner. He bowed graciously and said, "My dear, your party has exceeded my wildest expectations."

With a huge grin, Martha returned the gesture by standing and curtsying. "Why, thank you, kind sir."

Scrooge then raised his elbow to escort Martha to the dance floor. After a moment of hesitation, she put her hand under his arm and followed his lead. The couple danced to the delight of the other guests, who applauded when the dance was over.

When the music stopped, the lights began to dim. Chatter lowered to hushed whispers, as a tall man in full gentlemanly attire slammed the front door behind him and spoke loudly. "Marley was dead: to begin with. There is no doubt whatever about that. The register of his burial was signed by the clergyman, the clerk, the undertaker, and the chief mourner. Scrooge signed it: and Scrooge's name was good upon 'Change, for anything he chose to put his hand to."

The reading had begun. Guests eased toward the sound of Dickens's voice, while he continued reading from notes he'd written in shorthand.

As the author approached the place in his story where Scrooge first saw Marley in the door knocker, he pulled open the front door for everyone to see it hanging there, cold and silent. "Now, it is a fact, that there was nothing at all particular about the knocker on the door, except that it was very large."

Then, gesturing dramatically with his hands and adding a ghostly tone to his voice, "And then let any man explain to me, if he can, how it happened that Scrooge, having his key in the lock of the door, saw in the knocker, without its undergoing any intermediate process of change—not a knocker, but Marley's face."

The guests were mesmerized by the story and enchanted by the way Dickens dramatically brought each character to life. Even Scrooge was spellbound, as though he were hearing his own story for the first time. For two hours, the guests shuffled for position in the crowd, following Dickens up the stairs, in and out of Scrooge's bedchambers, then back down the stairs from room to room.

Some of the children clung to their mothers, as Dickens described the sheer terror Scrooge felt at the appearance of each of the three Christmas ghosts. In fact, one woman fainted and had to be carried by her husband to a spare bed in the house when Dickens described the *ghost of Christmas yet to come*: "The

Phantom slowly, gravely, silently, approached. When it came near him, Scrooge bent down upon his knee; for in the very air through which this Spirit moved it seemed to scatter gloom and mystery." The woman's husband, not wanting to miss a single word, promptly returned to the reading without her.

When the reading neared its inevitable conclusion, Dickens pointed to the lamps, which Richard promptly brought to full light. "…and it was always said of him, that he knew how to keep Christmas well if any man alive possessed the knowledge. May that be truly said of us, and all of us! And so, as Tiny Tim observed, God bless Us, Every One!"

The majority of the guests cheered and applauded vigorously, along with several shouts of "Bravo!" Some, however, were stunned into silence, while others patted their hearts.

"And so, my friends," Dickens concluded while he still held their attention, "go silently into the night with a renewed vow of peace on earth, goodwill toward all men, and Merry Christmas on your lips." Following the author's closing remarks, the quartet resumed a melody of Christmas carols, and the guests began to mingle amongst themselves. While some continued eating and drinking, a line started forming at the table where the publicist was taking names and accepting payment for a book that would see its first printing quite soon, on December the nineteenth.

Those attending the pre-publication reading who were, in fact, characters in Dickens' story found themselves being fawned over by the guests, but none more so than "Tiny Tim." Women, in particular, felt a strong desire to hug him, wishing more of the young gentlemen of London could be like him.

When the banter, merriment, and laughter were at their height, and the party seemed to be in full vigor, the quartet suddenly stopped playing. An abrupt silence fell over the room, with all eyes turning to the hushed musicians.

To everyone's surprise, young Tim Cratchit stood next to the cellist and called out, "Uncle Ebenezer!"

On the other side of the room, Scrooge responded just as loudly, "Here I am, Master Timothy!"

The guests remained silent, while the two carried on a not-so-private conversation.

"Do you recall last Christmas you promised I would walk one day?!" Tim rhetorically cried out at the top of his lungs. "Well, my dear uncle, this is my Christmas gift to you!"

As Tim unstrapped his leg brace and dropped it by his side, the crowd's quietude immediately turned to gasps. With Tim standing on both legs, unassisted by crutch or support for the first time in his life, the guests parted and moved to both sides of the room, clearing a path between Tim and Scrooge.

Lifting his right leg and extending it forward, Tim set his foot firmly down on his heel. Moving forward with his hips and rotating over the bottom of his foot, he shifted his weight to his right side and willed his left leg out in front of him. One careful step at a time, the boy who'd never been expected to walk progressed across the room in a determined fashion. When he passed in front of his mother, Emily could not contain her tears. By the time Tim had crossed the center of the room, there was not a dry eye in the house.

Still, he continued his slow, single-minded walk, one labored step after another. At one point, Scrooge leaned forward, but all present saw he rightfully resisted the temptation to make the distance between them shorter. When his 'nephew' finally reached him, Scrooge hoisted Tim into his arms and hugged him to the cheers and applause of the entire room. Robert beamed with pride at his son's magnificent Christmas gift to Ebenezer Scrooge.

The music shortly resumed playing, and the guests carried on with their conversations and revelry. When Dickens' publicist whispered in his ear, he nodded and moments later caught the attention of Scrooge and Tim, motioning for them to join him in a side room.

"Tim, my publicist just informed me of some marvelous news! He has already taken preorders for more than four hundred books!"

"Outstanding!" Scrooge proclaimed.

"That is good news, indeed, Mr. Dickens," Tim said, although seeming less enthusiastic than the men sitting on either side of him.

"Tim, are you somehow troubled?" Dickens asked. "We're a success. This is what Mary wanted, I'm sure. Once this story spreads, Christmas will take on new life! Don't you agree?"

"I hope so, Mr. Dickens. But there were two clergymen here tonight, and both of them left during your reading."

"But that is just two men, Tim. There are *many* important people here tonight and most ordered multiple copies. One gentleman ordered *one hundred* copies for his bookstore, on the condition that I sign them for his patrons."

"This was never about selling books, Mr. Dickens. Mary wanted us to save Christmas, to restore it as a day of celebration, to honor it as a glorious day of the most precious birth. If the church rejects us and rejects Christmas, then all we have is a book about a ghost story."

Scrooge spoke up, addressing his nephew in an encouraging tone. "Tim, we must let the word spread. This is only the first day! If it is passed from hand to hand, as I believe it will be, the churches will eventually have no option other than to recognize Christmas as a holy day of celebration, one which people in congregations both near and far truly wish to celebrate."

"I hope you're right," Tim replied. "I suppose we'll know on Christmas day. If the church bells ring in Christmas, then we'll have fulfilled the vision Mary put forward. If not, then I fear Christmas will be gone forever."

With the evening's festivities finally over, Martha stood alongside her mother at the front door with Fan bundled tightly in her arms, doing what she could to provide her baby with extra warmth against the frigid wind.

Buttoning her winter coat, Emily asked, "Are you sure you don't want me to stay and help you clean, my dear?"

"No, please, Mother! It's getting late. You all have a long walk home, and I need to get Fan to bed."

Emily and Robert both kissed their daughter and granddaughter before stepping off the front step with their children. Tim was the last of the Cratchits to leave, carrying his leg brace, instead of wearing it. Though Martha watched her brother walk away with a noticeable limp to his stride, she smiled proudly at his accomplishment and what she'd seen him do earlier in the evening.

Scrooge stepped up behind her and placed a hand on her shoulder. "The last of our guests, I dare say. This entire evening was magnificent and an outstanding success, Martha, so much of it due to you and your efforts."

"Not *entirely* successful, I'm sorry to say," she said, closing the front door.

"Why, whatever do you mean? The guests were thoroughly entertained. Mr. Dickens said the results following the book reading were second to none. Two of the guests even told me how they plan to defy the aristocracy by openly celebrating Christmas with their family and friends."

Martha turned to face Scrooge and said, "You should probably talk to your son. I believe you'll find him in your bedchambers."

Scrooge opened the door at the top of the stairs to find Chancy sitting in a chair next to the fireplace. "What ails you, son?"

In the flickering firelight, Scrooge could see the glistening red eyes of a young man who had been crying. Pulling a second chair close to the fire, he waited for Chancy to find his voice.

Finally, after a couple of false starts, Chancy blurted out, "I *hate* that book! The Ebenezer Scrooge portrayed in it is *not* the Ebenezer Scrooge who you are! I would *never* have become the son of such a hateful, stingy man as that."

Scrooge thought reflectively before responding. "The hateful, stingy man in the book would never have *asked* you to become his son. We've talked about this, you know, many times before tonight. Had I not been the man I was, I never could have become the person I am today. *A Christmas Carol* will serve me well as a reminder of my past, but more importantly, I hope it will show others a means to change their lives, as well."

"I am so grateful to be part of your life, Father, far more than words could ever express. But that book turns the name 'Scrooge,' a name I carry in my heart with honor and pride, into a name that will be despised by anyone who hears it. Mr. Dickens did not write about the man I love, the man who has opened his heart and home to a family of his making."

"The only good things I've done with my wretched life have come since last Christmas, Chancy. My greatest achievement occurred the day a humble street boy knocked me to the ground and picked me up again. Yet I feel there is so much more I must do-... so many people, more worthy than me, in need of a helping hand."

"But when is it enough, Father? When will your redemption be complete?"

"It will never be enough. As long as my body can take one more breath, then I have the power to offer a kind word to a passing stranger. When the time comes, I can only pray I'll have the strength and fortitude to serve a friend in need. So I charge *you*, Chancy, with the monumental task of making the name 'Scrooge' one that will be pleasant to the ears of those who hear it and sweet to the tongue of those who say it."

Chancy looked into his father's eyes for the first time since they'd started their conversation. After wiping the tears from his own eyes, he said, "That's a pretty tall order."

"Yes, and I chose the right man, the *only* man for the job."

Pulling his hand from his pocket, Chancy stood and said, "I have something for you." He stretched out his arm and placed five coins in his father's palm.

Scrooge looked at the coins. "Five bob?"

"The five shillings I stole from you when you first took me in. The five shillings I swore to repay. I've done what I could to compensate those who I wronged. I've now satisfied all of my debts, Father. Yours is the last."

Scrooge closed his fingers around the coins to form a fist and stared at his hand for a few silent moments. "Has there ever been a father more proud of his son?"

Standing up, he embraced Chancy in the glow from the fireplace. After relaxing his hug, he took one of the coins and placed it in Chancy's hand, saying, "Hold onto this coin, Chancy. Do not spend it or trade it. This coin represents everything you overcame from your past to get you to this day. When you feel overwhelmed, pull it from your pocket and rub it between your fingers. Remembering the challenges you faced in the past will help you confront those yet to come."

Scrooge stepped closer to the fire, then continued, "When Fan is older and encounters a day of insurmountable obstacles, give her this coin and explain to her the difficult road that *you* walked. Let it be a reminder to her, as it is to you, that no mountain is too high, no ocean is too deep, to keep you from facing another tomorrow."

Chapter 21

Just five days after the reading, Dickens returned to the office of Scrooge and Cratchit with a piece of paper rolled in his hand. Bypassing any pleasantries, he burst through the office door and proceeded directly to Scrooge's desk, upon which he slammed the letter under his fist. "Read *this*!"

Without a word, Scrooge lifted the paper and read the sheet twice. "Can they *do* this?"

"Can and will."

"What's wrong?" Robert asked, having been left out of their short, cryptic conversation.

Scrooge handed the letter to his partner and said, "It looks as though Reverend Potts has petitioned the Court of Chancery to stop the publication and printing of *A Christmas Carol*. He refers to it as 'an anti-religious work of propaganda designed to incite mass hysteria.'"

"He goes on to suggest the book is an attack on the Church of England," Dickens added, "and any such affront to the church is an assault on the British Empire, as well."

Robert handed the paper back to Dickens and asked, "How can we fight this?"

"I have been summoned to appear before the court the day after tomorrow for a preliminary hearing. Ebenezer, will you accompany me? I may need your testimony and support to back me up."

"Certainly, sir."

"The wheels are already in motion, gentlemen," Dickens said. "The plates are made, and the pages are printing as we speak. The printer has promised to have the books on shelves by the nineteenth."

Then, holding the injunction up in front of them all, he concluded, "If Reverend Potts is successful in stopping the distribution, we will have a warehouse filled with six thousand copies of a book that cannot be sold and I will be financially ruined."

Two days later, Dickens and Scrooge entered the Court of Chancery along with Mr. Chapman, co-founder of the publishing house of Chapman and Hall, all three wearing their finest suits. Within moments, Reverend Potts strode in, accompanied by two priests, one representing the Church of England and the other the Church of Wales. Everyone stood when the three-judge panel entered the court from their chambers behind the bench. When the judges took their seats, the judge sitting in the center said, "Please be seated, gentlemen."

After fanning through a stack of pages in front of him, the presiding judge looked at the six men in front of him and said, "This is just a preliminary hearing, gentlemen. No ruling will be decided today. No one is on trial here. Do each of you understand the purpose of these proceedings as I have stated?"

All six men agreed.

"Good, then let us proceed. I ask each of you to give your name and identify yourself as either a plaintiff or defendant."

One after the other, each man stood and gave his full name and position.

"Mr. Dickens," the judge began. "I am familiar with your work. Some of it is very good, but you do tend to dabble in some rather radical views, at times."

"I'm sorry, Your Honor. Radical views, you say?"

"Yes, Mr. Dickens. You seem to disregard a person's station in life. When I told my wife I would be meeting you today, she described your careless contempt of poverty and provision. Your characters seem to feel entitled to raise themselves to a higher standing than that to which they were born."

"And how is it a bad thing for one to strive to improve his lot in life, Your Honor?"

"When the poor read such fantasies, or have one read to them, I should say, they begin to believe they are better than their true selves. Such beliefs tend to lead toward civil unrest, sir."

Scrooge grabbed his friend's arm tightly, sensing Dickens was primed to lash out against the judge's accusations.

"Quite right, Mr. Scrooge," observed the judge. "Let's proceed with the hearing."

Turning his attention to the plaintiffs, he calmly said, "Reverend Potts, please present your case to this court."

Potts rose but did not keep his position, deciding instead to pace in front of the judge's bench, not wasting a moment's opportunity to use his cunning and experience in public speaking to hold their attention. "As a humble servant of the church *and* of the citizens of this fine city, I beseech the court to cease and desist the production and distribution of the book currently titled, *A Christmas Carol*, written by this man, Mr. Charles Dickens. It is my opinion, and the belief of religious leaders across these fair lands, that this book is designed to restore pagan practices that directly contradict church doctrine."

"Have you read the book, Mr. Potts?" the judge on the right asked.

"*Reverend* Potts, Your Honor," Potts said to clarify his title. "And no, Your Honor, I have *not* read it, but two of our finest clergy attended a reading of the manuscript by Mr. Dickens in the private home of Mr. Scrooge. From that reading, they determined the book contained satanic rituals and demonic possession, the likes of which challenge the very core of Christianity."

"That is woefully untrue!" Dickens shouted.

The presiding judge slammed his gavel and pointed it threateningly at the author. "See here, Mr. Dickens. I will remind you only *once* that this is a hearing. You will have your opportunity to speak after the plaintiff has his, but another outburst like that and I will close this hearing!"

Turning back to Potts, he said, "My apologies Reverend Potts. Please continue."

"Thank you, Your Honor. The book written by Mr. Dickens, and would sell if permitted, glorifies the pagan practice of sun worshiping and celebration of the winter solstice. I'm sure I don't need to explain to intelligent men such as yourselves the debauchery and depravity that was practiced by the ancient pagans. Animal and human sacrifice has no place in our modern society, but is exactly what we will have if books like this find their way into the homes of the spiritually weak, who know no better than to follow a cult offering of class warfare."

"Class warfare, Reverend Potts?" the judge to the left asked.

"Yes, Your Honor, class warfare. This book not only encourages pagan beliefs but typical of Mr. Dickens' past work, it glorifies the lower class, while degrading the working class. The entire premise of the book is to disgrace a hard-working business owner who intends to work on a pagan holiday while victimizing a servant who demands to be paid for a day with no work. Just imagine the chaos that would ensue if the masses were encouraged to revolt! I pray, Your Honors, for the good of the civilized world, you ensure this book will not see the light of day."

Potts returned to his chair, while the judges exchanged whispered comments. Eventually, the presiding judge looked at Dickens and said, "Your rebuttal, Mr. Dickens?"

After casting a brief, yet riveting gaze at all three judges, Dickens stood and flipped through a stack of papers, pausing somewhat dramatically when he came to the page of interest. "Your Honors, *A Christmas Carol* is a book about goodwill and redemption. There is not a sacrilegious word in it. To the contrary, it promotes Christian values, at least the way I learned them. I would like to read you a passage from the book that I feel sets the tone of the story."

"Make it quick, Mr. Dickens," the judge on the left said. "We have four other hearings to sit through after yours."

"I will, Your Honor. This is the nephew of Mr. Scrooge, Fred Holloway, speaking to his uncle:"

"There are many things from which I might have derived good, by which I have not profited, I dare say," returned the nephew. "Christmas among the rest. But I am sure I have always thought of Christmas time, when it has come round—apart from the veneration due to its sacred name and origin, if anything belonging to it can be apart from that—as a good time; a kind, forgiving, charitable, pleasant time; the only time I know of, in the long calendar of the year, when men and women seem by one consent to open their shut-up hearts freely, and to think of people below them as if they really were fellow-passengers to the grave, and not another race of creatures bound on other journeys. And therefore, uncle, though it has never put a scrap of gold or silver in my pocket, I believe that it has done me good, and will do me good; and I say, God bless it!"

"And so, Your Honors," Dickens concluded, "I assure you this book strives to instill good, wholesome, Christian values in each reader's heart."

After Dickens sat, the presiding judge asked, "Since this book appears to be based on recent events of your life, Mr. Scrooge, do you have anything to add?"

Scrooge stood and addressed the panel, "Your Honors, a year ago, you would have found me sitting at the table with our accusers. On more than one occasion, I was known to consider Christmas a 'humbug'. I despised the way it turned ordinary souls into merry children without a care in the world, feasting on the generosity of strangers and spending their meager resources like drunken fools."

"And now?" the judge on the right asked. "Why do you sit at the table with the accused?"

"And now, sir, I realize I was the humbug. The accusations brought forth in this hearing, are a humbug. The right of any man or institution to suppress a season that brings only happiness and joy to millions around the world, is a humbug. Mr. Dickens has captured the true meaning, the true *spirit* of Christmas in his book, and so, as my nephew so appropriately observed, I say God Bless It!"

Dickens leapt to his feet, next to Scrooge and applauded his friend's speech, before both men returned to their seats.

Addressing all three defendants, the judge to the right said, "The three of you are educated, upstanding citizens who surely realize Christmas is a relic from the past. The only ones who celebrate it are the very wealthy, those who never pass on an opportunity to put on their social airs, or the very poor, who, during this day, are cruelly tortured and reminded of their poverty. Nevertheless, we will consider all arguments. Please wait here, gentlemen, while we deliberate."

The judges retired to their chambers for consultation. Within a quick few minutes, they returned to render the results of their hearing. "Please be seated," the presiding judge said to the six men who stood before him. "Mr. Dickens, do you have a proof copy of the book that we can review?"

"I do, sir," he said, approaching the bench and handing over to the judge the loosely bound manuscript from which he'd earlier read.

"Both sides have made a compassionate argument," the judge began. "We do not wish to diminish religious values or moral fortitude, nor do we wish to stifle the creativity of our artists, especially a national treasure such as Mr. Dickens. Therefore, it is the decision of this panel that we should take this manuscript under advisement. The publication and distribution of the book known as *A Christmas Carol* are hereby temporarily suspended until we have had time to thoroughly review its content and assess the social and religious implications it may have on the readers."

Addressing the book's publisher, the judge said. "Mr. Chapman, in the morning, a letter will be sent to the publishing house of Chapman and Hall, formally informing you of our decision. In the meantime, I suggest you begin preparations to suspend operations."

Potts immediately began clapping his hands together, applauding the court's decision, and then shook hands with the two priests beside him.

"You can't do that!" Dickens exclaimed. "The book is already in production! How long do Your Honors expect this court's review will take?"

The presiding judge replied, "You will likely hear the results of our review within a few months."

"By then, it will be too late!" Scrooge argued. "You're not ruling on a book! You're condemning Christmas itself, and you know it!"

The presiding judge slammed his gavel on the bench and declared, "This hearing is now closed, gentlemen! Good day to you all!"

While Chapman, Scrooge, and Dickens were standing on the front steps of the court discussing what had just transpired, each holding an umbrella to block the cold rain on the gloomy, dreary day, Reverend Potts approached and gloated, "Tough break, gentlemen. Remember, a bell cannot ring without a rope to pull it, or a bell ringer to hold it."

He then proceeded down the stone steps with a triumphant grin, whistling a merry tune.

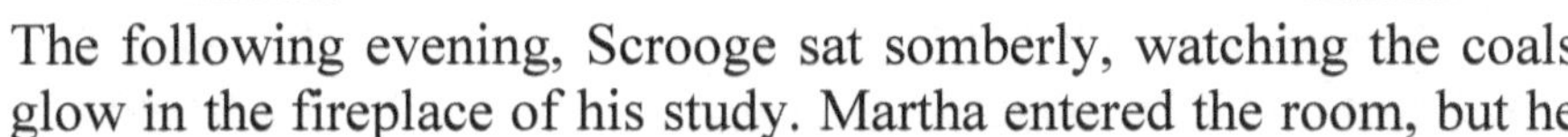

The following evening, Scrooge sat somberly, watching the coals glow in the fireplace of his study. Martha entered the room, but he remained silent, alone in his thoughts. He looked up, however, upon hearing Martha say, "Go ahead, tell him. Tell your father what you did."

It was only then that Scrooge realized Chancy had entered the room quietly behind her. "Tell me what?" he asked.

Chancy sat down in the matching wingback chair that faced the fireplace, mustering the courage to speak honestly. "Yesterday, it hurt me deeply to see how distraught you were, along with Mr. Dickens, after returning from the court hearing. Then, when you told Mr. Cratchit of the court's decision, I watched that poor man weep. It nearly broke my heart, knowing he had to tell Tim the book would not be distributed."

"What's done is done," Scrooge said, his face showing he'd resolved himself to what had transpired.

Chancy replied curiously, "I know I promised you I would never steal again, Father, but this morning I broke my promise."

Martha stood beside Scrooge's chair and took his hand in hers. "Go on!" she demanded.

Taking a deep breath, Chancy continued, "I went to find an old friend. I don't know his real name. We always called him Pinch. He was the best pickpocket of any of us. When I finally located him, I told him my plan, and the two of us waited outside the office of Chapman and Hall. We waited most of the day until the courier from the Court of Chancery happened by. Somehow I stumbled into the man and knocked an envelope out of his hand. Pinch picked it up from a snow bank and handed it back to the man. We both apologized and brushed the snow off his coat before parting ways."

"So nothing was stolen?" Scrooge asked.

Pulling a paper from his pocket and handing it to his father, Chancy said, "Well, somehow this must have fallen out of the envelope. Martha found it in my coat pocket."

Scrooge read aloud the document, which had been written on letterhead from the Court of Chancery:

It is the decision of this court that the book entitled, A Christmas Carol, shall not be published, produced, printed, sold or distributed until such time that the members of this court can rule on the social and moral provocations it may have on the British Crown.

Lowering the paper to his lap, Scrooge said, "So the publisher never received the court order?"

Chancy lowered his head in silence.

"But you said you returned the man's envelope. What did he deliver to the publisher?"

Chancy looked at Martha, who was now grinning at him, and then back to his father. "I'm fairly certain it said something like, 'Merry Christmas and Happy New Year!'"

"He meant well," Martha said. "Please don't be cross with him."

Scrooge stood up abruptly and burst into joyous laughter, tossing the letter into the air and raising his hands above his head in surprise. Relieved he was not angry with them, Martha and Chancy joined him in gleeful revelry.

Suddenly Martha stopped her celebrating and said, "But won't the court take legal action against the publisher, if the book makes its way to store shelves?"

"How can they?" Scrooge replied. "Chapman and Hall received no formal notice to suspend production."

"The court can still subpoena the publisher to stop production, can't they?" she asked.

"By then it will be too late," Scrooge said. "Once a book is sold, and the reader has read it, their actions will have no bite. You can't put the water back once the dam has burst, nor can you un-ring a bell once it has rung, my dear. Besides all of that, the Court of Chancery is a toothless lion."

"I was very angry with Chancy at first," Martha said. "Had he been caught, he could have been locked away for such an act."

Scrooge tempered his smile in agreement. "Yes, she's right, Chancy. Clearly, this was stealing. However, I see it as a crime of passion. This was a case where you broke the laws of man, but Heaven will judge you by what was in your heart. You stole for reasons of love and honor, not to line your own pockets. In fact, I believe, dear son, you may have just single-handedly saved Christmas."

"So you forgive me, Father?"

"I forgive you, and suggest we hold this secret between the three of us."

"But what about Pinch?" Martha asked. "He was involved, as well."

"I paid Pinch handsomely," Chancy said. "Besides, in his profession, secrecy is key to survival."

Martha wondered aloud, "Should we inform Mr. Dickens?"

"No need, I'm quite sure," Scrooge replied. "By now, Mr. Chapman has already informed him that the court has reversed its decision and offered their blessing to the book. Best we let it rest."

Moments before, the fire had seemed to Scrooge incapable of bringing warmth to his dampened spirits. Suddenly, though, it burst into a golden-yellow flame, brightly burning the handwritten note on letterhead from the Court of Chancery, he'd tossed onto the glowing coals.

Chapter 22

The morning of Christmas Eve Day, Scrooge awoke like a schoolboy on holiday leave. His first stop was the office of Fred Holloway. After stepping quietly through the door, Scrooge slunk in without being noticed and hollered, "Merry Christmas, Nephew! God save you!"

Fred flinched at the sudden interruption but immediately recognized the intruder. "Uncle Ebenezer!" he exclaimed, jumping to his feet to greet him. "Bless my soul, how are you this Christmas Eve?"

"I'm well, Fred. How are your good wife and your lovely children?"

"All quite well, and looking forward to a wonderful Christmas, despite the demands of our moral leadership."

"And tomorrow, on Christmas Day? You *are* bringing your family to my home for what promises to be a most gratifying Christmas dinner, are you not?"

"Ah, about that, Uncle," Fred said, turning solemn and lowering his eyes. But after a long, dramatic moment, he grinned and replied, "Of *course* we're coming, sir! We wouldn't miss it for the world!"

Scrooge laughed at his jesting nephew. "Fine, fine. I look forward to another stimulating conversation with both you and your good wife. I haven't dined with her since Christmas dinner *last* year. And please invite your friends and family. Mrs. Dilber and Martha have promised a feast second to no other, with games and music immediately after.”

Still, despite his best efforts and wishes, Scrooge saw that London seemed unaware of the holy day that followed. He stood at the front office window of Scrooge and Cratchit, watching as the snow danced and swirled in the street. A Christmas wreath of holly hung on the door to his business for the first time, but not one other shop in the neighborhood displayed holiday decorations. The carolers, who he had chastised and scorned in years passed were eerily silent for a December twenty-fourth, when they would have otherwise been most welcomed. No one solicited charity for the poor, as was commonly done, even though Scrooge’s pockets were heavily laden with coin suited to their needs.

“We failed, Bob,” he said. “We did all we could, but London is without Christmas this year, and I fear every Christmas yet to come.”

“But we still have Christmas, Mr. Scrooge, even if it lives only within our hearts.”

“In a genuine way, this would have been my first Christmas,” Scrooge confessed. “I prayed so hard that our book would make a difference-… that I could make a difference. I wish only to ease the burdens of those who suffer in poverty, and what better time than Christmas?”

“And you shall, sir, believe me, you shall, indeed. Please don’t despair so, Mr. Scrooge.”

Turning to face his partner, Scrooge managed a nod of his head and the start of a smile. “Yes, well, let’s not dally around here all day. We’ll close early, Bob. I have a family to get home to, I’m thankful to say, as do you. Maybe London will be open for business as usual tomorrow, but as for Scrooge and Cratchit, we will proudly display our ‘Closed’ sign, right Mr. Cratchit?”

“Right you are, Mr. Scrooge!”

After donning their overcoats, hats, and scarves, Scrooge took Robert’s hand in his and said sincerely, “Though the good old city may have forgotten, I never will again. *Merry Christmas*, Bob.”

"And a very Merry Christmas to you, as well, Mr. Scrooge."

The pair stepped onto the snowy stoop just beyond the office door, but before the key turned and the latch latched, Robert asked, "Do you hear?"

"I hear nothing."

"No, listen-…" Robert said, tilting his head.

Softly at first, as if whispered in a distant wind, the sound became familiar to them both.

"Over there!" Scrooge declared, pointing up the street.

Robert looked at Scrooge and smiled.

"Carolers!" Robert said. "And more voices than I can count!"

The two partners stood side by side, as the song being sung became a united band of people turning the corner next to the bakery onto their street.

"That's not a quartet or even a chorus of ten," Scrooge said to Bob.

The cobblestone road, indeed, was filled from one side to the other with dozens upon dozens of bundled-up men and women, singing with full hearts and voices, all heading directly toward them. Businesses, shops, and homes emptied onto the streets to join the gathering crowd in song and spirit. In the center of the first row, leading the multitude, was a tall, lanky fellow who stopped at the foot of the stoop, squarely in front of where Robert and Scrooge stood speechless.

"It's an absolute *miracle*, Ebenezer!"

Both Scrooge and Robert let out a surprised and jolly laugh.

"I can see that, Mr. Dickens! Wherever did you find so many well-meaning carolers?" Scrooge asked.

Dickens returned the laughter and exclaimed, "You don't understand, my friend. It's the book, you see! *A Christmas Carol* brought them all here to wish you, Bob and all of those who love you, a very Merry Christmas."

From the front stoop of their business, Scrooge and Cratchit stood three feet higher than the crowd, enabling them to gaze in awe at the expanse of people moving their way, all singing together.

"Ebenezer, Bob," Dickens continued, "I bring you good tidings! Tell that lovable, demanding Tiny Tim of yours that we did it. Gentlemen, at my own insistence, and of my own resources, I had *six thousand* first edition copies of the book printed, and by the grace of God, all six thousand copies sold in just a few days! This has *never* happened before, or will it again, I dare say."

Robert clapped his hands together and shouted, "Hoorah!"

"It looks as though you have many of the buyers with you this Christmas Eve!" Scrooge exuberantly teased.

"And for good reason, I might add," Dickens replied. "Every day, a group of people gathers outside my home before dawn, demanding my autograph, and every day the crowd grows larger. So on this day, there were so many that I decided to bring them here to meet you so *you* would be able to experience the enthusiasm spurred by *A Christmas Carol*. So gentlemen, turn yourselves about, warm your inkwells and fire up the stove. Many have, indeed, carried their book this Christmas Eve for autographs, and autographs they shall have!"

Dickens followed Scrooge and Cratchit into their office, where they set up a table facing the front door. For three and a half hours, the line moved slowly forward, one-by-one, into the office and back out, each grateful soul handing a book to Dickens, who would sign it and pass it on to Scrooge, who in turn autographed it and passed it to Robert, who would then apply his signature, as well. Many, too, asked Robert about a date on which they could return with their book for the opportunity to meet Tiny Tim and get his signature on their beloved copy of *A Christmas Carol*.

The sun had long set by the time Robert entered his home. "Good evening, my dear. Sorry I'm late," he said, kissing his wife while she cut open ripe figs.

"Good evening to you, love. How was your day?"

"A most amazing day, I must say!" After explaining the events that led to the book signing in their office, Robert said, "I'm really feeling the Christmas spirit, Em."

"I'm so glad to hear all of that! You know, my day went well, too. Normally around Christmas, I'm competing with the other ladies of the village for last-minute bargains and scraps. But this year, there was no pushing or shoving. The food pantries were full, and I had my pick of goose from the poulterer. So, even though most of London will forego the celebration, tomorrow's dinner will be a *Cratchit* success."

"The truth is, Em, in the midst of signing books today and being witness to the miracle of keeping the spirit of Christmas alive, my thoughts *often* turned to how much I'll enjoy your dinner tomorrow. It will *certainly* be a Christmas feast to remember."

Walking around the room, he greeted his children, but quickly realized his youngest son was not in his usual chair by the fire. "Where's Tim? *Surely* he isn't going to be late for Christmas Eve."

Emily stopped her chores for a moment. "I tried to stop him, but he insisted on going to the church. He said he always lights a candle on Christmas Eve, and this year would be no different."

Though Robert had an immediate sense of dread come over him, he held back any show of emotion. "I'm sure he'll be fine. But just to be sure he doesn't dawdle, I think I'll go find him so we can walk home together."

The dim streetlights made it challenging to distinguish the faces of those he passed on the street, but Robert was sure he would recognize Tim by his limp, that is *if* they crossed paths. When he got to the church, the building was dark, inside and out. For the first time since he'd been banished, Robert passed through the front doors and stepped into the sanctuary. The large room was as cold as the outside air. None of the coal burners were lit to warm the December chill. In the dim light, he could see the silhouette of a person kneeling at the altar in front of a single candle that flickered in the drafty sanctuary.

Walking down the aisle between the pews, Robert knelt next to his son. "You know we should not be here, don't you?"

"Yes, Father," Tim replied without lifting his head from prayer. "I just needed to make sure the bells would ring on Christmas morning."

Robert lowered his head and said, "Not this year, I'm afraid. Reverend Potts won't allow it. But Tim, I just had the most amazing day. The book has sold out, like *none* before it. Mr. Dickens has declared it a miracle in the world of literature. You did it, son! You, Mr. Scrooge and Mr. Dickens fulfilled Mary's wish!"

Unmoved by his father's news, Tim remained singularly focused on the bells. "Yes, we *did* do everything Mary asked-… and more. We gave Heaven a miracle, and I believe now Heaven will respond in kind. Tomorrow morning, the bells from this church and churches across London will ring in Christmas morning. *You'll* see, Father."

"But Tim, please understand. You and Mr. Dickens have won over the hearts and minds of thousands. There will surely be more printings and countless more sales. *A Christmas Carol* has taken on a life of its own. I saw it with my own eyes this very day! The people will *insist* that Christmas remains a holiday for all to enjoy, and the churches will be forced to recognize it as such. Reverend Potts and the others will have no choice but to withdraw their objections. I'm sure of it."

Tim looked at his father with moist eyes, straining to hold back the tears from falling, "When I asked Mary what sign I should look for to know Christmas is saved, she didn't show me a book. What she showed me was church bells all across London, ringing on Christmas morning."

Robert smiled, silently wishing he had half the faith his son possessed. Placing his hand on Tim's, he said, "Come, Tim, your mother is waiting for us. She'll be needing our help, I dare say, if she's to prepare a Christmas feast second to none."

"Yes, Father. We should go home."

The two walked together through the church's front doors, stepping out into a blustery cold wind, but stopped immediately before proceeding down the front steps. Before them, at the bottom of the steps and beyond, stood a mob of men, twenty strong. Some carried crude wooden clubs or burning torches, while the rest came armed merely with their spiteful anger and sanctimonious hate.

Standing at the front of the crowd next to a torchbearer was Reverend Potts.

"You're trespassing, Cratchit! You and that crippled blasphemer of yours!"

"We were just saying a prayer, Reverend," Robert replied. "Nothing wrong with that, I suppose, unless you have outlawed praying, along with Christmas."

"Perhaps you don't understand the meaning of excommunication, Mr. Cratchit. It means you are no longer welcome here! You and your clan have been banished! If you cannot understand my words, then maybe you will understand God's fury!"

Robert turned to his son and whispered, "When I move, I want you to run as fast as you can for home. And don't look back, no matter what."

Tim nodded in response.

"Now, Tim, run!"

As Robert yelled, he simultaneously ran down the stairs, flinging himself directly into the mob, pushing every man who stood in his way. Some of the men began pelting him with their fists, as he continued slogging through the gauntlet. Even though Robert did his best to draw all of the attention onto himself, the younger boys who were with their fathers saw Tim running away and gave chase.

"He's getting away!" one young ruffian cried out.

"Get him!" said another.

For several long minutes, the mob continued their beating, kicking, and thrashing, until Robert lay motionless on the ground, bleeding and barely conscious. Satisfied that sufficient punishment had been served, the crowd of men slowly dispersed. "Maybe next time you'll do as your told," he heard from an unrecognized voice, followed by one last brutal kick to his ribs.

As the last of the mob departed, Robert regained enough of his senses to remember hearing numerous boys yelling, *Get him!*

"Tim!"

Managing to stand, Robert tried to walk, but the extreme, searing pain from his attackers' blows and kicks had crippled his right side. Looking around, he could barely distinguish between the streets and the buildings that lined them. His right eye was swollen shut and the blood running down his forehead burned in his left eye. Still, he leaned forward with the singular purpose of finding his son and hobbled as quickly as his broken body would allow in the direction he knew Tim had gone.

It seemed to take forever, but within a block of the church, Robert came upon a group of boys, twice the size of Tiny Tim, standing in a circle. After pushing his way between two of the street-tough boys, he found Tim motionless, face down on the cobblestone.

"Honest, guv'nor, we never touched him," one boy said, as they watched Robert kneel by his son.

"That's a fact, mate. We started off chasing him, but he just collapsed and fell there, just as you see him now."

Swinging his left arm toward the circle of boys, he yelled through his tears, "Get back! Leave us alone!"

As he rolled Tim onto his back, he heard one thump, and then another, followed by a series of similar sounds. Only looking up halfway, he could see the boys dropping rocks that were intended for the lame boy who had come to the neighborhood church to say a prayer.

"Tim-… my Tiny Tim," Robert wept, as he lifted his son's head into his arms.

"Father?" Tim murmured weakly.

"Yes, Tim," Robert replied, pulling him closer.

"I'm sorry, Father," he whispered, before falling unconscious.

Fueled by emotion, Robert found the strength to stand and lift his son into his arms, plodding painfully forward toward their home. The circle of boys parted to allow father and son to pass. With each labored step, he found himself talking to Tim, hoping the sound of his voice would keep his son alive.

"Do you remember, Tim, when you were much younger, the days you would wait for me when I got off from work? How much fun you had riding on my shoulder? And do you remember how we'd wander through the markets?"

Robert tried to keep Tim's head against his shoulder as they walked, step by painful step. In the cold night air, mostly blinded by his own blood and swollen eye, he prayed earnestly that Tim would be alive when they passed through his front door if only for Emily to see him living and breathing one final time, or to share his last words.

At last, Robert found himself upon the stairs that led to their home. Able to use only his left leg to lift himself and Tim up each step, he climbed. Determined to carry his son home, even if this had to be the last time, he opened the door.

"Father, Tim!" Belinda cried out.

"Oh my Lord!" Emily screamed, seeing her husband bloody and swollen, carrying her youngest son like a rag doll. "Robert, what happened?!"

Ignoring his wife's question for the moment, Robert carried Tim to his bed and, with Richard's help, laid him down. "*Peter*," he called out, "as fast as you can, fetch a doctor!"

Without a word, Peter grabbed his coat and ran out the front door.

"Belinda," Emily said, "help me get your father into a bed."

Putting his left arm around her neck, Belinda lifted, while Emily supported his right side. She immediately backed off, though, when he suddenly winced in agony.

"It's alright, Mother, I've got him," Belinda said, helping him into Richard's bed, it being the closest to Tim's.

For well over an hour, Emily, Richard, and Belinda did what they could to clean the blood from Robert's wounds. Tim woke only for brief moments, before slipping away again, while Robert managed an occasional, barely conscious moan himself.

Finally, Peter returned with a doctor from the hospital, a tall, middle-aged physician who had been tending patients. Emily stood by silently, as the doctor first examined Tim and then Robert. The others stayed on the periphery, whispering a steady stream of prayers.

"Your husband has been beaten very badly, Mrs. Cratchit. Judging from the size and color of the bruise on his right side, he very likely has several cracked ribs. Time will heal him, but it will be a slow and painful recovery."

"And Tim?"

The doctor looked back at Tim. "He has a few scrapes and bruises, but it's his heart, Mrs. Cratchit. Its beating is very faint and erratic. I wish I could tell you otherwise, but your son-... he won't make it through this night."

"Can't we get him to the hospital? Dr. Owen could-..."

"Dr. Owen is a fine doctor, I agree. But please, believe me, Mrs. Cratchit, Dr. Owen is not God. There is no way to repair a heart, at least not in this world. Whatever happened to the two of them tonight was just too much for Tim's heart to handle."

Emily stepped forward to her son's bedside, knelt beside him and laid her face on his chest. Holding Tim close to her, she began sobbing in grief, knowing her son was slipping away.

The doctor turned to Peter and said, "Fetch me a towel. I'm going to lance your father's swollen eye to relieve the pressure."

Belinda knelt next to her mother with her arm across her mother's back. In the dimly lit room, Peter saw a stream of blood shoot up past the doctor's head, as he quickly pressed the towel over the blackened eye. After making two smaller incisions, he stood and handed the blood-soaked towel to Peter.

"There's nothing more I can do. When I get back to the hospital, I'll send word to the undertaker to come here in the morning. And then in a couple of days, I'll be back to check on your father."

"Yes sir, thank you."

Looking back at the two patients before leaving, the doctor quietly said to Peter, "I hope whoever did this to your family gets what they deserve."

Emily continued to kneel next to Tim, but said with a defeated tone in her voice, "Richard, please go to Mr. Scrooge's house. Bring him here-... with Chancy and Martha."

Chapter 23

When Chancy answered the knock at the front door, he took one look at Richard, standing breathless there on the porch, and knew something was amiss. "Come in, please!"

Hastily entering the sitting room, where Martha was rocking Fan near the fireplace, and Scrooge was napping nearby with a book on his lap, Richard blurted out, "Martha! Mr. Scrooge! All of you must come at once!"

Scrooge woke, as did Fan with the sudden commotion. "Richard, what's wrong?" Martha asked.

"It's Tim and Father."

"Catch your breath, Richard," Scrooge said. "You're not making sense."

"We've got to get back there! Someone beat our father to a bloody pulp, but Tim-…"

"What, Richard?" Martha asked. "What about Tim?"

Richard's face scrunched, and he broke into tears, not wanting to hear the words even from his own mouth, "Tim is dying! The doctor came and attended to them both, saying Father will recover, though you'd barely recognize him. But Tim, he said, won't make it through the night."

"Oh my Lord, no!" Martha cried out.

"Richard, run home and tell your mother we're on our way," Scrooge said. "Chancy, you and Martha take Fan to Belle's house and explain to her what has happened. She or one of her girls will care for the baby. I'll meet you at the Cratchit's home."

Scrooge changed from his nightgown into his day clothes and was the last to leave. Hurry as he might, he could not stop hearing Richard's words play over and over in his head, *Martha, Tim is dying-... Tim won't make it through the night.* The words rang louder with each passing step through the snowy streets. Suddenly he slowed his pace, and then completely stopped. Looking around, the familiarity of the buildings reminded him he was standing in the very spot where the Ghost of Christmas Present had vanished before his eyes, one year earlier that very night. And it was one year earlier, too, that the Ghost of Christmas Yet to Come, dark, mysterious, and foreboding, stood directly behind him.

Scrooge spun around, half expecting to have *another* ghostly encounter on the empty street corner. However, no one lurked in the shadows or doorways, and with his senses duly heightened, Scrooge knew he was positively alone. "What do you want from me?!" he shouted at the top of his lungs. Looking up in the stillness of the night sky, he was answered by only an eerily silent darkness.

"I did everything you asked, and then some! I am not the man I was! You told me if these things remain *unchanged*, the child will die! Well, I *changed* them, *didn't I*?!"

Pausing for an answer, he heard only the neighborhood dogs responding to his shouts. "*Answer me!* I changed my ways to alter the course of events, just as I promised! You know this to be true!"

Scrooge noticed a man who quickly pulled back from a ground-floor window inside a nearby building, someone who'd obviously heard him shouting like a raving lunatic. Angered with the ghosts who apparently had no intention of making themselves known this Christmas as they had in the past, he pointed directly toward Heaven, "This is *your* doing, not mine! I did everything I could to help Tiny Tim, even finding endless love in my heart for him! And now you want to take it all away?! Did it take you a whole *year* to punish me? If that is your plan, then take *me*, but leave the boy alone!"

Half an hour had passed before the door flung open and Scrooge hurried in. Martha and Chancy were already sitting with Emily, who kept vigil from a chair between the two beds where she could reach both her husband and youngest son. "Who *did* this?" Scrooge asked, both angry and distraught.

Looking up with tear-swollen eyes, Emily answered, "It doesn't matter who, or even *why*."

Martha knelt on the floor next to her mother and stroked Tim's hand. As her eyes adjusted to the dim candlelight, she gasped, "Mother, I can't even recognize Father."

Across the room, Peter explained the doctor's diagnosis to Scrooge and Chancy in hushed tones. Pulling a chair from the table, Scrooge sat next to Tim. Peter and Chancy stood at the foot of the bed, watching and waiting.

Just before it burned out, the candle on a wooden nightstand beside Emily was replaced with an oil lamp. Tim's breathing became more labored as the night waned. When Tim pulled in a particularly long, deep breath, Scrooge closed his eyes, for fear he was hearing his last.

"Uncle Ebenezer," the boy whispered slowly.

Scrooge opened his eyes to see Tim looking up at him through tiny slits. "I'm here, Timothy, never to leave your side."

Tim softly repeated. "My… fault. *My*… fault."

Tears dropped from Scrooge's cheeks onto Tim's blanket, as he pulled closer. "Tim, this is *not* your fault, dear fellow."

With labored breath, he whispered, "I prayed to hear the bells. Mary told me when I hear the bells on Christmas-…"

When Scrooge could no longer hear Tim, he looked to see that the boy had fallen asleep. His breaths, however, were now coming fast and short. Lifting Tim's hand with his, while looking over to the next bed, Scrooge begged relief from the man who lay battered and unconscious. "Oh Bob, how can we bear it?"

Laying Tim's hand back on the bed, Scrooge looked around at everyone who had been watching him. Suddenly, he stood up and headed quickly for the door. "Come with me, Chancy!"

In seconds, without a word to anyone else, the two were through the front door and striding quickly down the block. "Hurry, Chancy! We've not much time!"

"Where, Father? Where are we going?"

"To the church, my boy!"

Chancy caught up with Scrooge and held his arm to aid him, as they moved swiftly through the neighborhood, along cobblestone streets and snow-covered, empty lanes, finally reaching the churchyard where, just hours before, Robert had been brutally beaten. "We have to get into the bell tower!" Scrooge declared. "There's no time to waste!"

As the pair entered the bell-ringer's chamber and lit an oil lamp, the old man's heart sank. Looking up at the bells high above, he loudly grumbled, "Blast! The ropes-… they've been cut!"

Turning to Chancy, Scrooge grabbed both of his shoulders and said, "I'm too old to make it, son. I need you to run as fast as you can to the home of Charles Dickens. He told me last night that crowds gather outside his home in the pre-dawn hours, hoping for an autograph. I need you to rally them for Tim's sake. Tell them Tim's dying wish is to hear the bells ring out on Christmas. Urge them all to spread the word far and wide! Get them to ring every church bell and school bell, heralding the arrival of Christmas! Can you do that, Chancy?"

"I can and I *will*, Father."

"Good, my boy! *Very* good! I love you, son! Now, run like there's no tomorrow!"

Turning toward the chamber door, he heard his father yell, "My chains are gone, Chancy! I've been set free!"

Scrooge immediately began looking around the bell tower chamber for the steps or ladder leading upward. Seeing a set of steps carved into the inner stone wall, be began climbing without hesitation. Higher and higher he rose until he reached a catwalk that encircled the giant bells. Without a rope to pull, Scrooge realized his only option was to swing the bells manually, in hopes they would ring when they struck the clappers. Try as he might, the massive kettles would not budge, no matter how hard he pushed. Finally, he sat on the catwalk and pushed the largest of the six bells with his feet, while his shoulders pressed against the wall behind him.

As he pushed, then stopped, pushed, then stopped, the bell began a swinging motion. With each push, it swung a little further, until the clapper *finally* made first contact-... but only a barely noticeable "gong" sound emerged. Scrooge immediately kicked his feet to the next smaller one and pushed on it, just as the first bell returned. Soon, with one foot on each bell, rocking one and then the other, the two bells began to ring louder with each passing swing, until the tones were deafening! Not breaking stride for a moment, Scrooge pressed on. Moving around the tower, he began rocking the smaller ones with his hands-... and to his delight, found that due to their size, he could do so much more easily.

"Ha-ha! Do you hear it, Timothy?! You were right! The bells *are* ringing for Christmas, and for *you*, my boy!"

Scrooge continued to shout, unable to hear himself over the bells that rung loud and clear. Feeling inspired and strengthened by a force beyond himself, he moved from one bell to the next, scampering around the catwalk, swinging the bells onward in their rhythmic motion, so none would fall silent.

"Come back, Timothy! Come back to us and hear the bells!"

Blood ran from Scrooge's ears and down his neck after both eardrums had ruptured. He did not stop, though, nor did he realize he was completely deaf now and could no longer hear the bells himself. The potent, reverberating vibrations played throughout his body. "This is for you, Timothy! And for you, Jacob Marley! And you, Mary! Merry Christmas, London! Merry Christmas to you all!"

The bells swung before him, clanging triumphantly, all but one. The smallest was also hung the highest. Determined to ring all six, Scrooge struggled to hang onto the old wooden railing, as he stretched with all of his might to reach the rim of the sixth bell.

Through the darkness, Chancy dodged snow drifts and lamp posts. *I'm just one man*, he thought, as he ran through the streets. *It will take an army to do what my father has asked of me!* As he neared the front of the Dickens home, his spirit brightened when he saw before him the 'soldiers' of his army. No less than twenty men and women stood vigil, braving the frigid, early morning air. A small fire burned in a makeshift pit at the side of the street, which the crowd gathered around for warmth. As Chancy looked upon the group, he noticed one thing they all had in common: every person was holding a copy of *A Christmas Carol*.

Approaching an elderly man who held his hands over the fire's flames, he asked, "Why are so many of you gathered here?"

"We're hoping to get our copies of *A Christmas Carol* signed on Christmas morning!"

"You mean, you love the book so much that you would suffer this bitter chill for Mr. Dickens's signature?"

"The story changed my life."

Looking up at the darkened house where the Dickens family had not yet woken for Christmas morning, Chancy flipped an empty crate over to make himself a temporary platform. Standing above the crowd, he loudly said, "My friends, Mr. Scrooge sent me here to plea for your help! His partner's son, who you know from Mr. Dickens' *A Christmas Carol* as Tiny Tim has just this night suffered heart failure. He struggles this morning and is right now clinging to life."

The crowd gasped and gathered closer to Chancy.

"Mr. Scrooge has asked that we each say a prayer for Tim Cratchit, and for us to do what we can to grant his final wish. Before he leaves this world, Tiny Tim desires to hear the bells of London ring on Christmas morning."

Many in the crowd looked shocked and spoke amongst themselves.

"Please!" Chancy persisted. "Spread the word to family and friends! Wake everyone who carries the spirit of Christmas in their heart and beg them to ring any and every bell they can find! Ring out in every place of worship, every school and on every street corner! Make a joyful noise this Christmas morning-... for Tiny Tim!"

Finally, one man near the center raised his book high in the air and shouted, "For Tiny Tim!"

Chancy stayed on the box as the crowd rapidly dispersed. Every man and woman was gone from the Dickens home in less than a minute, running in every direction possible. Snowflakes fluttered around him, as he listened to the first faint bell, followed a minute later by louder rings. Reverberating tones spread from street to street and blanketed the city like a thick London fog.

Indeed, church bells and school bells rang from every township, along with hand bells and shop bells. Any bell that could be rung, by young and old alike, joined the chorus as the sun began to rise. Sleigh bells, door bells and dinner bells raised the melodies to the heavens.

Chancy laughed aloud when he saw women pouring into the streets, banging ladles against pots and singing a montage of Christmas carols. He spun around, still standing on the wooden crate when the front door of the house behind him swung open, and a tall man stepped out still wearing his night clothes.

"What is all this?"

Chancy threw his arms out from his sides and yelled over the glorious noise, "Merry Christmas, Mr. Dickens! Isn't it beautiful? They're playing Mary's song!"

"Listen, do you hear that?" Peter asked.

"I don't hear anything," Martha replied.

"Shush, listen! I heard a bell!" Peter insisted.

As the clanging grew louder and more frequent, Belinda lifted her head from her father's arm and said, "I hear it, too."

"And now, so do I," said Martha.

"Me, too," said Richard.

Even Emily let her thoughts leave her husband and son's bedside long enough to listen. "It's more than one church. I hear three, no *four*, now. Four churches ringing in Christmas!"

All of them rushed to the front door, and as Peter opened it, each saw the fresh blanket of snow under the dawn's first light. "It's really happening!" Martha gushed, as the sounds of more and more bells rose in the morning air.

"Do you think Mr. Scrooge and Chancy are doing this?" Peter suggested.

"There are more than just two men ringing," Emily responded, as she turned to step back inside, "I hear an entire *village* of-…" but before finishing her sentence, she shrieked and cupped her mouth.

The others ran to her side to see what had startled her so. Standing in the doorway to the bedroom, as he might on any other morning, Tim smiled and said to his mother and siblings. "Merry Christmas, everyone."

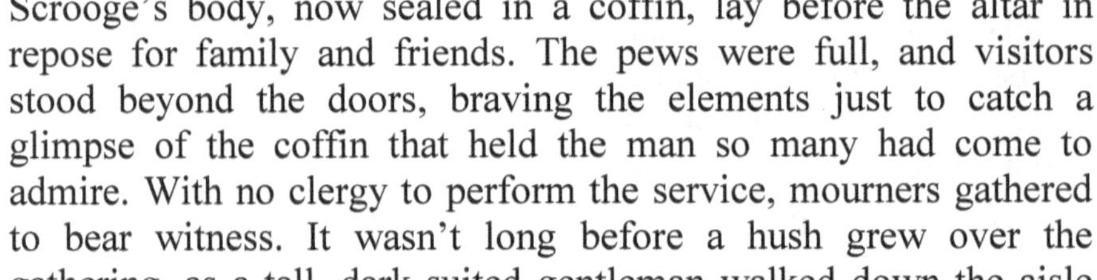

Scrooge's body, now sealed in a coffin, lay before the altar in repose for family and friends. The pews were full, and visitors stood beyond the doors, braving the elements just to catch a glimpse of the coffin that held the man so many had come to admire. With no clergy to perform the service, mourners gathered to bear witness. It wasn't long before a hush grew over the gathering, as a tall, dark-suited gentleman walked down the aisle and proceeded to the podium. Setting his hat and overcoat on the chair behind him, he stood solemnly for a few moments, just beyond the deceased.

In the front row, he was pleased to see Tim, Richard, Belinda, Peter, Rose, Chancy and Martha with Fan in her arms. Across the aisle, Emily and Robert sat, hand-in-hand, with Belle seated next to Fred Holloway and family. "For those of you who don't know me, my name is Charles Dickens."

"On Christmas morning, before first light, Chancy Scrooge stirred passion and zeal in the hearts of Christmas believers who silently waited near my home. Christmas rang in this year like never before, and the clergy of this town heard you loud and clear."

"Neither hide nor hair has been seen of Mr. Potts since Christmas Eve. He may have fled the area, knowing his crimes would eventually snare him by the tail. Because of his recent illicit behavior, Mr. Potts has been stripped of his license to preach. Therefore, this church no longer has a clergyman. Until a righteous minister can be found, services in this church will be conducted by lay leaders. The elders of this congregation have rightfully and unanimously bestowed deaconship upon Mr. Bob Cratchit. Once his body has healed, he will lead us on a journey of spiritual healing."

"I urge everyone, member or not, to attend this Sunday's service. I will do my best to deliver a sermon on forgiveness and reconciliation. The future of this body depends on your hearing this message. For the here and now, I have been asked to say a few words on behalf of Mr. Ebenezer Scrooge."

A number of parishioners behind the front row whispered and nodded, appreciating the message Dickens had just shared.

"One year ago, Ebenezer Scrooge lived alone. He would have died as he lived, had one thing not happened to change the course of his life. That one thing—was Christmas."

"He discovered through a series of events, that if he were to die, he would not receive a single mourner. Yet here we are one year later, and upon his death, the hall of this church is filled with those who wish to bid him a peaceful rest."

"Some of you have known Mr. Scrooge only a short time, myself included. Others have known him most of their lives. But it is his legacy that will live on. For Belle, the love of his life, his Christmas gift is the establishment of an endowment to fund her home for abused and unwed mothers. For his son Chancy, his Christmas gift is a name of which he can be immensely proud. For Timothy Cratchit, and for all of us, his gift is Christmas itself. Before they nailed his coffin shut this very morning, I placed his bible in his right hand, and in his left a first edition copy of *A Christmas Carol*. Inscribed therein, I wrote, '*To my friend who knew how to keep Christmas better than any man I know.*'"

"In one short year, Ebenezer Scrooge learned how to love, became an uncle second to none, a father, a grandfather, and a friend to everyone greeted by his warm smile and hearty handshake. In one short year, Mr. Scrooge lived a lifetime."

At this point, Dickens took a step back and gazed for a few moments at the coffin containing his now deceased friend.

"Perhaps some of you aren't aware of this, but on Christmas morning, Ebenezer Scrooge climbed the bell tower of this very church to ring the bells of peace and goodwill. He fulfilled Heaven's desire for Christmas to thrive in the hearts of all good men. And for his act of selfless courage, he was rewarded with a final wish. Timothy Cratchit described the events of Christmas morning to me like this: As Tim's life was slipping from this realm, Mr. Scrooge had just passed, having fallen from the tower. On what was to be his last breath, Tim opened his eyes to see Ebenezer Scrooge standing next to his bed, his face glowing with joy and a smile of ethereal peace. He placed his hand over Tim's failing heart and said, *Merry Christmas, Timothy*. And you see, after that, Tim's heart was restored to good health in what the doctor who examined him can only describe as a miracle. As for myself, I conclude: '*Greater love has no one than this: to lay down one's life for one's friends.*'"

"I have always considered myself to be a man who knew how to keep Christmas as it were, but it wasn't until I met Ebenezer Scrooge and Timothy Cratchit that I fully began to understand the love that binds us together. Mr. Scrooge has given us an immeasurable gift by sharing his personal odyssey in *A Christmas Carol*. And now by this, his final act of selfless love, he has fulfilled Mary's desire and Timothy's wish for all of us to know the true meaning of Christmas."

"Tim asked me, when we first met a few months ago, why I never finished the poem I had started writing for my wife's sister, Mary, upon her death. My answer, Tim, is that I had a beginning, but no ending."

Stepping forward, Dickens looked upon those in the front row about whom he'd been speaking and addressed them directly.

"So for you Timothy, and for Mary, I stayed awake last night to finish her poem. Early on Christmas morning, in front of my home, Chancy gave me the title I'd been searching for: *Mary's Song*. I feel it is appropriate to read the poem now, as we celebrate the life, and mourn the loss, of Mr. Ebenezer Scrooge."

Mary's Song

The pure, the bright, the beautiful
That stirred our hearts in youth,
The impulses to wordless prayer,
The streams of love and truth,
The longing after something lost,
The spirit's yearning cry,
The striving after better hopes—
These things can never die.

The timid hand stretched forth to aid
A brother in his need;
A kindly word in grief's dark hour
That proves a friend indeed;
The prayer for mercy softly breathed,
When justice threatens high,
The sorrow of a contrite heart—
These things shall never die.

Lose not a chance to waken love
And find one to admire,
For heaven's host will share with thee,
Thy one true love's desire.
So shall a light that cannot fade
Beam on thee from on high,
And angel voices say to thee—
"These things shall never die."

The bells once silent, ring again,
For glory will not wait;
No man this season can upend,
His Son gave us in grace.
So rest my angel, near my heart,
Your wish I have obliged,
That Christmas be forevermore—
This thing shall never die.

Epilogue

Ebenezer Scrooge was buried in the cemetery of the very church in which he died, in the plot nearest the tower from which the bells rang. A number of those who knew the man, as well as those who knew him only from *A Christmas Carol*, placed holly wreaths, instead of flowers, on his grave on the day of his burial, and countless others came back and did the same for years to come. Charles Dickens himself wrote the epitaph for Scrooge's stone, which read: *Here lies the man who died so that Christmas may live*.

Two months after the funeral, in late February, Emily went to the grave of Rebecca Cratchit to view the newly carved headstone. Cupping a hand over her mouth, she turned to see if anyone was watching her. Tears fell silently on her fingers before she allowed herself to laugh aloud, as she stared in amazement at the thick blanket of Winter Aconites that had miraculously overcome the salted soil and flourished. Their small yellow blossoms carpeted the grave from end to end.

Charles Dickens continued writing novels throughout his career, even dabbling in plays and acting from time to time, but none of his works would have such a dramatic impact on his life and career as did *A Christmas Carol*. His readings were in high demand, especially near Christmas, and he traveled extensively across Europe and the United States to give such to his audiences.

Robert refused to change the sign above the business to place his name first, even though he became the senior partner to the younger Mr. Chancy Scrooge. The business of Scrooge and Cratchit flourished in the wake of a Christmas revival, the likes of which grew out of a seed, planted by a young crippled boy who truly believed.

Eighteen months after *A Christmas Carol*'s initial publication, Edward Chapman, Dickens' publishing liaison at Chapman & Hall received an unexpected letter by courier from the Court of Chancery, which simply stated:

After a thorough review, the court cannot find reason or cause to delay the publication of the book titled A Christmas Carol.

To Tim's delight, the bells of Christmas had, indeed, rung that year, and continued to every year thereafter, heralding peace on earth and goodwill toward men.

And so, as Tiny Tim observed, God Bless Us, Every One!

ℌistorical ℜeferences

(Author's Notes)

Mary Hogarth:

Mary Hogarth was a sister to Catherine Hogarth (wife of Charles Dickens). She died in the arms of Dickens at the age of seventeen on May 7, 1837. The cause of death is believed to have been either heart failure or a stroke. Upon her death, he slipped a ring from her finger and wore it for the rest of his life. She was buried on May 13 at the Kensal Green Cemetery, London. Dickens wrote the epitaph on her tombstone, which says, "Young, beautiful, and good, God numbered her among his angels at the early age of seventeen."

As a result of Hogarth's death, Charles Dickens missed the publication dates for *The Pickwick Papers* and *Oliver Twist*. It was the only time in his life that Dickens missed publication dates. As a reason for missing the publication dates, he wrote that "he had lost a very dear young relative to whom he was most affectionately attached, and whose society has been, for a long time, the chief solace of his labors."[1]

---

[1] https://en.wikipedia.org/wiki/Mary_Hogarth

Smoking Bishop:

When Robert returned to work after Christmas to find Scrooge a "changed man," they enjoyed a piping hot (or smoking) Bishop. Together they toasted the season and each other as they made plans for the days ahead. Typical of the time, if you bought a Bishop on the street, you brought your own cup or bowl.

Smoking Bishop was made from port, red wine, lemons or Seville oranges, sugar and spices, such as cloves. The citrus fruit was roasted to caramelize it, and the ingredients then warmed together. There is a persistent myth that the name comes from the shape of the traditional bowl, shaped like a bishop's miter and that in this form, it was served in medieval guildhalls and universities.[2]

Gingerbread:

When Scrooge invited himself to dinner at the Cratchits, he did not show up empty-handed. He presented Emily with a standard, yet often cherished dessert: a loaf of gingerbread.

Ingredients:

- 4 oz (110g) butter
- 4 oz (110g) brown sugar
- 8 oz (220g) golden syrup (molasses)
- 8 oz (220g) all-purpose flour
- 1 level teaspoon baking powder
- 1 level teaspoon mixed spice (personal taste: consider equal amounts of allspice, cinnamon, and nutmeg)
- 2 level teaspoons ground ginger
- 2 eggs
- 4 fluid oz (120ml) milk

---

[2] https://en.wikipedia.org/wiki/Smoking_Bishop

Procedure:

1. Put the butter, sugar, and syrup in a pan. Heat gently until the butter melts.
2. Place the dry ingredients in a bowl. Pour the melted butter mixture into the bowl, and beat thoroughly.
3. Warm the milk in a pan (so it will dissolve the syrup).
4. Add the milk to the bowl, and beat thoroughly.
5. Beat the eggs, and then stir them into the mixture.
6. Pour the mixture into an 8-inch (20cm) greased square cake tin.
7. Cook at 325°F (170°C) for one hour.
8. Cool in the tin for 15 minutes, then remove.

Leave sitting and covered at least one day before cutting into squares.[3]

Ether:

Tiny Tim was very fortunate to have surgery in 1843, the same year Charles Dickens wrote *A Christmas Carol*. It was merely a year sooner, March 30, 1842, Dr. Crawford Long, an American surgeon, made the first known use of ether as a general anesthetic. Previous attempts at general anesthesia were not effective, and now for the first time, major surgery could be accomplished without pain.[4]

A Christmas Carol Timeline:

By mid-1843, Dickens had begun to suffer from financial problems. Sales of *Martin Chuzzlewit* were slowing, and his wife, Catherine, was pregnant with the couple's fifth child. Matters worsened when Chapman & Hall, *Martin Chuzzlewit*'s publishers, began to talk about reducing his monthly income by £50 if sales dropped further. He began to write *A Christmas Carol* in October

---

[3] https://en.wikibooks.org/wiki/Cookbook:Gingerbread

[4] https://www.historyandheadlines.com/march-30-1842-first-use-ether-anesthesia/

1843. Michael Slater, Dickens's biographer, describes the book as being "written at white heat;" it was completed in six weeks, with the final pages written in early December. He built much of the work in his head, while taking nighttime walks of 15 to 20 miles around London.[5]

The First Edition:

A Christmas Carol, published by Chapman & Hall on December 19, 1843, was an immediate success and the initial print run of 6,000 copies sold out within a matter of days. Dickens had hoped the book would clear his debts with Chapman & Hall, but the lavish production, including four woodcuts and four color plates by John Leech, meant Dickens only made £230 from the first printing.[6]

The Regent's Park:

The Regent's Park is adjacent to Camden Town. The park includes the London Zoo, where Tiny Tim worked and first met Charles Dickens. The author was known to frequent the park and its many animal habitats while living nearby at No. 1 Devonshire Terrace, Regent's Park. Prince Regent (later King George IV) commissioned architect John Nash to create a master plan for the area. Nash originally envisaged a palace for the Prince and a number of grand detached villas for his friends. But when this plan was put into action beginning in 1818, the palace and most of the villas were dropped. However, most of the proposed terraces of houses on the park's fringes were built.[7]

---

[5] https://en.wikipedia.org/wiki/A_Christmas_Carol
[6] https://www.bl.uk/collection-items/first-edition-of-a-christmas-carol
[7] https://en.wikipedia.org/wiki/Regent's_Park

Oliver Twist:

Martha's cherished magazines containing the chronicles of Oliver Twist were her most prized possessions. The novel was originally published in monthly installments in the magazine *Bentley's Miscellany* from February 1837 to April 1839. It was originally intended to form part of Dickens's serial, *The Mudfog Papers*. George Cruikshank provided one steel etching per month to illustrate each installment. The novel first appeared in book form six months before the initial serialization was completed, in three volumes published by Richard Bentley, the owner of *Bentley's Miscellany*, under the author's pseudonym, "Boz." It included 24 steel-engraved plates by Cruikshank.[8]

Paganism vs. Christianity:

Reverend Potts protested vehemently to the celebration of Christmas as a Christian holiday, believing instead it was rooted deeply in pagan beliefs and practices, and therefore had no place in the modern church.

Paganism is the worship of the physical universe, particularly the sun, moon, and stars. Sun-worship formed the basis of Mithraism, Zoroastrianism, other Roman religions and many other pagan traditions. It is the reason Sunday ("Sun-day") is a holy day in many religions, and why major festivals are held at spring and the solstices. [To pagans,] the real meaning of Christmas is sun worship, a reminder to all life on Earth that we owe everything to the sun. Sun worship is actually one of the main pillars of many religions, especially older religions. Sun worshippers and nature religions held major celebrations at the Winter Solstice, the victory of the strength of the sun over the forces of darkness that try to suppress it. [9][10]

---

[8] https://en.wikipedia.org/wiki/Oliver_Twist
[9] http://www.humanreligions.info/christmas.html
[10] https://en.wikipedia.org/wiki/Christmas

Court of Chancery:

When Reverend Potts took legal action to prevent the publication and distribution of *A Christmas Carol*, he turned to the Court of Chancery.

The Court of Chancery was a court of equity in England and Wales that loosely followed a set of rules to avoid the slow pace of change and possible harshness (or "inequity") of the common law. The Chancery had jurisdiction over all matters of equity, including trusts, land law, the administration of the estates of lunatics and the guardianship of infants. Its initial role was somewhat different, however. As an extension of the Lord Chancellor's role as *Keeper of the King's Conscience*, the Court was an administrative body primarily concerned with conscientious law. Thus, the Court of Chancery had a far greater remit than the common law courts, whose decisions it had the jurisdiction to overrule for much of its existence, and was far more flexible. Until the 19th century, the Court of Chancery could apply a far wider range of remedies than the common law courts, such as specific performance and injunctions, and also had some power to grant damages in special circumstances. With the shift of the Exchequer of Pleas towards a common law court and loss of its equitable jurisdiction by the Administration of Justice Act 1841, the Chancery became the only national equitable body in the English legal system.[11]

Mary's Song:

The poem, *Mary's Song*, was originally written by Charles Dickens (though there is some debate that the author was Sarah Doudney) under the title, *These Things Shall Never Die*.[12] I modified the poem slightly to fit the storyline while doing my best to preserve the beauty and intent of the author's words.

---

[11] https://en.wikipedia.org/wiki/Court_of_Chancery

[12] https://allpoetry.com/poem/13111731-These-Things-Shall-Never-Die-by-Charles-Dickens

About The Author

Dixie Distler was born in Germany and later moved to the United States with her family. She earned her certification as a Radiological Technologist in Lexington, Kentucky, and currently resides in Huntsville, Alabama with her husband and children. A mother of three and grandmother of three, Dixie has proudly served her local church as a teacher for over thirty years. It was through her love for children and storytelling that she found her passion for writing fiction and reading the classics.